David Burnell comes from York. He studied maths at Cambridge and taught it for several years to sixth formers in West Africa. After returning to the UK, he applied it to management problems in health, coal mining and the water industry. On "retiring", he completed a PhD at Lancaster University on the deeper meaning of data from London's water meters.

He and his wife split their time between Berkshire and North Cornwall. They have four grown-up children.

Cornish Conundrum Author Reviews

Doom Watch: "Cornwall and its richly storied coast has a new writer to celebrate in David Burnell. His crafty plotting and engaging characters are sure to please crime fiction fans." Peter Lovesey

"A well-written novel, cleverly structured, with a nicely handled subplot . . ." Rebecca Tope

Slate Expectations: "combines an interesting view of an overlooked side of Cornish history with an engaging pair of sleuths, on the trail from past misdeeds to present murder." Carola Dunn

"An original atmospheric setting which is sure to put Delabole on the map. A many-stranded story keeps the reader guessing, with intriguing local history colouring events up to the present day." Rebecca Tope

Looe's Connections: "A super holiday read set in a super holiday location!" Judith Cutler

Tunnel Vision: "Enjoyable reading for all who love Cornwall and its dramatic history." Ann Granger

Twisted limelight: "The plot twists will keep you guessing up to the last page. A thrilling Cornish mystery." Kim Fleet

"A clever, exciting story of modern-day skulduggery and romance on the beautiful north Cornish coast." Roger Higgs

Forever Mine: "An intriguing mystery set to the backdrop of a wedding in sleepy Cornwall, where all is not as it appears." Sarah Flint

Crown Dual: "A page-turning contemporary thriller with a deeply compelling narrative." Richard Drysdale

Unsettled Score: "A stack of mysteries to solve, including an unusual murder, all in a wonderful Cornish setting." Stephen Baird

Peter Lovesey holds multiple awards for his crime writing, including a Crime Writers' Cartier Diamond Dagger.

Carola Dunn pens Daisy Dalrymple and Cornish Mysteries.

Rebecca Tope pens the Cotswold and other Mysteries.

Judith Cutler created the DS Fran Harman crime series.

Ann Granger authors the Campbell and Carter Mysteries.

Dr Kim Fleet, poison expert, writes the Eden Grey Mysteries.

Dr Roger Higgs is a Bude geologist and local guide.

Sarah Flint authors the DC Charlotte Stafford series.

Richard Drysdale pens thrillers on Scottish Independence.

Stephen Baird, a Truro Cathedral Guide, is author of "Fire in the straw".

BEYOND
REACH

A Cornish Conundrum

David Burnell

Skein Books

BEYOND REACH

Published by Skein Books, 88, Woodcote Rd, Caversham, Reading, UK

First edition: May 2022.

This book is a work of fiction, though the settings around Bude are real. There was a pioneering canal in the nineteenth century and a steam railway up to 1963. Cleave Camp operates today as part of the security services. The names, characters and current incidents portrayed are from the author's imagination. No character is based on any real person, living or dead; any resemblance is purely coincidental.

ISBN: 9798443359922

The front cover shows the viaduct on Trelay Farm, which once carried trains to Bude from London and Exeter. In the background is a belfry at a local Church. Thanks to my wife, Marion, for the viaduct and author cover photos; and to Dr Chris Scruby for the belfry photo, Hartland and Stanbury Beach (pages 187, 1 and 237) and refinements to all the originals.

OUTLINE

Moonlit lighthouse at Hartland Point

PROLOGUE   July 1944

Occasionally there was a glimpse of a moon but most of the time the silvery shimmer was hidden behind rain-filled clouds. A blustery night, the sound of the wind was rising steadily. But the weather was not bad enough to disrupt the operation this time: the exercise was deemed too important to allow further postponement.

'I guess it could be a lot worse,' shrugged Chuck, the American pilot, as he adjusted his helmet and snuggled himself into his harness.

'You're lucky to be flying tonight,' responded Bert, his navigator, seated behind him. 'The storm was far worse two weeks back.' That had been a trial all round. But his pilot on that occasion, Dennis, was now held in solitary confinement, charged with by-passing key protocols. 'Right, I'm ready when you are.'

There was no excuse for delay. Chuck waved to the landing crew, just visible beyond the wingtip in the subdued lighting, as the sound of the piston engine rose in intensity. The plane inched slowly forwards, heading for the main runway. That was hardly lit at all: it was taken for granted that the flyers' eyes would have gained a measure of night vision – as well as having seen the airfield layout many times before, in the cold light of day.

At least there was no need at this point to worry about other aircraft. This would be the only flight from here tonight. The plane reached the far end of the runway and the craft turned towards the main levelled pathway, stretching ahead. The pilot could see a light at the far end, six hundred yards away, directed towards him. It wouldn't be there for long: it would go out as soon as they were airborne.

Everyone knew it was impossible to keep their activity totally secret from the local population, but this was a rural area, lightly populated, and the airfield's Commanding Officer made sure that not many clues were on offer.

Two minutes later, the muffled engine had reached its peak revolutions and the aircraft bumped its way down the grassy runway and into the night sky.

The first part of the flight was to head north, up the coast towards Hartland Point. The aircraft took a position out over the sea, half a mile out from the cliffs but a few hundred feet higher. No lights were visible, either inside the cockpit or at the extremities of wings or tail.

And not a single light was showing from the occasional cottage along the coast.

Chuck could just see his instruments in the gloom. The main task for now was to maintain height. It would be easy enough to allow the craft to drift slowly down towards the sea: you wouldn't realise the peril you were in until it was too late. But the American had plenty of flying experience from pre-war days, though he had never flown a mission like this. He was relying on his seasoned navigator behind him to guide them through the high-stress activity when the crux came.

Chuck had arrived at the base scheduled for "light duties only", to aid his recovery. He'd only been drafted into this mission because the established pilot, who should have been flying the plane, was locked in an airbase cell serving his time.

'We'll be off Hartland Quay in four minutes,' said the voice behind him.

Chuck wasn't yet familiar with every local landmark. 'OK. So what happens there?'

'There's a single anti-aircraft battery. All being well they should have been warned that we'd be coming this way tonight. They probably can't see us anyway.'

It was a modest consolation, thought the American. Then he noted the downside: it implied any enemy aircraft exploring this part of the Cornish coast would be equally invisible. With some effort he managed to restrain the barbed comment that had come to mind. He knew it was important to maintain allied co-operation.

Bert was also conscious of the need to guard his tongue. He didn't know the pilot well, he found his fellow traveller abrasive, though he'd been told Chuck was as well-qualified as anyone. Even so, it wasn't the same as being with a fellow-Brit – especially someone from this less-known corner of Cornwall. On previous flights, with a local compatriot, the two had shared many reminiscences of their wartime "adventures", most of which had no connection with the official enemy.

Outside there was silence. It seemed that the Hartland Quay crew were either forewarned or else off their guard. 'We'll go on as far as the Hartland Point headland, then head back,' said Bert. 'That's another minute.'

Suddenly, the rainclouds cleared and for the first time on the flight they were into clear moonlight.

'Hey, look down there, Chuck. All those rocky spines, sticking right out into the sea,' urged the navigator. 'It goes on like that for mile after mile. You can see why they've had so many shipwrecks on this stretch of coast over the centuries.'

The American was less impressed. Or rather, he could see a downside arising from the unfriendly coastline below. In truth, he had less confidence in his aircraft than had his navigator; maybe he was oversensitive, but he sensed an occasional

3

faltering in the engine's rhythm. The Hawker Henley was not the most modern aircraft deployed by the Royal Air Force in 1944. There weren't any beaches along here that he'd fancy trying to put down on, even with the most modern machine, if it came to an emergency. But for now he managed to suppress his anxieties.

'It's time to head back,' stated the voice behind him, a moment later. The high, rugged cliffs of Hartland Point were visible over to their right. And there was the lighthouse, almost at sea level, far below – though no beam came from that source in wartime.

Chuck's restless mind went over all the other things that could go wrong. 'So Bert, you've got the gear?'

'Don't worry, Chuck. It's already loaded.'

Managing not to worry was easier said than done.

Just as they turned back along the coast, the moonlight disappeared; they were in total darkness once again. Chuck wasn't sure if that was a benefit or an extra handicap in what was coming next. He was an all-action man; he longed to be the centre of attention.

There was ten minutes of silence. Chuck concentrated on maintaining their height. He could hear Bert scuffling about behind him.

'Right,' said the navigator. 'I reckon we're in position. You hold her steady, Chuck, I'll let out the drape.'

There was the sound of the cockpit floor being unbolted and opened up behind him. Then came a jerk; something heavy was thrown out of the aircraft, followed by a pull as its connecting rope tightened.

For a second the plane reacted with a wobble of its own, followed by a lunge upwards. After that the additional weight now being towed behind them started to slow everything down.

Suddenly there was a huge explosion in the sky above. It was impossible for eyes conditioned by ten minutes of pitch darkness to take in any detail, but the sound was certainly that of a live shell, bursting not far away.

Chuck knew the sound well enough from his previous tour of duty over the English Channel. That had ended with an unpleasant five-hour swim before he'd been picked up by a passing fishing boat. It hadn't been warm but at least it wasn't winter. It was the main reason he wasn't meant to be flying at all.

If anything, the aircraft was more troubled than the pilot. The airspeed dropped alarmingly; now the altimeter showed they were only a few hundred feet above the blustery waves below.

But that wasn't all. There was a second explosion, this one only just behind them.

'They've got the target,' shouted Bert. For some peculiar reason that Chuck couldn't understand he sounded pleased.

But whoever was shooting at them was not content just to hit the target. For the next shell, whether by accident or design, came further forward. This one hit the Hawker Henley in mid fuselage, just below its fuel tank.

This time there was an even bigger explosion as the aircraft blew into a thousand tiny pieces. Neither Chuck nor Bert would ever grace the skies of North Cornwall again.

PART ONE

PETER TRAVERS INVESTIGATES

MERRIFIELD MANOR

NOVEMBER 7th – 9th 2021

The old Merrifield Station: next stop Bude

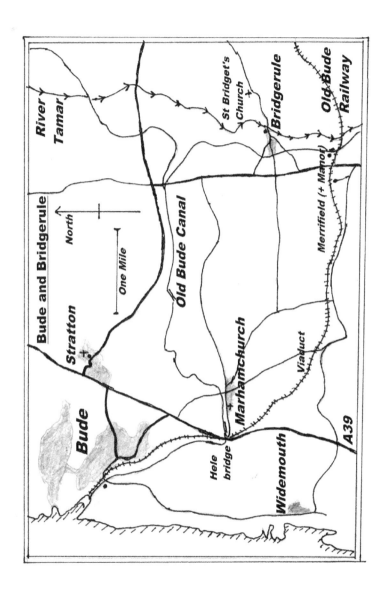

CHAPTER 1   Sunday Nov 7ᵗʰ 2021

The call came just before seven o'clock on a November Sunday morning. Peter Travers, senior policeman at Bude Police Station, took a while to respond; he was at home, in bed, enjoying what was supposed to be a day of rest. His wife beside him was still sound asleep.

Peter's first reaction was to ignore the call, hope it would go away, but it persisted. Eventually he reached out and grabbed his device.

'Inspector Peter Travers here.'

'Thank goodness,' a quavering voice responded. 'Your Station operator said they could put me through, but it's taken a while to reach you.'

'How can I help you, sir?' There were other questions he needed to ask his staff – like why on earth was he being rung at all on his day off? – but those were for later.

'My name is Wilfred – Sir Wilfred Gabriel, in fact. I'm the master of Merrifield Manor. That's five miles out of Bude, near Bridgerule.'

Travers knew Bridgerule, on the Cornwall-Devon border, though he'd not heard of Merrifield. He presumed it was one of many tiny hamlets surrounding Bude, half of which didn't even justify a road sign. 'And what's the problem, sir?'

'Well,' said the voice, 'it all started with the firework display. It normally happens at Bridgerule Primary School but this year they didn't want it because of Covid. But it's always a popular event, so after some thought I offered the use of the Manor instead.'

Travers wondered why he needed to know any of this but held back for the moment. 'Go on, sir.'

'The event seemed to go off smoothly. But afterwards there were two disturbing consequences. Firstly, because of fresh damage to an outbuilding door, I believe someone had attempted to burgle the Manor. And secondly, more seriously, the reason I'm ringing this early, my wife has disappeared.'

Travers glanced across the bed. His own wife, Maxine was still fast asleep, but it would be cruel to disturb her. They'd had plenty of disturbed nights from their baby daughter and she needed as much rest as she could manage.

Still clutching his phone, the policeman slid out of bed and moved onto the landing.

'The second of those sounds serious, sir. I'm not up yet but I can be with you in half an hour. It'd be better for us to talk face to face, I think.'

There was a relieved sigh from the other end. 'Thank you, Inspector. I'm here on my own at this moment. I promise I won't touch anything. See you soon.'

Peter and Maxine Travers lived in Poughill, just north of Bude; Bridgerule was a village to the east. As he heaved on his uniform and grabbed a sustaining banana, the policeman decided that, if this event was as serious as Sir Wilfred had suggested, it would be as well to take someone with him. The obvious candidate was his brightest police officer, newly promoted Sergeant Holly Berry, who lived not far away in Stratton.

He made a quick phone call to alert her – she had young children, so was already up – and then he was on his way.

When he got to Holly's house, ten minutes later, he found his colleague was already standing by the roadside, awaiting his arrival.

'Morning, Holly,' he began, as she climbed in. 'Sorry to muck up your day off.'

''S'all right, guv. Gives my husband a chance to spend time with the kids. So what excitement have we got today?'

'I had a call early this morning from the owner of Merrifield Manor. It's near to Bridgerule. That's where we're heading. They hosted a firework display of some sort in their grounds last night. No problem with that. But after it was all over, he found that his wife had disappeared.'

Holly pondered for a moment. There was virtually no traffic on the road to Bridgerule, but she saw that her boss wasn't hanging about. 'We don't often respond this quickly to a Missing Person report.'

'The thing is, Holly, the owner told me he also suspected they'd been burgled. It was the two items presented together that made me think his call warranted urgent attention.'

'You mean, the wife might have caught sight of the burglar or something, that made him need to get rid of her?'

Travers grinned at her enthusiasm. 'Best not to get too far ahead of ourselves, Holly. Till we know more details. But if there are complications it'll be good for us to be on the case quickly. Missing Person cases are always hard to assess when they first arise: is it a false alarm or must you respond quickly? I've known them be resolved before we've even had time to visit the person reporting. But that seems less likely this time.'

There was little more to be said and Travers concentrated on his driving. It was only fifteen minutes later that they turned down the main road from Bridgerule to Launceston and then off to the hamlet of Merrifield. The Manor, a robust-looking stone building, was up a side-track with a commanding position on a gentle hill.

'This was probably valuable property in its prime, Holly,' commented the inspector as they turned into the drive. 'But I reckon it's got a lot worse for wear in recent decades – needs a new coat of paint for a start. The man who rang me up is called Sir Wilfred, by the way.'

'Doesn't worry me who he is, as long as he's not expecting me to curtsey,' Holly replied. 'Better than a Duke or Lord, anyway.'

Sir Wilfred had seen the police car pull up outside and had the front door open to welcome them before they'd even had time to ring the doorbell. Holly saw an older man, probably in his early seventies, casually dressed but with an elder-statesman air of gravity and purpose. His most obvious feature, though, was a strong sense of anxiety.

'Thank you for coming so quickly,' he began.

'Can we go inside, sir?' asked Peter Travers. 'It's not exactly warm out here. I'm Inspector Travers and this is Sergeant Holly Berry. I take it you're Sir Wilfred?'

The man nodded. The three went inside; the two police officers were led into a spacious lounge and sat themselves at either end of a well-worn settee. Sir Wilfred took the armchair opposite.

'Right, sir,' said Travers. 'Tell us, please, exactly what happened.'

Sir Wilfred braced himself and took a deep breath.

'Usually, the local school, up the road at Bridgerule, organises the fireworks around November the fifth. It's always a popular event, most of the village turn out and there are all sorts of refreshment stalls inside the school hall, as well as the fireworks in the playground. But this year they didn't want to risk holding it. They'd been badly hit by Covid rules this time last year, you

11

see. So I offered to stage the whole thing here.'

Travers nodded but chose not to interrupt the flow.

'My wife, Daphne, agreed to take charge of the refreshments. She was a bit apprehensive, not done that sort of thing for years, but she knew the kitchen, of course, and the Bridgerule school cook – a lady called Sheila, who Daphne knows well through church – offered to work with her. I'd say the catering side of the event seemed to go well.'

Sir Wilfred paused, obviously trying to reconcile the need to be succinct against the need to cover the key details. 'I spent most of the evening outside, in the yard or the garden, keeping an eye on the kids and the fireworks. I wasn't lighting any of the things myself, of course, but the school had given me a couple of names of locals who'd done it before. I got in touch with one of them and ended up with them both – they seemed confident enough. They were big on safety, anyway.'

'What period of time are we talking about, sir?' asked Holly.

Sir Wilfred considered. 'The whole thing, including the stalls, the eats and the mulled wine, was meant to start at six o'clock and go on till nine. That's what the school usually did and was what was printed on the tickets. But it was all very re-laxed. People arrived or left at all sorts of times within that time frame. If they had young children, for example, they might not want to stay right to the end. The last firework went off about eight forty-five. After that there was lots of chattering and hus-tling about – I mean, there was still plenty of wine to be drunk.'

Sir Wilfred paused for thought then continued. 'I think it was then that I was first told that Daphne was no longer scurrying round the kitchen. But it took a while before it bothered me. There were so many people here to look after, you see. We'd opened all the downstairs rooms – and left windows open, so there was plenty of ventilation. It was good to see the place being

12

used. But I was mostly talking to guests outside till the crowd had gone and the fireworks team had started taking down their launch stands.'

Travers could see that the manor owner was starting to lose focus amongst the detail, tending towards verbal diarrhoea. 'About what time would this be, sir, before you started any search for Daphne?' If a search was needed, it was important for the police to establish some hard facts.

Sir Wilfred mused. 'Around nine thirty, I suppose. At first, I wasn't particularly bothered. I mean, wives don't go missing halfway through a social event. It took me half an hour to go quietly on my own through every room inside the Manor and check that Daphne wasn't in any of 'em. It was at that point when I started voicing concerns out loud.'

'Were there many left by this stage?' asked Holly.

'No, not many. There was my son, of course. Edward. He'd come to stay with us for the fireworks. And our farm manager, Brian. He lives in a cottage by the main gate, he was here to supervise the crowds. And Sheila was still here, she was organising the washing up in the kitchen.

'The men immediately set out to search the stables and the gardens by torch light. But they came back half an hour later. To the best of their belief Daphne wasn't to be found in either.'

'Mm. So that's around ten pm. Where are they now?'

'Well, Inspector, last night was pretty dark: heavy cloud and not much moon. We don't have much outdoor lighting, so it was hard to spot anything. The men agreed it would be better to start again at first light and search the whole estate. The River Tamar's down in the valley, you see. Daphne might just have gone down for a walk by the river or something.

'If she hadn't turned up by dawn, I said I'd phone the police and wait to deal with whoever came – and take any other calls –

inside the house.'

He glanced at his watch. 'They've been gone for an hour now, should be back soon enough.'

There was an uneasy silence. Peter Travers mentally went over the first moves in his manual on a Missing Person case. There were a few obvious steps, but these needed to be set alongside the advice "don't over-react too early", and the need not to upset Sir Wilfred any more than was strictly necessary. The owner was no spring chicken and obviously extremely worried anyway.

'Right, sir. What you've told me is rather disturbing. It's good you've called us so quickly. There might be some perfectly innocent explanation, and we'll need to consider the possibilities carefully in due course. But in the meantime, in case the search party doesn't come back with anything, I need to ask you one or two questions.

'Firstly, can you tell me what Daphne was wearing yesterday evening? And has her outdoor coat disappeared?

'Secondly, does your wife possess her own mobile phone; and if so, has she taken it with her? And for that matter, sir, have you tried to ring her?'

'And thirdly, do you have a recent photograph of Daphne that we could, if necessary, hand out to the media?'

Travers gave a sigh. 'We're going to need that, I'm afraid, if the search has to be widened.'

CHAPTER 2

After an unrelenting hour of enquiries, Peter Travers' concern had intensified. This certainly didn't look like a Missing Person case that would be resolved on its own.

With a little prompting, Sir Wilfred had produced a recent photograph of Daphne that he'd taken on his phone, walking along the cliffs above Bude. A tall, blue-eyed woman with a cheerful smile, her grey hair tied in a bun. For someone in their seventies she looked fairly fit. He had emailed copies to Travers and to Holly.

The police officers had established that Daphne had been wearing a dark blue dress, a thick cable-stitch cardigan and outdoor shoes. A quick check had shown, though, that her outdoor coat was still hanging in the manor hall.

At that point the inspector had asked if they could see the missing woman's bedroom. The room was tidy enough – no sign of hastily-emptied wardrobes or missing suitcases. This didn't look like a case of "flight". Daphne did indeed own a mobile phone: it was lying on her bedside table. The inspector seized it. In the worst case, Daphne's outgoing or incoming calls might need to be examined in forensic detail.

'I'm afraid I don't know the password,' admitted Sir Wilfred.

'Don't worry, sir. If we need it, I'll pass it on to one of our techies,' replied the inspector.

Holly was on a different track. 'What was Daphne's usual means of transport, sir?'

Sir William explained that he and his wife owned just the one car between them. 'We're both here most of the time,' he said. 'We go into Bude together for the weekly shop. It was out of sight during the firework display, of course.'

'Can we check it's still where you left it, sir?'

The three had walked round to the stable annexe behind the manor. Sir Wilfred unlocked one of the doors, revealing a ten-year old estate car in what he said was its usual position.

'And that's your only source of transport?' repeated Travers. Sir Wilfred nodded. But the whole business was making less and less sense.

'Ah. Did Daphne own a bicycle, sir?' asked Holly.

'That's a good thought,' replied Sir Wilfred. 'She didn't use it much, but she certainly had one. It speeded up her visits to Bridgerule and she even went occasionally as far as Bude.'

But Travers could see that Sir Wilfred was looking puzzled. 'Ought that to be in here too, sir?'

'Ideally. Daphne would sometimes leave her bike propped up against a manor wall – if she came back late, for example.'

'Could we have a quick look around now, sir? If her bike is really missing, that would be a clue as to how far she might have gone.'

It was as they paced around the Manor that Travers remembered Sir Wilfred had mentioned a second item of concern.

'When you first called me this morning, sir, you spoke of a suspected burglary?'

Sir Wilfred gave a bitter laugh. 'I'm afraid that's sunk right down my concerns, Inspector.'

'Even so, sir, I'd like to take a look at what you'd seen. Then I can decide whether or not to leave it for the time being.'

The owner shrugged. 'As you prefer. It's round the back here.' He led them onto the next corner. There they saw an oak door in the far corner of the wall, almost hidden by rampant ivy. As they got close, it looked to have been attacked repeatedly with something like an axe.

Travers bent down for a closer look. At least the lock on the door was still in place. 'It doesn't look as though they managed to force it open, sir. So there's no reason to think they got in. Might this have been done during the fireworks?'

Sir Wilfred nodded. 'Probably. We had several rockets with multiple big bangs towards the end. This wall would be out of sight for any audience focussed on the fireworks.'

At that point Sir Wilfred's son, Edward, and farm manager, Brian, returned from their search of the Manor estate. Travers saw that they weren't carrying anything.

'We've walked round the whole estate boundary,' stated Edward. 'That gave us the chance to look across every field in turn. Fortunately, at this time of year, there are no crops growing.'

Brian took over. 'There's just one wood on estate land. We checked the main footpath running through it. We'll go back for a more thorough check in a moment. That's unless there's anything more urgent you want us to do?'

Though he didn't say so, Travers was impressed. They shared the owner's worry over Daphne, though they were practical and level-headed in their response. The two had been together for the whole search. If they couldn't find anything then the policeman accepted that there was nothing obvious to be found.

Both men looked fit enough to tramp the countryside for hours. Edward was tall and thin, Brian older and more burly. He guessed the latter was kept fit by all his practical work on the farm.

But while they were with him, before they went back to comb

the wood, Peter Travers took the opportunity to interview these fresh witnesses of the fireworks.

'If Daphne can't be found on the estate, gentlemen, is one possible explanation that she slipped out toward the end of the evening with one of the guests?' the policeman suggested. He turned to Sir Wilfred. 'Did you have anyone guarding the entrance to the firework party, that might have seen her leave?'

To his surprise, Edward was the one to answer. 'I can answer that, Inspector. Yes, I was the one on duty. At the entrance to the driveway. I was there from six o'clock onwards. Most of the guests already had tickets – they'd been on sale in the Bridgerule Post Office and the local pub, the Bridge Inn, for a couple of weeks – but I also had tickets on sale at the gate.'

'Did you recognise everyone that you let in?'

'I don't live here much of the time, Inspector. The villagers were well wrapped up. And there's not much light down there. I half-recognised most of those that already had tickets, though I'd be pushed to give you their names.'

'That doesn't matter,' interjected Sir Wilfred. 'The post office and the pub were both asked to keep a note of all who bought tickets. They could give you a list of names if you wanted.'

Travers turned back to the son. 'But what about the tickets sold at the gate? Were there many?'

Edward considered. 'Probably not more than a dozen. But I didn't know any of them.'

'Could anyone else have slipped past you while you were selling tickets?' asked Holly.

'Oh, I wasn't doing it all on my own,' replied Edward. 'I had a friend helping me. She sold a few tickets as well. Between us, I don't reckon we missed anyone at all.'

'And did you get their names?'

Looking crestfallen, Edward shook his head. 'No-one asked me to do that. We just collected their money. The prime aim was to cover the cost of the fireworks, you see. They were quite expensive.'

Travers tried again: 'But most importantly, sir, did you see your mother leave the estate? She might have been on her bicycle.'

Edward shook his head again. 'She certainly didn't come out early on. To be honest, we didn't stand at the gate all night. By half past seven it seemed there were no more new arrivals, ticketed or otherwise. Besides, I wanted my friend to see the fireworks – and to have her glass of mulled wine. I mean, our key task had been to watch for new arrivals. We'd no reason to worry about leavers at that point.'

'That seems clear enough, sir,' conceded Travers. 'But could you give me the name and address of your friend? It would be good to have her account of the evening as well. She might give us some names.'

'I'm afraid she's not local, Inspector. I doubt she'll be able to give you any names at all.' He paused. 'Actually, she's someone I only met recently. She lives down near Tintagel. I don't have her exact address, but I can give you her phone number.' He smiled. 'Her name is George.'

Peter Travers knew one George who lived down towards Tintagel but decided that for the moment Edward's "friend" wasn't a priority.

He addressed the assembled household. 'Given what we know at the moment, gentlemen, the most likely outcome seems to be that Daphne walked out of the estate sometime after half past seven, maybe pushing her bicycle. But it could have been entirely innocent. Maybe she met a friend from the village who offered to show her something of mutual interest and the two left together?'

He turned to Edward. 'Before we cast the net too wide, I'd like you and Brian to go and search that wood carefully, please. Daphne was last seen wearing a blue dress and we've checked: her coat is still in the manor. So if she's tripped and fallen under a bush or something, she should be fairly easy to spot - though she'll be very cold.'

Then he turned to the owner.

'Sir Wilfred, you were outside with the onlookers most of the evening. I'd like you to make a list of everyone you can re-member who was here last night. And a second list of any rela-tives or close friends that Daphne might conceivably have gone to stay with. After that, I'd like you to get on the phone and contact all those on the second list: check if she's there.'

'Meantime, Holly, can you take the car and visit the post of-fice and the pub in Bridgerule, obtain their lists of ticket-buyers. Bring them back here; we can check the names against those that Sir Wilfred has given us. It might not be a complete list of attendees at the fireworks, but it'll give us most of 'em.

'Then I need you to go and find Daphne's friend - Sheila, I think you said. Get her account of the evening and find out when she last saw Sir Wilfred's wife. We need to get her disappear-ance time as tight as possible.'

'What will you do, guv?'

'For a start, I'll get onto Bude police station. Tell them what we're doing and get someone to do all the usual checks for a missing person - contact local hospitals and so on. Then I'll need a couple more here, to help us do visits in Bridgerule.'

The inspector didn't say so, but he feared this was starting to look like a major incident.

20

CHAPTER 3   Monday Oct 25th

Edward had first met his new friend George on a London train from Exeter, two weeks earlier. It had happened like this.

George Gilbert, industrial mathematician and occasional amateur sleuth, was not usually late for her train to London from Exeter station. But there had been an accident on the A30 which had halted eastward traffic for half an hour, after which the vehicles ahead of her were bunched up and incredibly slow-moving.

George had dumped her car in the long-stay car park and ran into the station as her train drew in. It, too, was late; the guard was hustling passengers on board at speed. Purely because she grabbed the nearest door and jumped aboard, George found herself in a first-class carriage. She didn't normally travel first class, but it wasn't the end of the world. She shrugged; was this her chance to catch up on reading, without the distracting sound of small children clamouring to be fed?

The train started to inch forward, and George glanced around. The first-class carriage was far less crowded, anyway. She grabbed the nearest empty seat, slipped off her rucksack, plonked it on the seat beside her and started to relax.

Opposite her was a slim, confident-looking man. His attention had been caught by her slim figure and dark, curly hair, but he couldn't help smiling at her discomfiture. 'I don't like waiting ages for trains either, but I don't normally cut it that fine,' he observed.

'Traffic accident on the A30,' she replied. 'That lost me half an hour. I come this way regularly. I don't usually cut it this fine either.'

'Was the accident somewhere near Launceston?'

'That's right.' George guessed he was another motorist. 'I presume you didn't drive in that way?'

'I've come from Bude, so I cut straight across to Okehampton. I was delighted to see my bit of the A30 was completely clear. Now I understand why.'

George had intended to read but the man had sparkling grey eyes and seemed to take delight in the twists and turns of life's rich tapestry. It was a decade since she had lost her husband. Perhaps the reading could wait.

There was a few minutes' silence as the train picked up speed and George settled herself, recovering her composure. But she was a sociable woman, not used to keeping silent when there was someone to talk to.

'I'm heading all the way to London,' she said. 'I'm glad I made it. The is the fastest train of the morning: it's not one to miss.'

'I know,' replied the man. 'I've been doing this same journey quite a lot recently. Mind, I don't have much choice right now.' It seemed a flicker of sadness crossed his face.

George wondered to herself what sort of problem might require so much travelling. She was too polite to ask but would be happy to listen if the man chose to say more.

'I need to meet my lawyer again, you see,' he added.

George was surprised. 'Aren't there any good lawyers in Bude? Or at least Exeter?'

He nodded. 'There probably are, I haven't looked. But I had a good one when I was working in London, so that's where I started. I didn't realise I'd need to see him this often.'

There was silence for a moment. George glanced at the autumnal Devon countryside as it sped past them. This was a beautiful time of the year in these parts.

'Trains are by no means cheap,' she commented, 'but it's more relaxing than driving on your own. I'm on a visit to check up on my house in London. I let it out to post-graduate students. Nowadays I spend most of my time down near Tintagel. But my work is spread around Cornwall. At least that's quieter than London.'

'I can imagine. What kind of things d'you do?'

George smiled. 'It's hard to pin down, I've developed quite a repertoire. Basically I try to solve people's problems. Usually when there's a mathematical or statistical element – or at least it's complicated enough to require hard thought. Sometimes I develop a computer model. For example, I've spent much of the last year working for the Director for Public Health for Cornwall, helping her to design and analyse surveys.'

Her listener looked a little surprised. 'Wow. I'd have thought all that sort of thing was done at national level.'

'A lot is, of course. But Cornwall has special problems. For a start, because of the tourists, in normal years the summer population is twice that in the winter. That gives some awkward decisions for the Council. My team's role has been to gather hard data, to help them with rational decision-making.'

The man laughed. 'Well, I'm glad there's some logic in the process. It's not always obvious, I must say. Are all the problems you tackle large scale ones?'

She nodded. 'Mostly. Though for my own sanity I try to keep a variety of projects on the go. Sometimes the smaller ones are the most interesting.'

George judged that if the man wanted to say anything about

his own problems, she'd given him an opening. She paused for any reaction.

Her companion seemed to be weighing options. Then he spoke.

'If you're willing to listen, I'll sketch out what forces me to keep repeating this wretched journey. See if anything overlaps with your expertise or your skill set. My name's Edward, by the way.'

'And I'm George. London's two hours away. If you want to share, Edward, I'm very happy to listen.'

'I presume, George, that you're familiar with Bude?'

'I know it well enough. One of my projects started there, a few years back. To do with the man who invented the steam-powered motor car.'

'Good. Even so, I doubt you'll know where I'm from. It's called Merrifield Manor – over by Bridgerule. Five miles east of Bude.'

George frowned. 'Mm. Should I have heard of it?'

'Don't think so. It's fairly small, not National Trust or anything. Not yet, anyway. But the estate is quite big. That's part of the problem.'

George looked at Edward more carefully now. His well-trimmed, dark beard made it hard to be sure, but he couldn't be more than fifty. He might have parents in their eighties – if they were still alive. Maybe there was some issue with handing on the property?

'Is this something to do with inheritance tax, Edward?'

He looked surprised. 'My, George, you're quick. That's part of the problem, certainly. But by no means everything.'

'Please, go on. I'll try to stay silent, I promise.'

Edward was quiet for a couple of moments, weighing up how

best to tell the part of his story that he was willing to share.

'My family have lived in Merrifield Manor for over six hundred years. No doubt there were fiddles of one sort or another that helped them hang on to it down the centuries, but they must also have been good at assessing which way the wind was blowing; and who to stay on good terms with. That couldn't be easy, for example, during the Civil War.'

George smiled and nodded but did not speak.

'One reason it survived, I suppose, is that it's a manor rather than a mansion. No battlements or anything, and well off the beaten track. It's a pick and mix design, every generation added something or other – one a moat, another a wing, a third a new kitchen. Rooms for troops during the war. Always driven by pragmatism, not fashion. My ancestors were farmers rather than adventurers. They didn't want to etch their names on the public mind.'

Edward paused to make sure George was following him. She nodded again; this was intriguing.

'It was the last century when things fell apart. Governments had tried to collect some form of wealth tax ever since the seventeenth century: there were always wars to be financed and empires to be won. But they left umpteen loopholes and my ancestors were good at wriggling. Prime Minister Gladstone tightened things up, but the charge rate was still modest. In the late 1800s the estate was a valuable employer in the neighbourhood.'

He sighed. 'It was Attlee's post-war Labour Government that saw wealth tax as a way of "levelling up" and removed many of the loopholes. Denis Healey did more in the 1970s. Finally, Nigel Lawson streamlined it into Inheritance Tax - the rate on that's now 40%. On my Manor, with land worth millions, that's going to be crippling when my father dies – there's not that much in the kitty. He's healthy enough right now, but that won't always be the case.

He paused to allow some sort of response.

'I don't want to sound unsympathetic, Edward, but shouldn't he have consulted his lawyers earlier?' asked George. 'I'm no tax expert, but what you're saying is hardly a big surprise.'

'Trouble is, my father's not the most forward-thinking man on the planet. I'd often try to talk to him about it, but he just wouldn't listen – stuck his head in the sand. I wasn't there much of the time anyway, I had a job in London.' He shook his head. 'I suppose, looking back, that was another form of escapism.'

There was silence for a moment, then George ventured a question. 'Do you have brothers or sisters to share this with?'

Edward shook his head. 'I was an only child. My father had a sister and I've a couple of cousins, but they all emigrated to Australia years ago. I sometimes wish I could join them.'

Edward stopped talking. He seemed to have run out of steam. But George didn't think he'd shared everything. She gave a coaxing smile, encouraged him to keep going.

'Let's leave the tax details to the lawyers, Edward. You said earlier that inheritance tax was only part of your difficulties – though it sounds tough enough. Is anything else bothering you?'

Edward gave himself a shake. Like the chair of BBC's Mastermind, he'd started so he'd finish. Perhaps this chance encounter with a friendly woman was a last offer from providence. She was easy to talk to, anyway.

He glanced down the carriage. It was first class; all the occupants looked peaceable. And the seat behind him was unoccupied: he wouldn't be overheard. There was no excuse for clamming up.

'I don't want to go into detail,' he began. 'Not here, anyway. But I have other financial difficulties. In summary, before Covid came along, I owned a small publishing house in Holborn. It was aimed at minority academics with controversial views. It never made huge profits, but it kept me afloat. But all these lockdowns we've seen over the past two years haven't helped my business at all.'

'You mean, no-one wanted your style of publishing anymore?'

Edward sighed. 'More that my market drained away. Or at least, those who used to publish with me no longer itch to do so.'

George pondered for a while. 'Covid has had all sorts of effects on society. For one thing, far more people will work from home in future. That might make them keener to critique online, rather than through published media.'

Edward nodded. 'That's what my fellow publishers think – they're struggling too. But none of us can turn back the clock, can we?'

George smiled. 'I don't think so. But what we can do, perhaps, is to try harder to think ourselves into the future.'

'What on earth do you mean?'

So a second phase of conversation began.

The train had passed non-stop through Taunton and was racing through Wiltshire. Conversation was helping the journey pass speedily. As Edward slipped to the toilet, George extracted her coffee flask and had a drink. She also took out her notebook and turned to a fresh page. As soon as Edward returned they could begin.

'Forget about inheritance tax and publishing for a while, Edward, we'll let our imaginations flow. Never mind the problems, your dad's stubbornness and all the rest: we'll give the left side of our brains the reins. The sky's the limit. So what might be done with your Manor house as a fund-raiser, or a source of extra income?'

Was Edward stuck in the same rut as his father, or open to fresh thought? She saw the faint glimmer of a smile. Promising enough, anyway.

'One possibility that I've mused on occasionally in my sleepless nights,' said Edward, after a short pause, 'would be to turn the Manor into a hotel, or some sort of bed and breakfast outfit.'

George scribbled the ideas down. 'We're not going to discuss anything yet,' she explained. 'I want a list that's as long as possible. Right. What's next?'

Edward frowned. 'Isn't it your turn, George?'

George grinned. 'I'll put something down shortly. Remember, I've never seen your Manor or its surroundings. One or two more ideas from you will help me focus – and maybe provoke a response.'

There was a thoughtful silence. Two brains harnessed to the same task. Then Edward spoke again.

'The Manor has an interesting hillside kitchen garden, facing west. With sections constructed in different eras, from early Tudors through to the Victorians. It might be a place of historic interest – perhaps a North Cornwall version of Trelissick?'

'That sounds possible.' George scribbled the idea in her notebook, then glanced at her companion. 'Any other distinctive aspects of the Manor that you can think of?'

'Mm.' Edward was thinking harder now, mentally pacing his home and land. The trouble, thought George, was that it was all far too familiar. It needed fresh eyes.

Then something came. 'There's the remains of the old railway.'

The comment caught George by surprise. She knew about the North Cornwall Railway that once ran through Camelford and Delabole, then down to Padstow. But this was obviously different. 'Which railway?'

'The line to Bude from Okehampton. Built in the 1880s, I think, and closed in the 1960s. I'm too young to have seen it running, of course, but my father used to talk about it a lot. It came via Holsworthy.'

He paused as he recalled his father's enthusiasm. 'They've taken up all the track now, but you can still see various embankments and cuttings where the line used to run. Actually,' he gushed, 'part of it went over our estate.'

'Wow.' George thought for a moment. 'Are there any traces of machinery left to exhibit? Or signal boxes? What happened to the engines and the rest of the rolling stock?'

Edward shook his head. 'There's nothing like that, George. I guess any working items would be taken back for use by British Rail, or whatever they were called. Why are you asking?'

'Well, I was just wondering if there was space for a railway museum at your Manor. There's nothing like that in Bude, I don't even know where the old station was. But there's still plenty of interest in old railways among the general public.'

George hastened to write the idea down. The exercise was proving more productive than she had expected.

The thought experiment continued for some time. Edward and George were of similar age and interacted well together. They sparked various ideas off one another, both enjoying the process.

Time flew by. Suddenly Edward realised that they were passing through Reading and would be at Paddington in twenty minutes.

'Hey, George, this is a disaster. We won't finish this before the journey's over.'

29

George giggled. 'We're not even halfway through the brainstorming. We've still got to take each of these ideas, make them specific, then analyse them further. Some of them will just be pipe dreams. We need to distinguish those from the real possibilities.'

Edward pursed his lips. 'The trouble is, I'm in London for the next few days. But I was really enjoying the exercise. Maybe I'm too much of an optimist, but it was starting to give me hope that all may not be lost.' He looked at her imploringly. 'Is there any chance we could meet again to complete this, when I get back to Bude?'

'I'll be back in Tintagel tonight. I'm more or less between projects right now, so I'll be there for the rest of this week. I'd be happy to tidy up our ideas, give us something to take a bit further if you wanted.'

'I'd invite you to the Manor, George. Trouble is, my parents would cross-examine me afterwards. I'd prefer to meet for a meal in Bude. Say Friday evening at the Falcon Hotel. That's beside the Bude Canal. At my expense, of course.'

'I'd be happy to come over to Bude for a meal. But given what's happened to your publishing business, you're certainly not going to pay the whole cost. I insist on splitting the bill.'

The details of a further meeting were agreed and phone numbers exchanged. Two contented passengers emerged from the train a few minutes later. It looked like the start of a productive friendship.

CHAPTER 4   Thursday Oct 28th

It was Monday mid-evening by the time George Gilbert arrived back home. She was far too tired to give Edward Gabriel's Manor any more thought. But their free-ranging conversation around Bude made her realise, with a pang of guilt, that it was a while since she had seen her old college friend, Maxine Travers.

Maxine lived in Bude, was married to a policeman. Worst of all, George had been so busy with her own project work during lockdown that she'd hardly had time to build a relationship with Maxine's one year old baby girl, Rosanna.

An apologetic phone call was called for. After a little grovelling she was forgiven; Maxine had been busy too. Half an hour later George had managed to wangle an invitation to afternoon tea on the coming Thursday. Convenient; she would go over to Bude for the day and find out what was going on in the town.

Offering Edward thoughts on what to do with his Manor was never going to be a major project, but she could at least aim to be as informed as possible.

Thursday was another cold-but-fine autumn day. George was in a cheerful mood as she drove up the "Atlantic Highway", as the A39 was now styled. As she came over the hill at Box's Shop, the coast stretched out ahead, a mile or two over to the west. The white buildings of Bude were four miles on and the assorted satellite dishes of Cleave Camp a few miles beyond that. The whole scene was striking in its autumn colours.

There must be something distinctive that Edward's Manor

could offer tourists who came this way – if he was minded to pursue it.

First stop was the Bude Visitor Centre. In summer this was thronged with tourists but today was quiet. Soon George had the ear of an attentive, bespectacled, young woman at the far end of the counter. Her label said she was called Annie.

George gave her a smile. 'Good morning, Annie. I'm on a local history hunt. Can you tell me about the railway that used to terminate here?'

The woman smiled back and shook her head. 'I'm afraid that was long before my time.'

'Actually, that doesn't surprise me,' said George. 'But do you have any leaflets about it? Or a museum where I could learn more?'

It was soon clear from Annie's replies that the old railway was not a Bude highlight. Crooklets beach and harbour, and the surrounding rugged cliffs, were of far greater interest. Disappointing in one way, but it might leave possibilities for Edward.

'What else is there around here of historic interest?'

'There's the Limelight Museum,' said Annie. 'Inside the old castle. That's got all sorts of odds and ends. A whole section about the local geology. And a café that overlooks the seafront. It doesn't even charge for entry.'

George smiled. 'I know something about that. I once had a project based there. That was to do with Goldsworthy Gurney. You know –'

'He's the man who invented the steam-driven motor car?'

'That's right. Trouble was, it was just the time the railways were starting up. To be honest, he didn't have a chance. But Gurney was an inventor: he also developed limelight. That was big in the nineteenth century. Gurney's devices and mirrors lit the Houses of Parliament for half a century.'

'At least till they discovered electricity?'

George was pleased that Annie used the word "discover" rather than "invent". But she wasn't making much headway on other ideas for Edward. 'Can you tell me, is there anything else that Bude is famous for?'

The guide mused for a moment. 'There's the Bude Canal, of course. That's even older than the railway. You can still see the lowest reach, just beyond the car park. A few years back the Council strengthened the gates on the sea lock. Those are a rare sight, I believe. You can hire a rowing boat and row up it for a mile or two if you want. Or even walk the towpath.'

George wrinkled her nose. 'It's cold for rowing at this time of year. Do you have any leaflets on it?' she asked. 'How far does it go?'

Annie found a short leaflet and glanced at it before handing it over. 'I'm afraid that these days it's only a real canal for the first couple of miles – up as far as Helebridge.'

'And there are no museum for the canal, either?'

Annie shook her head. 'Sorry. Mind, we're hoping for more visitors next year. Maybe that'll encourage someone to be more proactive.'

It took George a second to pick up the clue. 'Why more visitors, Annie?'

'Haven't you heard? They're re-opening the railway line from Exeter to Okehampton. By December, all being well, there'll be a regular two hourly service to and from Exeter.'

This was new information. It would increase her options for reaching Exeter. 'But why should that give Bude more visitors?'

'They are also planning express buses from Okehampton to Bude. Linked to the trains, I presume. It won't help travellers coming by road, but it'll make the town more accessible to everyone else.'

'Well, thank you, Annie. That's useful. Right. I'd be happy to spend time with anyone you can recommend, on the old railway, or the even older canal. Who would you suggest?'

Annie thought for a moment. 'You could always try the Post Office, just across the road. The postmaster's lived in Bude all his life. He'd be good for a chat, anyway.'

George hesitated but Annie's commendation gave her hope. At worst she'd just be sent on her way.

The name read "Crescent Post Office: established 1936". The post office counter was at the far end; the shop also sold many other items, including home-made cakes. She'd buy one for Maxine.

A few minutes later George was heading the queue. A cheerful, middle-aged man was serving behind the counter. He had neatly combed white hair, a small beard and rimless glasses.

'Good morning,' George began. 'I don't want to buy anything but the Visitor Centre suggested you might be able to help me.'

The man smiled. 'I'll do my best. But you can see the queue. Tell you what, it's my lunch hour in forty minutes. If you came back then, we could maybe have lunch together.'

'That'd be wonderful. My name is George, by the way. George Gilbert. Right, I'll be back by 12:15.'

George used the gap to check on nearby cafés where they might lunch. The nearest one, facing onto the Canal, was the Olive Tree. Once she'd found this, she jotted down a few ideas.

Before long it was time to collect her mentor. The postmaster was happy to lunch at the Olive Tree. Introductions were made as they walked round there; he was called Mike.

'I thought I knew Bude fairly well,' George began, as they grabbed seats in the bay window. 'But I seem to know very little of its history. I'm woefully ignorant about the old railway here, and even more clueless on the Canal. Could you help me on either of these – or suggest where else I might go?'

The waitress came at that point and took their orders. That gave Mike a moment to assemble his thoughts.

'Let's take the railway first,' he began. 'I'm old enough to remember it, though I never had cause to use it. It was a single-track line, came in from Holsworthy, the station was on the Kingshill Road. You could see the trains arriving from what was then my dad's Post Office. The best views were from upstairs.'

'Were there many trains?' asked George.

'Not a lot. Even in high season there were only half a dozen a day. From a small boy's point of view, the great joy was that they used steam engines right to the end. When he had time, my dad would take me to the station and we'd watch 'em coming in. They were majestic, you know, with the steam and smoke and the pounding pistons. Made you feel you were in the presence of something significant.'

George had brought the Bude Explorer map with her and a pair of highlighter pens. 'Could you mark where the line went?'

This took a while. Their lunch arrived as he tussled away, but he was obviously used to eating and thinking at the same time. Eventually a dotted orange line was plotted, leading from Bude to Holsworthy.

'Are you hoping to create another cycle trail?' he asked. 'Looks like there's plenty of the old route still visible.'

'Well, I did think I'd drive around it, see how much looked passable. But that'd be a massive project. I'd be happy to support it, but it'd need local backing. Of course, the new railway link to Okehampton might give it more appeal.'

'Only if the cycle trail reached Okehampton, I'd say. And that's a long way. But there might be other modes of transport that could run on a public bridleway.'

There was silence as the pair finished their toasted sandwiches. 'How long's your lunch hour? Time for a dessert?' asked George.

'You're wanting to quiz me on the Canal.' Mike replied. But he spoke with a grin. 'That was all well before my time: it won't take long.'

Chocolate brownies were ordered and the conversation resumed.

'I'll give you the edited highlights,' said the Postmaster. 'But the real expert on this is a friend of mine, James Gibbon.' He gave George the man's details; he was also a Bude citizen.

'The Canal was devised in the late eighteenth century,' Mike told her. 'The idea was to link Bude to the River Tamar, so boats could pass from Plymouth to the Bristol Channel without going round the whole coastline. It never achieved that. But by the 1820s it reached Launceston, and up to the Tamar Lakes. Then came the railways: the Canal could never really compete. It battled on delivering sand to farms, then it had to close.'

Mike took a bite from his brownie. He'd said all he knew.

'I don't suppose you could mark the line of the Canal for me,' asked George, unfolding her map once more.

The postmaster studied the map for a few moments. 'There are far fewer signs of the Canal. James might be able to do it,' he replied. 'There were at least two branches. Goodness knows where they met.'

George felt she'd made some progress, anyway. She'd have something to share with Edward. She had no idea that, soon, something far more challenging would take all their attention.

CHAPTER 5   Sunday Nov 7th

It was ten thirty at Merrifield Manor before Edward and Brian returned from their detailed search of the estate wood. But they had no good news. No trace had been found of the missing woman.

By now Inspector Travers had set various initiatives going at the Bude police station which would take some time to complete. In the meantime, he decided, he would conduct more searching interviews with the various members of the household now present.

'Right, sir,' he addressed the owner. 'Before this case goes any wider, I'd like to interview everyone who might be able to help us and to record their answers. Is there a room we can borrow for the purpose? And is there any chance of coffee, please?'

There was no shortage of rooms. Soon Travers and Sergeant Berry were sitting in a plush, panelled dining hall with their backs to the wall and a polished table before them. 'I'll call you in one at a time, when we're ready,' he announced.

Once they were alone, Peter Travers turned to his colleague. 'At this stage, Holly, I'm assuming Daphne's disappearance is legitimate. Of her own will. Maybe with encouragement from someone she met at the fireworks. We need as complete an account as we can of the main events here last night. But if her flit's genuine, we need to explore reasons why it might have happened. That may force us to push witnesses further than they want to go.'

37

'Am I here mainly to take notes, guv?'

'I'd like you to do that as we go, please. Straight onto your laptop if possible. But please feel free to add extra questions if you think I'm missing something. We'll have to play some of this by ear.'

A few minutes later the policeman called in Sir Wilfred to begin the process. He sat on an easy chair facing them, looking a little nervous.

'Sir Wilfred, so far you've told us you were mainly monitoring events outside, while your wife was supervising refreshments indoors. You first suspected she'd gone missing – at least from her role in the kitchen – by half past nine. But it took you half an hour to check the Manor, room by room, to be sure. At that point you asked the remaining guests for help. Edward and Brian set out to explore the garden by torchlight, but without finding anything of value. Have we got all that correct, sir? Is there anything you'd like to add?'

Now that the interview was underway, Sir Wilfred started to relax. 'I'd say that's a good summary, Inspector.'

'Right. At this point I'm assuming that, for some reason or other, Daphne decided to leave of her own free will. I'd like to find out if there's any reason why she might have decided to do so. Have you any ideas? Any ideas at all?'

The interviewee started to look stressed again. He didn't seem to have expected this line of questioning, though it was hardly a surprise.

'I'm not quite sure what you're after, Inspector.'

'For example, sir, how have relations between you and your wife been recently? Have there been any rows? Or ongoing disagreements?'

Sir Wilfred started to look uncomfortable. 'Inspector, my wife and I get on perfectly well, practically all the time. Like any couple, we've had the occasional difference – for example, she would moan about me coming into the kitchen from the garden with muddy boots – but there was nothing going on between us to make her leave home.'

Travers gave a nod. 'That's reassuring, sir. But was there any other reason why she might leave? For instance, had she any ambitions to go travelling? Were there any special places that she was hoping to see? Or relatives that she was pining to catch up with?'

At this point Holly intervened. 'For example, sir, we've all been messed up by Covid. Right now much of the world is more or less out of reach. Did Daphne ever speak of frustration at the places she'd like to visit but couldn't?'

Sir Wilfred mused for a few minutes.

'Daphne had occasional flights of fancy, I guess. Like most women who haven't travelled that often. But I never thought they were remotely serious. For example, she sometimes talked about visiting my sister, Alicia, in Australia. We went out there to sidestep the Brexit referendum and she revelled in it – the warm beaches and coral reefs and all the rest of it. But she would never go back on her own. For a start, I doubt she'd have the confidence to cope with the ins and outs of air travel. It's even worse now you know, with all the complications of Covid.'

'D'you know where she keeps her passport, sir?' asked Holly. Sir Wilfred nodded. 'Well, when we've finished, would you mind going to check it's still there? It would be a relief to all of us to know she's not got it with her.'

'I'm sorry to be so intrusive, sir,' added Travers. He could see Sir Wilfred was looking irritated. 'Our only goal is to narrow the places we need to look. One other reason why she might have gone off, I suppose, is if she had any issues relating to health?'

Sir Wilfred gave a clipped laugh. 'Daphne wasn't much older than me, Inspector, but she was a lot fitter. She often went for long walks on the cliffs. She knew this part of the coast very well.'

'How about her mental health?' asked Holly.

'Ah. Well, she had the occasional wobble. Forgot what she'd come in the room for, or the name of an old friend. As I've done myself. We would laugh about it. "First sign of old age," we would tell one another. But it wasn't serious enough to bother the doctor – he's too busy to see people at present, anyway.'

Travers nodded. There was nothing in what he was being told that sounded like a good reason for Daphne to run off. Not on her own, anyway.

'Can I just ask, sir. Have there been any incidents where Daphne has disappeared before? Even just for a short while?'

Sir Wilfred paused and frowned. 'I don't think so. From time to time, I recall, when we were working in the garden, Daphne would say she was heading off to another corner after some obscure plant. Then she'd be gone for ages. But that's different, isn't it?'

There was silence for a moment.

'Would you say you two were close, sir?' asked Holly.

'Close enough, I'd say. My favourite activity is doing the gardening around the Manor here, she spent more time with friends in Bridgerule. She was in the church choir, for instance. Also a bellringer. But she won't be in church this morning.'

A few minutes later, without any strong revelations emerging, the interview came to an end.

'I'll try and get us another coffee,' said Travers, as he went out to call in Edward. A few minutes later he returned with mugs in both hands and the owner's son behind him. The next interview could begin.

'Right sir,' began the policeman. 'What we're doing this morning is to assume that for some reason or another, possibly along with a friend, your mother chose to go missing. We can't rule that out, anyway. It might emerge from one of your guests when we talk to them later. But if so, we want to know why. That's a question that we can best hope to answer from her close friends and family.'

Edward nodded. The questions might be painful; but it was a necessary part of the search process.

'Were you and your mother very close?' began Travers.

'I thought we might get into this at some point,' replied Edward. 'I suppose the honest answer is "not particularly"'.

'Could you elaborate?'

Edward reflected for a few seconds. 'Well, I always felt a bond with my father, though there were plenty of things we disagreed about. What he expected to happen to the Manor after he died, for example. But with mother I always had a sense that she was holding back.'

'D'you mean, she had a mystery background of some sort, sir?' asked Holly.

'Well, she wouldn't talk about her origins or her family. Not to me, anyway. Our conversations were always perfectly civil, but I'd say they were generally shallow. She didn't share much of her past; equally, though, she didn't delve much into my present.'

'Had she met your friend – the lady who helped you sell tickets?'

'George? Good heavens, no. We only met a fortnight ago. Thrown together on the London train from Exeter.' Edward smiled. 'I wouldn't rush to bring any new friend of mine to meet my mother. She'd have all sorts of expectations, things no

41

modern woman could ever hope to satisfy – or would even want to.'

'So what happened to George, once the fireworks were over?' asked Travers.

'She got into her car – it was parked outside – then drove back to Tintagel. She won't yet be aware that my mother has gone missing. I'll ring to tell her later on, of course. Right now I need to support my father.'

There was a pause. Travers glanced at his interview notes.

'How would you describe your mother, Edward? In character, I mean.'

Her son mused for a moment. 'She seemed quiet. But I would say that under the surface she was a strong woman. She'd push for things she wanted, anyway. And if something got in the way, she would push even harder to work round it.'

'So from that point of view, sir, she might have decided to slip away from home – if it related to something she really cared about?'

Edward nodded, reluctantly. 'Yes. But it would need to be something very unusual for her to take that drastic a step. And I for one have no idea at all what that something might be.'

CHAPTER 6

Once the household interviews were over, including the estate foreman, Peter Travers itched to move off site for lunch. His absence might also make Sir Wilfred feel less nervous.

By now it was approaching midday and, after his paltry breakfast banana, he was in need of a substantial lunch.

'Come on Holly, let's try the local pub. If we get there as soon as it opens, we should find a quiet corner to talk things over.'

The Bridge Inn was just opening as they drove into the car park.

'Good morning, sir,' said the inspector to the landlord, once they'd put on their masks and headed inside, 'are you serving Sunday lunch today? And if so, have you a quiet corner we could eat in? We're looking into the disappearance of Daphne Gabriel.'

'Ought we to have told him our business?' asked Holly, once they'd been shown to a small table in a side alcove.

'I wouldn't have dreamed of it, Holly, if we were investigating a clear-cut crime. Right now we need all the local support we can get. He's probably heard about it, anyway.'

'Actually, I spoke to his wife when I came in earlier to collect the ticket list. So, assuming they talk to one another, he must have. Right, guv. What sort of roast d'you fancy?'

A few minutes passed while they studied their menus, ready to place orders. Then Travers moved on to the case under investigation. 'Let's give this some thought, Holly. Without needing to worry about Sir Wilfred's feelings. What scenarios should we consider?'

Holly pondered for a moment. 'The only case we've given any time to so far is the "Innocent Disappearance, for reasons unknown". The trouble is, we have no idea what issue Daphne might have been seized by.'

'Right. That's one idea. But the only hint we've had on it is Edward's impression that there was something odd about his mother's distant past. But even if there was, why on earth should she start worrying about it now?'

'There's something else, guv. What would be so secret about it that she slipped away; wouldn't even share it with her husband? We had no hint of any trouble between them, did we?'

At this point their order arrived and they took a while to make sure they had all the sauces needed. Two halves of Healey's cyder also appeared. The inspector had ordered roast beef and his colleague roast lamb with mint sauce. Once the meal was properly under way, discussion could resume.

'One variant of Innocent Disappearance, Holly, would be if Daphne was trying to escape from the Manor. In that case, running off in the middle of a crowded firework party might make some sense. Mind, she would need help with transport.'

'But she'd only need to do that if Sir Wilfred was an outrageous bully. Or a control freak. We saw no signs of that today.'

'In any case, he told us she went for those long walks on the cliffs on her own. It would have been much easier for her to slip away on one of those.'

'And if she went, she would be sure to take her phone with her. She'd need that to set up a fresh life elsewhere.' Holly shook her head. 'No. I'm afraid "Escape from the Manor" is even less likely than "Innocent Disappearance".'

There was a pause while they each started their lunches.

'Let's leave Innocent Disappearance and its variant for now, Holly. What other options can we devise?'

The sergeant speared a roast potato hungrily as she considered. 'Could we be facing an abduction?'

'The couple seem wealthy enough,' responded Travers, taking a mouthful of beef. 'That's assuming they own the whole farm estate and haven't already used it to back a previous loan. We'd better check. If he had to, I'd say Sir Wilfred could surely raise the money needed to meet a ransom demand.'

'But guv, wouldn't the mechanics of an abduction, in the middle of a village fireworks party, be very difficult? I mean, they could hardly grab Daphne in the middle of the crowd. Once she started screaming, people would notice. It would be a major disturbance.'

Holly paused to consider the alternatives. 'No. They'd need to lure her somewhere quiet and then silence her – I dunno, perhaps round the back, next to the stables. Then load her into a car to drive off in. Which might easily be spotted, as it went down the drive. It's not so easy.'

Travers shook his head. He had a more strategic objection. 'If someone wanted to kidnap Daphne, it would be much easier, surely, to seize her on one of her cliff walks.'

'Yes. But that would need someone in the household to warn the kidnapper that she was out for the day – and to say which bit of the cliffs she was exploring. Alright, what other options do we have?'

There was silence as the two tucked into their roast lunches. 'The residents of Bridgerule do very well if they eat here. This meal is good. I wonder if Sir Wilfred comes here often?'

They'd finished their main courses before the conversation resumed.

'I've got one more idea, Holly. It's pretty outlandish, but I'll say it anyway, then you can dismiss it.'

Holly smiled. 'Go on, guv. We're not exactly awash with likely ideas so far.'

'Well. Suppose this whole disappearance is some sort of inside job?'

Holly looked puzzled. 'Whatever d'you mean?'

'D'you remember, when we first drove into the Manor, I observed it looked a bit run down. Well, suppose it's worse than that: maybe the Gabriels are losing money hand over fist. Perhaps practically bankrupt. So, in desperation, they need a scheme to change that.'

'Like what?'

Travers paused to put his thoughts in order.

'Well, how about if Daphne hasn't disappeared at all. She's just hidden away somewhere in that rambling manor. Next Sir Wilfred claims she's gone missing. Organises a fruitless search. Even calls the police – but notice, he didn't do that until next morning. He needed a chance to put her in a more secure hiding place late at night, once the guests had gone.'

'And this is a scheme that's supposed to raise money?' Holly was dismissive.

But Travers hadn't finished. 'Hold on. The next thing to happen, I reckon, is some sort of ransom request. Made up of letters cut out from recent newspapers, perhaps.'

'But on this scenario, guv, Wilfred has no resources to meet the demand anyway.'

'Precisely. But he has strong local support from all the guests from Bridgerule who were here last night, enjoying his hospitality. And he might expect the police to start using the media to publicise the event. I mean, I've already asked him for a photograph. Daphne is attractive enough for a woman in her seventies. There'd be enough publicity for him to start a crowd-funding scheme. What'd that be worth, d'you reckon? Could it raise a hundred thousand?'

Light started to dawn. Her boss hadn't lost his marbles after all. 'And the amount raised is paid over in a remote spot to the supposed kidnapper. . . After which, after some delay, Daphne reappears. Looking the worse for wear. . . But in the end, when the fuss dies down and the kidnapper hands his takings back over to Sir Wilfred, the pair have made a hundred grand and they are solvent once again.'

Travers looked at her and grinned. 'So might it work?'

Holly knew her boss wanted her to be realistic. He was not a man who took much notice of hollow praise. She pondered.

'They'd need to work hard on the details, guv. Daphne might have to be hidden away for weeks – she'd need a really secure hiding place. She couldn't just be kept in the Manor's attic or cellar. When she finally emerged, she'd need to look like some-one who had suffered a lot in the whole episode. And she would have really suffered, that couldn't be fake. She's over seventy, you know. We haven't even asked yet about whether she was on regular medication. High blood pressure tablets, for instance. Running short of those might scupper the scheme anyway.'

There was a pause as the idea was evaluated from different angles. The author himself had increasing doubts.

'Trouble is, Holly, it sounds to me like a plot for a crime fiction story. There are so many things that could go wrong. You'd have to be desperate even to try it. I wonder if the Gabri-els have any acting experience? And another thing, do you reckon Edward would need to be in on the plot?'

'That might depend on how much of the time he's living at the Manor. My guess is that they'd try to keep him out of it.'

'They'd also need some hard wisdom on crowd-funding.

Nothing that's been told us so far makes me think Sir Wilfred is any sort of internet wizard. In fact, the more I think about it, the more complicated it seems.' He gave a frustrated sigh. 'Right, Holly, shall we treat ourselves to a pudding?'

'I'm not really sure we deserve this.' Holly was eyeing her Crème Brûlée; she wasn't sure what her expenses were meant to cover.

Travers smiled. He always enjoyed Eton Mess, a plate of which had just been set before him. For some reason he never had this at home. But the hard thinking wasn't over yet.

'What we haven't taken into account, Holly, is the only piece of hard evidence in the whole case – the suspected burglary.'

'You're assuming that happened during the fireworks?'

'Unless Sir Wilfred did it himself. Which would make him devious beyond measure. Practically crook of the year.'

Holly had a mouthful of dessert before essaying a response.

'Assuming it was the same villain, the axing of the door must have happened before anything occurred to Daphne. It might have been a first attempt to force a way in.'

'Mm. Which would give the two events something in common. But it's impossible to guess what, without more information.'

'Mind, it wouldn't hurt to know what's the other side of that door. It can't be the kitchen or someone would have heard the banging from inside the Manor.'

Holly had more of her dessert then had another thought. 'Incidentally, guv, we could try Sheila again on our way back to the Manor. She's the one person who was mostly in the kitchen last night; and is a friend of Daphne. She wasn't in when I tried earlier; her neighbour said she'd gone to church. But they don't have long sermons these days. She must be back by now.'

CHAPTER 7

As Peter Travers and Holly drove back through Bridgerule, they were relieved to find Daphne's kitchen co-worker, Sheila Townsend, was finally at home.

'Yes. It was announced at church that Daphne had gone missing,' she confirmed, as she welcomed them into her tidy cottage. 'Caused quite a stir, I can tell you. More than the usual notices. No-one knew what to make of it. I was expecting you here before long. It's all very peculiar.'

It was good to know that the village grapevine was humming. If it had been announced in church (presumably Sir Wilfred had called the vicar as part of his quota of phone calls), then by now almost everyone living nearby would know the key facts. And if Daphne was staying with one of the congregation she would certainly know she was wanted. But she hadn't made herself known.

'Can you tell us about your evening in the Merrifield kitchen,' began Travers. 'How did Daphne seem? Did anything strange happen during the evening?'

Sheila paused to gather her thoughts. 'It was certainly a busy evening. Sir Wilfred had told me he expected over a hundred guests. I think it was the biggest thing that had gone on at the Manor for years.'

She drew breath and continued. 'But Daphne was calm enough. We were organised. She and I had spent several afternoons cooking away, preparing for the event. We'd plenty of cakes and so on in the fridge – they'd hired a catering fridge for the occasion. And that kitchen is a good size and fairly well equipped.'

'How did Daphne seem?' repeated Holly.

'She was absolutely fine. In her element, you might say. Like she'd been hosting big parties for years. The Mary Berry of Merrifield. Or perhaps I should say, the Nigella of North Cornwall.'

'Right. You'd no clue that she was about to disappear?'

Sheila shook her head. 'None whatsoever. She'd not said anything. It was as much a shock to me as to everyone else.'

'So the evening went on . . . till about nine thirty?'

Sheila frowned. 'Around then, anyway. By now demand had started to fall away. Appetites had been satisfied. For sausage rolls and cakes, anyway. The guests were still drinking the mulled wine, but that wasn't our concern. Sir Wilfred and his farm manager were handling that on the terrace.'

'And then?'

'Some time around then Daphne got a phone call. She'd left her mobile on the work surface, close to the door. Mind, she looked a bit surprised as she picked it up.'

This was new information. 'Did she give any indication of who was calling?'

'None at all. She just said, "Hold on a minute." Then slipped out the kitchen door into the hallway. I haven't seen her since.'

There was silence for a moment.

'You didn't go to look for her?'

'Well, I couldn't leave the kitchen unattended. By now there were waitresses coming in with empty plates. There was plenty of tidying up to be done. And Daphne was in her own house. I hardly thought about it at first, assumed she'd met someone out in the hall and been waylaid. I mean, she was an event host.'

'So when did you start to worry?'

'Only when Sir Wilfred started asking where she'd gone.

Which was probably around ten o'clock. But even if she'd gone off, the kitchen still needed to be left in good order. That kept me busy till gone eleven. I felt slightly aggrieved that I was doing it on my own, but I was there as the official caterer. By the time I'd finished I was dog-tired. Not surprisingly; I mean, Daphne and I had been on the go since before five.'

'You didn't offer to help with the search?'

'I'm afraid I didn't. I was bushed. I just said good night to Sir Wilfred and slipped away. Didn't realise anything was seriously wrong till I heard the notice in church.'

Peter Travers took stock for a moment.

'Can I take you back, Sheila? From what you've just told us, it sounds as if Daphne chose to leave Merrifield of her own accord. But without telling anyone – not even her husband – where she was going or what she was aiming to do.'

He sighed. 'But if so, it would be good to confirm that. Can you think back to recent conversations you've had with her? Is there anything she said – anything at all – that might suggest what caused her to slip away? Anything that would give us a clue as to where she might have gone?'

For a few minutes Sheila sat still, pondering.

'The only minor oddity I can recall happened a few months ago.'

'Yes?'

'Daphne and I were at St Bridget's – that's the Bridgerule church, up on the hill – we were doing the flowers together. There's a rota and we're on once a month. It must have been in late August. One of those times when Covid restrictions were being relaxed.'

'And what did she say?'

'It was as we walked up the path. Daphne happened to notice one of the gravestones. That of a previous vicar. He was famous, or maybe notorious, for having been vicar here for seventy years. He died in office, the plaque said, in 1958.'

'That's a long time ago.'

Sheila nodded. 'It's over sixty years. Anyway, Daphne turned to me and said, did I know anything about her early life? It was an odd question. I mean, I'm only sixty, she's at least a decade older than me. There's no way I could remember anything of her childhood. That's what made it such an odd question.'

Travers mused while Holly jotted down Daphne's question. 'And she never mentioned this again?'

'Not to me, anyway. Apart from that, our friendship has trundled along steadily for years. As far as I know she has no health issues. And no sick relatives. She and Sir Wilfred seem very happy together and obviously they've no financial issues. I'm sorry, Inspector, I can't think of anything else at all.'

A few minutes later the two police officers were in their car, heading back towards Merrifield Manor.

'Sheila seemed a sensible, down-to-earth woman, guv. And she was clear enough. It sounds as if Daphne was summoned away by her caller. Does that change things?'

'I'm not sure, Holly. We still don't know if she'd been hoping for the call and responded willingly; if she was lured away; or even if the call took the form of a threat.'

Holly frowned. 'To me it sounds like a willing departure. She must have known who was calling. No-one would set out at that time of night to meet a complete stranger. Not a seventy-year-old woman, anyway – at least she'd tell someone where she was heading. But exactly where she was going, who she was hoping to meet and what she was hoping to discover, is anybody's guess.'

The inspector paused for a moment, reflecting, as he waited

to turn onto the main road that ran from Bude towards Launceston.

'The timing, half past nine, suggests it was probably someone who knew about the firework party and when it was due to end. Half an hour earlier, say, and Daphne would have been too busy to pick up the phone, let alone respond. Whereas a little later and she'd have been in the throes of washing up.'

'Yes. It's a pity we don't even know if it was a man or a woman. Or if the call was local or came from miles away.'

'But we've a chance on that, Holly. D'you think the call came through on the phone that we saw in Daphne's bedroom? If it did, and assuming that's her only phone, then there's hope. Even if Sir Wilfred didn't know it, someone back at the station must be able to unpick her password in a day or two. Then we could work out where the call came from. We know the time of the call, at any rate.'

CHAPTER 8

'Has anyone managed to find Daphne's bicycle yet, sir?' asked Inspector Travers. He was addressing a downcast-looking Sir Wilfred, back at Merrifield Manor.

'I'm afraid not, Inspector. I've been busy contacting names from Daphne's address book. Without success. Meanwhile Brian and Edward have spent an hour going round all the nooks and crannies where the bike's ever been left before. It's certainly not on the estate.'

'Right, sir. Now we've just heard from her friend Sheila Townsend that Daphne received a call at about nine thirty. She moved out into the hall to take it. Our working hypothesis must be that this call led her to move off the estate, taking her bicycle with her.'

Sir Wilfred nodded slowly. 'And how does that affect our search, Inspector?'

'Two of my officers are working through Bridgerule, inter-viewing guests from the party. Perhaps one or other of them walked down your drive with Daphne and saw her leaving. But the mechanics don't matter much. The crucial thing is whether she left of her own accord; or because of some form of pressure, reinforced by that phone call.'

'Hm. I see.' It didn't look to Holly as if Sir Wilfred "saw" at all. 'So what can I do now? To me neither of those seem re-motely likely. This is my wife of nearly fifty years, Inspector. And I've known her even longer. She's a simple country woman. Not a member of the Mafia.'

Belatedly, Travers realised that more logic was called for. 'If the caller was nearby and had a car, he (or she) could have picked her up on the main road, taken her off anywhere. Anywhere in the country.'

He could see that Sir Wilfred was shocked. Would that loosen his tongue? 'But it's just possible, sir, that if we could work out a reason why Daphne chose to leave, one with some evidence behind it, that might tell us where to look for her.'

'What would happen then?' asked Sir Wilfred doubtfully.

'Well, once we found her, a police officer could talk to her. If it was her decision, the need for official intervention would be over. You and she might have an argument about whether she was coming home, but it wouldn't be a police matter.'

Travers sighed. He felt for the old man; this was heavy going. 'So what I'd like you to ask yourself, sir, one more time, is: what possible reason might Daphne have had for disappearing like this?'

There was silence in the room. But he could see that Sir Wilfred was struggling to answer. Perhaps more help was needed.

'For example, can you recall any odd conversations with Daphne in the past few months? Did she ask you any peculiar questions?'

The master of the Manor mused in silence.

'Or were there any disputes between you, say on a place she wanted to go on holiday? Were there any exhibitions or museums that she was hoping to visit?'

He paused, stuck for ideas. Holly took over with some ideas of her own. 'Were there any new hobbies that Daphne was itching to take up? Did she ever mention, say, windsurfing, or skydiving? Or did she hanker after any particular West End play?'

There was a longer silence in the lounge, but Travers felt it was a constructive stillness. Sir Wilfred was certainly doing his best. Then he responded.

'I recall one rather odd conversation we had a year ago. Daphne started asking me about her early childhood.'

'And how did you answer?'

'I told her we were children at much the same time: I'd no first-hand memories. All I could do was to repeat the official family line that I'd been told by my parents: Daphne was the child of one of the servants at the Manor. The father had vanished before she was born, and the mother died while she was very young. So in fact she was brought up in and around the Manor as part of our family, more or less together. But she didn't seem to want that answer at all.'

'She probably knew that already,' surmised Holly.

'In any case, memories from seventy years ago are hardly likely to cause strange actions today,' added Travers. 'I mean, it wouldn't be a reason for running away now.'

The silence resumed but this time it was totally unproductive.

'The trouble is,' said the inspector after a while, 'if it's not a voluntary disappearance then it must be involuntary. Something's happened to her which makes it a police case. Is there anyone Daphne fell out with recently? Or old enemies that have reappeared?'

If the policeman's previous challenge had almost stumped Sir Wilfred, this one was an unreachable long hop.

'Inspector, we're talking about a seventy odd year old woman who has lived around here all her life. She used to help with the Women's Institute in Bridgerule and is a regular member of the congregation at St Bridget's. There might have been the occasional disagreement but nothing on this scale. She helps with the flowers at church and is a regular bellringer.'

He paused. What else could he say? 'Daphne's a fit woman.

She swims in the outdoor pool at Bude, when it's open. When it's not, she goes on regular walks in the Tamar valley or along the coast. She doesn't do anything to make enemies. It just doesn't make sense.'

There was a longer silence. It seemed he had nothing else to say.

Travers sighed. 'The trouble is, sir, if it's not a voluntary departure and it's not a malicious kidnapping, the only other possibility is that it's accidental. But that makes no sense either. This is North Cornwall. It's not the Bermuda Triangle.'

As the two police officers drove back to Bude later that Sunday they both felt highly dissatisfied. The officers interviewing firework party guests in Bridgerule had found nothing significant. Progress had been minimal.

'Isn't it time for the Regional Crime Squad, guv?'

'Not until we're sure it is a crime. I mean, where would they start? We've no hard evidence at all. It might just be a Missing Person.'

'I don't suppose you had any reason to disbelieve Sir Wilfred, did you?'

'I just saw an older man, Holly, who'd lost his lifelong companion and was desperate to find her again. His memory might not be that brilliant, but I had no sense he was hiding anything.'

They drove in frustrated silence for half a mile.

Holly spoke again. 'If we're not calling in the Crime Squad, guv, we've got to act as if we've some hope she left of her own accord. Perhaps she fell off her bike and is lying somewhere badly injured. Or . . . maybe she's lost her memory? In either case, haven't we got to continue the local search?'

'Trouble is, Holly, there are no hard boundaries. Daphne's a fit woman and she knows the area. On a bike she could be twenty miles away, in any direction. More if she keeps going for a second day. You could spend a month searching with dozens of officers up and down the Tamar valley and not find anything. It's a well-farmed area in well-wooded countryside.'

'But in that case, guv, shouldn't we involve the media? At least get every farmer in North Cornwall to search their own land, like Sir Wilfred did for his own estate?'

'Sir Wilfred's a very private man, Holly. I suggested wider publicity to him, but he didn't want every newspaper in the land tramping the area. This is rural Cornwall. No doubt there are skeletons hiding in cupboards here, waiting to be found. Anyway, I agreed to keep quiet, at least for a couple of days. I mean, Daphne might just turn up. She's not been gone twenty-four hours yet.'

CHAPTER 9   Monday Nov 8th

Peter Travers did not sleep well that Sunday night. He continued to wrestle with the conundrum of the missing Daphne Gabriel.

He would have discussed it all with his wife, Maxine. Except that they had learned over the years that it was best not to bring work problems home. There were too many potential issues over confidentiality. In any case Maxine was about to restart work at Cleave Camp. She had enough challenges of her own.

He was having an early breakfast – a large bowl of porridge, more substantial than the single banana he'd had the day before – when it occurred to him to examine the Merrifield location on his Explorer map. And that gave him an idea.

He was still clear in his own mind that attempting to search the local countryside offered diminishing returns, on what he knew. But he had spotted something more promising, no more than half a mile from the Manor. There was some sort of campsite or caravan park marked, between the road and the dismantled track of the old railway.

It was November, he reminded himself. No-one stays in caravans this late in the year. If there were any static vans on the site, they would almost certainly be empty.

But that, surely, offered a tempting hiding place for someone trying to hide away?

He pondered the notion for a few minutes. He had no alternative, anyway. Ten minutes later he had rung Holly Berry again. She was already up – he could hear the sound of her children arguing in the background – as he outlined his idea.

'It's worth a visit to the campsite at least,' she agreed, after a few moments debate. 'Can you give me a lift again?'

Fifteen minutes later they were driving back again towards Merrifield. Travers was pleased to see that his colleague still looked enthusiastic. Perhaps she'd slept better than he had.

They found the campsite on a sideroad, not far from Merrifield Manor, marked by a rather battered sign on the roadside. There was no gate on the entrance drive, so they drove in and down the sloping, rutted track towards the camp office.

'This whole place is bigger than I realised,' muttered Travers. There was no doubt that the site catered for caravans: they could see forty or fifty static homes on the pitches around them, and there were probably more still in the field beyond the hedge.

'The question now is, is the office manned at this time of year?' asked Holly.

'Trouble is, Holly, it's only half past eight. The manager might not be here this early. Not with the place this deserted, anyway.' A minute later Travers' comments were confirmed: the office was closed.

'We could still drive around the whole site, guv. See if there are any homes with signs of occupation. Or if any of 'em have a bike left outside.'

Now they were here, Travers agreed, they might as well do something. He started the car and the police officers drove slowly up and down each lane in turn.

Most of the caravans were rather forlorn, looked like they hadn't been occupied for months. Then, at the far end of the fourth lane, they passed a couple of homes with one or two signs of life. One had a half-full dustbin, the other had some washing hanging outside. Neither, though, had a bicycle left nearby. They didn't look very promising. Even so, Holly made a note of the caravan numbers.

It took forty minutes for them to drive painstakingly round the whole site. 'OK. Let's go back to the central office,' muttered the inspector, glancing at his watch. 'It's after nine now.' He feared the visit had been a complete waste of time. Would he be the butt of ridicule, once they were back in the police station?

But as they got near to the office, they were encouraged to see a light on inside. Someone was there after all. Half a minute later they were inside and introducing themselves to the well-wrapped up woman at the desk. She muttered "I'm Moira, Moira Jenkin" in response.

'We're looking into the case of Daphne Gabriel, from Merrifield Manor. She went missing on Saturday night after a firework party.'

The woman put her hands to her face. 'Oh, no. I was at that,' she said. 'I took my lad. It was a good event, too. Plenty of mulled wine on sale as well as rather too many noisy rockets.'

'D'you know Mrs Gabriel?' asked Holly.

'Vaguely,' she replied. 'But I didn't see her on Saturday. Sir Wilfred was managing all the outside activities. Maybe his wife was in charge of the catering. So how can I help you?'

'It occurred to us,' said the inspector, 'that your campsite at this time of year is a plausible place to hide. Especially for someone who'd slipped away from the Manor. We'd like to check each of your mobile homes, either for traces of Daphne herself or for her bicycle.'

Travers was relieved to see that the woman wasn't fazed by the request. No doubt it helped that she knew Merrifield Manor and was acquainted with both of the Gabriels.

The woman rummaged in her handbag, then produced a

key. But it wasn't the key to any caravan. She stood up and turned to the painting of Hartland Point on the far wall. Then she swung it out to reveal a small safe doorway hidden behind.

'Some of our summer guests need a safe for their valuables. So I also keep my spare caravan keys in here.' She opened the door and pulled out a dozen sets, each a large ring of Chubb keys.

'I'm only here till lunchtime,' she added. 'Will that be long enough? If not, I'm afraid you'll have to bring them back here, then come and check the rest tomorrow.' She handed all the key rings over to the inspector. 'You two are very privileged to borrow these, you know. I don't normally let them out of this office.'

As the police officers set out on the laborious task of checking every caravan, Holly observed, 'That was serious security, you know. It would take some effort for Daphne to obtain a key.'

'We'll worry about that once we find some evidence she's been here,' replied her boss. He examined how the keys were arranged. 'Right. We'll take each lane in turn. But I reckon we can split up and check opposite sides. That'll speed things up a bit.'

'So, to be clear, I'm looking for any evidence of Daphne's belongings, including her bike?'

'That's right. Call me over if there's any doubt. I'll do the same for you.'

They decided to check the lanes nearest the office first. Once they got into a routine it didn't take too long. Most of the caravans were completely empty and could be dismissed at a glance. Only occasionally did either of them come across belongings and most of these, for example beach gear or children's toys, could be rejected with just a moment's thought.

By half past eleven the two had inspected all the caravans in the lanes around the office. This left just the ones in the next field, behind the hedge.

'If you were planning to hide here for any length of time, you'd go for one of these,' said Travers, as they reached the second field. It wasn't clear if he believed this or was simply trying to encourage his colleague. For he could see that Holly was starting to look weary.

Once more they worked the lanes. The result was much as before. Steadily they worked on. Until they came to the last caravan on the furthest lane.

Peter Travers glanced at his watch. Not yet half past twelve. He felt relieved. They wouldn't need to come back another day after all. He wondered if the Bridge Inn served food on a Monday. He'd had an early breakfast and was starting to feel hungry.

The discovery happened on the side where Holly was working. Once more, carefully, she picked out the key whose number matched the caravan and opened the door. The home looked much like all the others, unoccupied and virtually empty.

But best to be thorough. The police officer stepped inside and prowled steadily along the length of the caravan. Then, at the far end, on the floor beside the bed, she saw it.

A long, dark blue dress. Exactly the colour they had been told Daphne was wearing, two evenings before. It wasn't neatly folded, though. It looked rather as if it had been dropped on the floor after being taken off in a hurry.

Quickly, Holly went back to the door and called to her boss, who had just come out of the caravan opposite.

'Guv, come here. I think I've found something.'

CHAPTER 10

On that Monday, in the end, Peter Travers didn't get any lunch at all.

He didn't say anything, but he was as excited as his colleague by the find of the blue dress. Swiftly he took a large evidence bag from his jacket pocket and slipped on some thin nylon gloves; Holly did likewise. Then, carefully, they bundled the folded dress inside the bag and the inspector slipped the bag inside his all-purpose rucksack. At last, possibly, they had some evidence.

Quickly they scoured the caravan but found nothing else of interest. A hunt of the immediate vicinity found no bike either. But there wasn't time for a protracted search. Mrs Jenkin was wanting her keys.

Travers managed to hand back the keys without giving anything away: there was no point in starting fresh rumours. Then the officers drove the short distance to Merrifield Manor. They needed to see if Sir Wilfred would confirm that the dress was the same as that worn by his wife on the previous Saturday evening.

Nothing much seemed to have changed at the Manor. Sir Wilfred was pottering about in a distracted manner. He had obviously run out of ideas or friends to ring. He was alone: the estate manager was off somewhere, managing the property; his son was no longer around.

'Any progress?' he asked eagerly, once he'd let the officers in and settled them into the lounge.

'We found this, sir.' Peter Travers was equally eager to show off their find.

'That's . . . that's Daphne's.' Then the implications struck him and his face clouded. 'Where did you find it?'

'It was locked in one of the caravans in the campsite down the road.' Travers didn't try to explain the magic combination of hunch and persistence which had allowed them to locate it. 'Did you or Daphne ever go over that way?'

'I've never been there myself. Never had cause to. In my experience, locals and campers don't have too much in common. Whether Daphne ever passed that way on one of her walks I couldn't say. She never mentioned it if she had, as far as I can remember.'

There was a pause. Then, 'Where does that takes us, Inspector?' he asked.

Travers rubbed his chin. He was facing an old man in great distress. He needed to choose his words carefully.

'I'd say, sir, that it tends to support the theory that Daphne left the Manor of her own accord. With her bicycle. But she would find it extremely difficult to cycle properly in a long, flowing skirt. So I'd say it's likely that that she took something like a pair of jeans with her, changed in the caravan and then cycled on.'

'We've no idea how she got hold of the caravan key,' added Holly. 'But for the moment that's not too important. Our strongest conclusion is that, for reasons unknown, Daphne has headed off, away from Merrifield Manor.'

'At the very least,' concluded Travers, 'it suggests that there's no point in having a media campaign and asking every farmer between here and Launceston to search their fields and woods for her.'

There was a pause as Sir Wilfred tried to make sense of the

latest finding and the officers' words.

'But if she's riding her bicycle, Inspector, can't you at least look at your traffic cameras, see if you can see her?'

'These days, I'm afraid, we don't have that many cameras operational at any one time. And the ones we have are all located on main roads. But I agree, it's something to try. I'll get my traffic officer onto it, once we're back at Bude police station.'

He gave the owner a studied frown. 'In the meantime, sir, we need you to man the phone here in the Manor. I need to know at once if Daphne rings you. Or if there's any sign of life from her debit card. Don't worry, Sir Wilfred. We're not out of ideas completely.'

A few minutes later the officers were heading back down the Manor drive. After that, the lane into the hamlet of Merrifield took them over a narrow, single lane bridge before turning right towards the main road. In a moment of insight Holly realised what they were doing.

'Hey, guv, does this bridge go over the old railway line?'

Her boss smiled. 'It might. So is this the route taken by Daphne? It'd be off the beaten track. Come on, let's have a look.'

Travers pulled in beside the hedge and the pair headed back to look over the bridge walls. On the side that faced towards the campsite was a cutting, filled by a mass of overgrown bushes.

'She wouldn't have gone that way, guv. I doubt even Tarzan could make much headway through that lot.'

But the other side was more open. They were looking down towards what they almost immediately realised was the remains of the old Bridgerule railway station. The traditional wooden canopy over the old platform was still there, now embedded into a house, but the overall layout of the area was clear. This was one place where parallel tracks would have allowed two trains to pass one another, on the largely single-track line.

'This way is passable for a cyclist, Holly. Trouble is, it's going in the wrong direction.'

They were no further forward in following Daphne's route. As they sat back in the car, Holly seized her boss's map to orient herself. This must be the line from Bude to Holsworthy and beyond. So where did the old railway actually go?

It took a moment to work out where they were. 'Hey, guv, if we go along this side road that goes to Marhamchurch, the old railway track should be alongside us. But at one point it disappears altogether. D'you reckon that could be a tunnel?'

Travers peered over her shoulder and shrugged. 'It's not far out of our way. Let's go and see.'

They set off, crossed over the main road and headed along the side road. As they drove Holly tracked their progress on the map. Satnav wouldn't help them here.

'Can you stop? This is where we might find a tunnel.'

They stopped, got out and peered over the hedge. But there was nothing to see but a field and a few cows.

Travers frowned. 'I'm afraid it's not a tunnel after all, Holly. The farmer has just covered over the railway line completely. To be fair, it must be over half a century since the trains last ran.'

Disappointed, they continued their journey. But a few moments later they went over another bridge. Holly still had her nose in the map.

'Can we stop, guv? We've gone over the railway again. But you wouldn't need a long tunnel, you know, you could shelter for a night under a railway bridge. That's provided you could get down to it.'

Once more they peered over the bridge wall. On one side was the other end of the abortive tunnel that was no longer a tunnel at all. On the other was another deep, bush-filled cutting, heading through a wood.

But this time the bushes seemed to grow less densely as the line ran under the road. And they could just make out a rough path, down beside the bridge.

'We might as well have a quick look, Holly.'

It didn't take long to scramble down to the level of the old railway line and then to peer under the bridge.

'You could shelter in there you know, guv. It'd be cold but at least you'd be dry.'

But Peter Travers wasn't interested in habitability. For he had seen something else under the bridge, on the far side.

'Look, Holly.'

Then she saw it too. A lady's bicycle. It was a dark green Raleigh, old fashioned but in reasonable condition. There was no rust evident, it hadn't been there for long.

'I got a bike description from Sir Wilfred, guv. That bike exactly matches his description. It must be Daphne's. I wonder why she abandoned it.'

'I can tell you that, Holly. Look at the rear wheel.'

And when Holly looked carefully, she knew as well. For the rear wheel was completely flat. Daphne had been beaten by a puncture.

PART TWO

MAXINE TRAVERS

CLEAVE CAMP AND MORWENSTOW
NOVEMBER 1st – 17th

St Morwenna's Church, Morwenstow

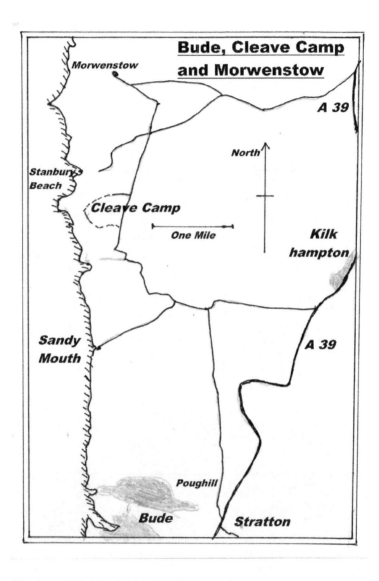

Bude, Cleave Camp and Morwenstow

CHAPTER 11   Monday Nov 1st

The invitation – which, when she thought about it, was really an instruction – had come out of the blue the week before.

Dear Maxine,

I noticed that you are about to restart work at Cleave on a part-time basis next week. Had you thought of bringing your little one to visit us at Cheltenham? Several of your friends here have very happy memories of you and would love to meet the next generation.

And if you are coming, I would value a few words (with you) myself.

Best wishes,
Jeremy

"Jeremy" was Maxine Travers' former boss at GCHQ Cheltenham. He had been a wise mentor. Since her transfer down to Cleave Camp, near Bude, almost a decade ago, he had risen fast in the hierarchy, was now a senior manager. Of course, he wouldn't put any requests that might claim on her time in the Camp in writing. But Maxine found it exciting that someone high up still had confidence in her.

Maxine was reaching the end of her maternity leave. It had been complicated for both herself and her new daughter, Rosanna, by Covid. With her daddy often working long hours on police business, the little girl had had a surfeit of her mummy's company for the first year of her life. But it didn't seem to have done her much harm; in fact, it had allowed Maxine's maternal instincts to flourish.

Arrangements were made and mother and daughter drove over to GCHQ a week later. The usually tight security was relaxed for the one-year-old and a happy time ensured.

The conversation with Jeremy took place once it was clear Maxine's friends, many of whom had children of their own, could easily cope with a little one for an hour or so.

'Hasn't your office got larger?' Maxine asked, once Jeremy had emerged from his lair and invited her to join him.

He smiled ruefully. 'Some Civil Service rules still apply: the higher you fly, the more carpet you need beneath you. But it's not worth the bother of fighting them all. You're looking very well, Maxine. Cornwall obviously suits you.'

There were just a few minutes of opening chatter. Both knew this time was precious – and it was limited.

'Right,' said the senior manager. 'Here's what I was hoping you could help us with. This isn't official, yet, but I understand from the Bude Commanding Officer that the person who's been covering your position during your maternity leave has blossomed in the role. Management don't want to lose that. So they are intending to promote you to the Camp management team – and, of course, pay you accordingly. That's something they'll talk to you about once you get back.

Maxine was pleased but slightly surprised. A pay-rise was always welcome, especially with the extra costs of a new baby. Mind, she wasn't sure she was cut out to be an administrator.

She gave him a cautious smile. 'So where do you want help?'

'It's like this, Maxine. For a long time, one or two senior managers here have sensed that something is not perfect at Cleave Camp. The operational level is fine. We get our regular reports and there's no reason to suspect they are incomplete.

Whenever we can, we cross-check with reports from elsewhere; there's the occasional gap, but almost never a discrepancy.'

Maxine nodded. 'Good. So, where's the problem?'

'Well. Relationships always seem to be rougher than they need to be. There's less positive support than you'd hope for. Some of that's in the links between ourselves and the Americans. It's hard work to get joint ventures off the ground. We are meant to be on the same side. Even so, there's always some reason why things don't work out as well as we had hoped.'

'So the problem is simply between us and our so-called allies?'

Jeremy sighed. 'I'm afraid not. There are also less positive relations than I would like, between the Camp and the surrounding area. Worse than other outposts around the UK.'

Maxine was silent for a moment. If this was the Civil Service, they'd blame underlying problems on the man at the top. Could it all be down to the man at the top of the Cleave totem pole?

'Does Cheltenham appoint the Commanding Officer at Cleave?'

'We have some say. But the final choice is always made by the Ministry of Defence. It was their site in the first place, you see. They still see it as a military location: Cleave was actually an airfield in the Second World War. But I've been happy enough with what I've seen of the current Commanding Officer, Bill Oakshot. In any case, our worries go back long before his time.'

There was a short pause.

'What I don't quite understand, Jeremy, is why you're entrusting any investigation to me. I mean, I've not even been on the site for the last year. Before that I was a technical guru, leading the decoding team. Taking as little notice as possible of the high-level politics. Working around them where I had to.'

Jeremy looked at her closely and grinned. 'It's precisely

because of that attitude that I thought of you. You see, you're not a political animal, Maxine. Your ambition is for the UK to have the best possible intelligence it can obtain from around the world, to keep us all safe. That's what drives you. Not where you fit in the hierarchy. You're as impatient with inefficiency as I am.'

He took a deep breath and then continued. 'I'm not saying there's anything fundamentally wrong. If there was, National Security would shut the place down. But there's something. It needs a top-class analytical mind to discern what's wrong.'

Maxine had one last try to dodge the poisoned chalice. 'In that case, Jeremy, shouldn't you find a consultant to advise you?'

The man sighed. 'I don't want a short investigation, concluding with a whizz-bang Powerpoint display by some outside consultant. Whatever's wrong there is deep-seated. It'll only be spotted by someone who knows most of the staff, works regularly on site, been there a few years themselves. And who has good interpersonal skills. Someone, ideally, with a Cornish background, who understands local problems. I would say that all of this applies to you.'

It was now Maxine's turn to sigh. She'd tried, but there was no easy way out. 'You're very persuasive, Jeremy. Alright, I'll give it my best shot for a month or two. As long as you understand that I might fail completely. But now, in the time we've got left, could we consider how this research might be done?'

Jeremy smiled; he had won his agent to the cause. 'Before we do that, let me get us some coffee.'

'Clearly, Maxine, you'll need to keep this project to yourself – as far as possible. But you'll be in a unique position, coming back to a place on the Camp management team.

For one thing, that'll be a reason for you to spend time getting to know each of the team. One thing to ask, in those meetings, is where the boundaries lie on their spheres of influence. Are there any big gaps, which a newcomer to the team like yourself could help with?'

Maxine saw the line he was suggesting. 'I could offer to review the paperwork at the Camp setting out current boundaries. If these aren't properly recorded that's a source of trouble anyway.'

Jeremy nodded. 'Or if there's a discrepancy between records? Say, two managers with conflicting briefs. That could run on for years. And explain why there've been so many misunderstandings between them.'

Maxine mused for a moment.

'I'm not doing this entirely on my own. Does GCHQ have any questions about recent reports from Cleave that they'd like investigating? Something that would give me an excuse to keep in direct touch with you?'

Jeremy considered. Then he reached for a file from his steel cabinet and pulled out an item.

'I've one observation on the Cleave report from last week that might help. About a recent energy bill.'

'What's wrong with it?'

'Well, it's way higher than the bill for the months before. With no explanation to account for it. How about if I ask the Cleave Commander about it? If I phrase my request carefully, there's a good chance he'll pass it on to the newest member of his management team – i.e. to you.'

Jeremy pondered, then nodded sagely. 'Yes. That'd give you something to investigate for him. And a reason, if you need it, to keep directly in touch with me.'

CHAPTER 12   Monday Nov 8th

Maxine's first full day back at Cleave Camp, a week later, was by no means as relaxed as her one-day visit to Cheltenham.

She was used by now to seeing husband Peter cycling off with Rosanna strapped into the seat behind, taking their child to nursery. But seeing her daughter taken away and waving good-bye still brought a lump to her throat.

Today it also brought a tear to the eye. She was facing a new phase of motherhood: how would she handle it?

Once the analyst reached the Camp, located on a level, grassy area, four hundred feet up and half a mile inland, with a barbed wire topped fence all round, she had to pass through security. This was her first visit here for over a year and, of course, there'd been staff changes here as well. Despite having worked here for close to a decade, she was not even recognised.

Fortunately, all Maxine's paperwork was in good order and after various checks she was allowed in. But the process was very impersonal. Remembering her hidden remit from Cheltenham, she asked herself if the formality was all necessary. What would this sort of welcome do for local tradesmen? They must call regularly to discuss catering orders and aspects of maintenance.

For herself, she missed any mention of her precious one-year-old. She'd had a letter telling her to return to work today, it was hardly a surprise. It wouldn't have taken much for Personnel to send a note to the guards, explaining who she was and why she'd been away.

Cleave Camp had various buildings on the surface as well as thirty listening satellite dishes above, of varying sizes. All the analysis was carried out in purpose-designed structures, buried well below ground. This was where regularly downloaded signals were decrypted and suspicious new messages given preliminary analysis.

She had had no further directions. Maxine went first to the room where her desk had been before she went on leave, but the desk was now occupied by her replacement. Even her former decoding colleagues, eyes glued to their computer monitors, looked extremely busy.

Maxine felt a spark of irritation. Five minutes welcoming her back, after a whole year away, surely wouldn't have been that difficult? Was this the long-term effect of a military command structure, she mused, being imposed on a civilian workforce? Or just that she'd been off the production line for too long?

As she stood, wondering, a cheerful-looking woman of around her own age strode along the corridor behind her.

'Maxine,' she said, 'welcome back. I'm sorry I wasn't here for you; we hadn't expected you for another hour. Didn't you see the time in the letter? You've probably forgotten me: I'm Samantha, from Personnel – widely known as Sam. Please, do come with me. The management team has a new corridor of their own, well away from the rest. You've even got your own office.'

It turned out Maxine's new office wasn't large (compared with Jeremy's in Cheltenham, for instance) but it was freshly painted and adequately furnished. It had its own coffee-brewing machine and a couple of easy chairs as well as a desk with a telephone and computer. A blank whiteboard hung on one wall and a sizeable monitor screen was attached to a second. There was a wooden bookcase on the third, but it was currently empty.

'I'll give you ten minutes to settle yourself, Maxine. Then I'll come back to welcome you properly.'

Maxine used the time to acquaint herself with the coffee machine and make a carafe of coffee. She also checked the recall letter. Sam was right: she'd appeared too early for her first day back.

There was a knock and Sam reappeared. This time she carried a sheaf of papers with her. The two women grabbed their coffees and sat down in the easy chairs. Sam noticed her companion was small and slim. She still had shoulder-length, honey-blonde hair and looked keen to return to the fray.

'I was planning to be in the security hut to welcome you back, Maxine. I'm doing my best to humanise the place but it's a long haul.'

Maxine smiled. 'I've checked my letter: I was an hour too early. I'd just assumed the Camp's day-shift hours wouldn't have changed. Sorry.'

Sam grinned in response. 'You're upper management now, Maxine. Not many perks round here but there are a few. Make the most of them. That's my strategy, anyway.'

'You're upper management too?'

'For the time being. There is a Personnel Director, but right now she's off with long Covid. I was her deputy. When she was away, they quickly found they needed someone at the top table to handle people issues, so I'm her formal stand-in. Most of the Directors aren't terribly people-sensitive, if you know what I mean. They're horribly task-oriented.'

Maxine frowned. 'How d'you know what I am?'

'You're a new mum and working here part-time?'

Maxine nodded.

'Case proven. As far as it needs to be, anyway. There aren't many part-timers here at the Camp. That's why I'm so keen to prove it can work. We can't be that different to the rest of the country.'

There were echoes here of the analysis from Jeremy. Maybe Sam would be a useful ally?

'I'm sure we'll come back to this, Sam. But maybe we'd better start with the usual notices. Where's your office, for a start?'

The rest of the morning passed pleasantly enough. Sam was thorough but not over-intense. She went through the management team person by person, giving her own personal view of each one's strengths and weaknesses, as well as a summary of their nominal areas of control.

From time to time, Sam would ask Maxine about her earlier career in decoding and her critique on what was expected of her team. Especially the (limited) amount of feedback they'd had on what they'd found and where it might lead.

Sam also had plenty to say about the impact of Covid.

'By and large, staff here haven't much time to be sociable. They work hard all day, then go home for a rest. It's relentless, month after month. But what about their days off?'

'Well. As you know, Maxine, there's not much indoor entertainment in Bude. One cinema, the Limelight Museum and umpteen pubs. The best places are out of doors – on beaches, the sea or the cliffs. As a result, our level of Covid infection is relatively low. And management insist: if you think you've been infected, stay at home self-isolating. So far Covid has been a problem we can handle.'

'I reckon the most likely way for me to get Covid,' said Maxine, 'is from my little girl Rosanna at her nursery. She's only been going for a few weeks; there've already been a couple of times when I've had to keep her at home because another child's tested positive.'

Sam sighed. 'And that will happen again. Whatever we do, we must take account of the virus – and its variants. At least you'll have more chance to work at home on reports than your decoders will. Most of what goes on here can't be taken off site at all.'

Which made Maxine think about exactly what she would be doing. And led Sam to open another of her files.

'The Commanding Officer, Bill Oakshot, will see you straight after lunch. He'll tell you what he wants. I'd best not pre-empt that, though you can come back to me afterwards if you want. But in the meantime, I've got an overview document for you about the management team and how it's meant to operate. You can't take it off site but it's yours for reference in this office.'

Maxine took the document. 'Thank you. By the way, what happens about lunch for people like us? Do we have our own cordon bleu restaurant?'

'I wish. Well, the team all have lunch together once a fort-night. It's something I started once I had the authority. I would say it's improved the underlying spirit. The rest of the time you either use the Camp restaurant or bring your own.'

'Do the team ever go off site? There are plenty of interesting pubs round here. My husband's a police inspector. They often eat out when they're on a case. He says that's another way of building his team.'

Sam gave a grin. 'I like the idea. But it's not done very often, if at all. Everyone in authority here is caught up on security. They act as if there's a member of Al Qaida or the FSB lurking in every bar.'

She mused for a second. 'As far as I know, there's nothing in the rules to stop it. Why don't you and I give it a try, say on Wednesday? See what happens. Apart from anything else, I'd love to see a few pictures of your Rosanna.'

CHAPTER 13

Bill Oakshot, Bude Camp Commander, was an imposing figure of upright bearing, well over six feet tall and, she guessed, in his mid-fifties. Despite the heavy demands of his role, he was generally of a cheerful disposition. Maxine had met him before, but this time was different: now he was her direct boss.

'Welcome back, Maxine,' he began, giving her a strong handshake. 'I hope you're happy with your new position. I'm glad to see your analytical and logical skills added to our management team. Right. Let's sit down. Would you prefer tea or coffee?'

'Tea, today, I think.' She'd been about to call him "sir" but was that still appropriate?

He glanced at her, guessed her confusion and smiled. 'Call me Bill, please. Unless it's a camp-wide meeting, of course. Or a Royal visit. Though the last one of those was back in 2016. Mercifully, Princess Anne didn't hold us up for too long.'

He phoned their beverage choices to his secretary and the meeting began, seated either side of the coffee table.

'I have two goals for the next hour,' Bill began. 'First, I'd like to tell you something about the management team. After that we need to discuss your tasks for the first month or two. At the end you might have one or two questions.'

If she was a full member of the team, there was no way Maxine was going to restrict her contribution to the final few minutes of the meeting. "Analytical and logical skills", if recognised, needed to be exercised. She threw out an opening question.

'How well does the team work, Bill? In your opinion?'

The Commander frowned and then smiled. 'Well done, Maxine. Stalling my standard address before it had even begun. What I deserved, anyway. OK, we'll make the whole thing interactive. But obviously, this is a private conversation: not for wider dissemination.'

'Sam went through the official descriptions of what you all do with me this morning,' she said. 'Team members, one by one. Where they came from and what they did. I know more than she did about decoding, of course. The whole lot sounded sensible enough, as far as it went. But in real life, how d'you reckon it's going?'

Bill mused for a few seconds. 'If I had to give you a one-word description, that word would be "silos".' He gave a sigh. 'I mean, we don't have duffers on the management team. They've each been hand-picked. Each one's competent in their own field. My frustration is more subtle. What we never seem to do that well is to work closely together. In fact, we try hard, not even subconsciously, to keep one another out of our own spheres of influence. I sometimes think that we're hardly a team at all.'

Bill's secretary brought in the tea tray at that moment and settled it between them. That gave Maxine a chance to think.

'Can you give me a specific example, Bill?'

'Well, since I mentioned it a few minutes ago, let's go back to the visit by Princess Anne. At one level it was a successful Royal outing. She flew in by helicopter, spent a couple of hours touring the Camp and meeting each team leader, got high-level summaries from each. After that she had a rather splendid lunch and then flew away.'

Maxine frowned. 'So why was that frustrating?'

'It was a lost opportunity. The view of Royal Intelligence for years has been that Anne is the brightest of the Queen's children. But when we had the chance for a grown-up conversation, we treated her as a numpty. We made no attempt to relate to her own experience of Security, here in the UK and around the world. No attempt to get her to understand – and interact with – the life and death issues we wrestle with, here every day.'

Bill sighed. 'I bet she went away thinking, "Gangs of boys and their toys. Playing satellites keeps them happy, but I don't really know what they do. And why are there so many of them?"'

'OK. The Royals won't properly understand us. But they aren't an active branch of government. Does that matter?'

Bill looked shocked. 'Maxine, it does. I bet there was almost no positive feedback from the Princess's visit. We'll carry on battling with government to receive ever smaller portions of a shrinking financial cake. Our Prime Minister talks about "having our cake and eating it". But our share of the cake is getting steadily smaller.'

The posh façade had faded and Bill was sounding angry. Maybe, thought Maxine, that could be a step forward?

'With hindsight, Bill, how might the visit have gone better? What lesson did you learn?'

Bill supped his mug of tea as he reflected.

'I'd say that we, the Camp team, are all too task-driven. It's a huge effort to keep regular intelligence going. Keeping track of all those signals, watching for new messengers, making sense of encrypted messages – it's all intellectually demanding. It matters. And because that's the sort of people we are, we knuckle down to doing it. We're never fully on top: that's impossible. All we can hope for is to make good judgements on what signals warrant our attention. We can't possibly always get that right.'

It was almost a council of despair. But it raised a wider question. 'And in all that effort, Bill, what gets missed out?'

'I'll tell you what gets missed out the most. That's helping one another along. Recognising that a small fraction of time spent encouraging one another, making us each feel valued, will pay off in the end.' He paused again, reflecting.

'It's almost, I'd say, Maxine, like we've lost the bigger picture.'

Maxine felt that Bill had opened up better than she'd dared hope on their first one-on-one management conversation. There were questions that had been raised that she needed to think about and hoped to return to. But, in the meantime, she must leave the Commander feeling positive and upbeat.

'Don't be too hard on yourself, Bill. It's not an easy balance to strike. On the one hand you're carrying a huge burden of the national security, which often calls for intense, high-level secrecy. Not easy to share. On the other hand, we live in a functioning democracy. Transparency and clarity are part of our values. We operate on a knife edge. No wonder we sometimes fall off.'

Maxine suddenly noticed the clock above the monitor on the wall beside her. She'd already had more than half an hour of Bill's precious time. She needed some goals of her own for the next few weeks.

'I think we were also going to talk about what you wanted me to do, as I settle back to life here?'

Bill smiled. 'Good idea, Maxine. Before we do that, would you like a second mug of tea?'

'I could do with more challenges like we've just romped through,' admitted Bill. 'As I said, there are massive gaps between our silos. I need help with an overview. Coming to see me every month or so, for a chat like we've just had, could be a valuable part of your remit.'

Maxine smiled but did not dissent. She had enjoyed their debate too. And the ideas tossed about might contribute to her enquiry for Jeremy, in Cheltenham.

'What I'd like you to do first, Maxine,' Bill went on, 'is something to help you grapple with these issues with a fresh pair of eyes; and to find ways to handle them better. So how would you like the challenge of preparing an account of the camp's history since it became an outpost of GCHQ?'

Maxine gulped. 'To do that properly would take a serious historian some years, Bill. Could I leave out the finer details like decoding?'

'That is one of our better-recorded silos. Cheltenham realise we have some very clever people here, they try hard to understand our new ideas. A decoding archivist visits every few months. Leave all that to her for the time being.'

Maxine was glad of the concession, but the task still felt unmanageable. 'Couldn't I identify key stress-points for the Camp over the last half century? Once I'd done that, I could try to deconstruct them in detail – a bit like we tried to do earlier with Princess Anne?'

Bill mused. 'Let's make the topic sharper still. Why don't you start with key battles here between the British and the Americans? There are plenty of issues to go at. But what underlying reasons make things go wrong – things that keep happening again and again? And how might the Camp avoid them in the future?'

At last, a manageable objective. But how could it be done?

'Are there Camp diaries for past years that I could work from? Would I need higher security clearance?'

'I've plenty of records in my safe here. Daily logs, financial records and so on. But they might be too detailed for a broad history.'

Maxine pondered. 'Could I interview some of your predecessors, then?'

'I can give you their names,' offered Bill. 'The most recent ones, anyway. But I can't guarantee they'd talk – even to a senior insider like yourself. Or even remember what really happened. Some might choose to forget the gory details as they move on.'

Maxine pursed her lips. 'Alright. What if I start with old hands who are still here? That'd keep me going for a few weeks, anyway.'

She noticed there were now only a few minutes left of the hour she'd been promised.

'Were there any specific issues you wanted me to look into?'

Bill nodded. 'There was one. It's last month's energy bill. Cheltenham queried it: it's about three times as high as usual. They wanted to know why.'

'Does that happen often?'

Bill sighed. 'Well, usually Martin Jordan, the Energy Director, would have added a note, accounting for any glaring anomalies. But this time, for some reason, he hasn't. So would you check this out for me, please, with Martin or his staff? Come back with your explanation, say, in a couple of weeks.'

Overall, the meeting had gone well, thought Maxine, as she strode back to her own office. No doubt Bill would want to be personally convinced that she could probe carefully and bring him back answers.

But first she needed to check with Sam. What was the Personnel view on Martin Jordan, and the best way approach him?

CHAPTER 14 Tuesday Nov 9th

Martin Jordan, the Camp's master of energy, was able to see Maxine next morning. He was an old hand; she'd often seen him around but never had much to do with him in her techie days.

He was welcoming enough. Her formidable technical reputation as a decoder must have gone before her. He ordered coffees and they chatted amicably for a short while. He was clearly happy to have her on the management team. But also keen to broaden her expertise.

'Shall I sketch out the energy scene?' he began. 'Our biggest need is for electricity to run all our thirty-odd satellite dishes and the computers. They're greedy beasts. When all's going well, we're happy to rely on the National Grid, use the same electricity as everyone else. But we need an alternative, in case that falters.'

'We're a twenty-four-hour operation,' agreed Maxine. 'There'd be panic in Whitehall if there were any gaps at all.'

Martin nodded. 'Hence, we have our own generating capacity. That's hidden away, well below ground level, and it's really well maintained. Over maintained if anything.'

'D'you know, I've never seen or heard it operate in ten years.'

'Not many staff have. We don't advertise it. You and I can go to see it later, if you like?' He smiled. 'I like to appear there unannounced from time to time, not least to check on the engineers. Make sure they are still awake. Not just doing

87

crosswords.'

'I'd really appreciate that, Martin. The more I know first-hand, the more likely I am to add to the management team. But first you need to finish telling me about the energy landscape. Presumably the generators need their own fuel?'

The master of energy sipped his coffee before replying.

'That's heavy fuel oil – essentially diesel. We have massive tanks storing that, even further below ground.' He shuddered. 'It'd be a disaster if they were ever disrupted – or sabotaged. It could blow up the whole site.'

'And where does that fuel come from?' Maxine was a bright woman. She wanted the whole picture.

'It's brought in from a Ministry of Defence establishment, in a huge oil tanker. As required. And always at night.'

Maxine drank some of her coffee as she constructed the next question. Was she hearing a defensive tone?

'And this whole arrangement never goes wrong?'

'It's worked fine over the years.'

Maxine realised she'd reached the point of decision. She could simply accept his answer. But she was on the management team; and had been asked to find a full answer for Bill Oakshot. And she knew that, for some reason or other, not so far explained, there had been a massive energy overspend in October.

She tried to think of problems that might have disrupted the arrangement.

'What happens if the MOD establishment itself is low on fuel?'

Martin looked less confident now. 'That hardly ever happens.'

'But when it does?'

He sighed. 'In the last resort we'd simply use a regular commercial supplier of fuel oil. There are plenty of them. After all, it's the same fuel as they use across industry.'

'But is it the same price? Bill Oakshot mentioned that the Camp's energy bill was three times as big as usual in October.'

There was a delay. Martin seemed to be weighing up options. Then he spoke.

'You know, Maxine, I was afraid someone high up would spot that,' he murmured. 'I can explain. But it'll take some time.'

Maxine smiled at him sweetly. 'One of the benefits of starting a new job, Martin, is that you're given time to get stuck in. Right now there's nothing else I really have to do. So, please, do explain. I always like a good story.'

Martin rang for more coffees and did not begin speaking again until it had been delivered.

'Maxine, let me first stand back a little. Did you know that 2021 has been one of the least windy years ever recorded?'

'I can't say I'd noticed. But go on, how much lower is it?'

'The average wind speed in the UK this year has been 15% below the long-term average.'

'Wow. So the energy from wind is 15% lower?'

Martin sighed. 'I'm afraid it's worse than that, Maxine. It's not a linear relationship, you see: the green energy produced is even lower. Everyone's been affected, including military establishments. So at the start of October the fuel stored here wasn't as high as we'd like it; we had to take emergency action. Call in commercial tankers.'

'Ah. And they charged a lot more than the MOD?'

'Well, they did. You might recall, diesel prices for ordinary customers rose by 25% towards the end of September. With fuel shortages at many garages. We had a heck of a struggle to find a tanker firm willing to bring all their load to this site. There are one or two reliable ones we've used before, but this time, with all the pressures, they couldn't help us. In the end we had to hire unknown tankers starting from the Pembroke refinery. And pay a premium for the privilege.'

Maxine sipped her coffee and pondered. A 25% increase might be justified. But Martin still hadn't accounted for the full discrepancy.

'Did something else go wrong?'

Martin sighed and grimaced.

'One of these tankers lost its way. Eventually turned up at three in the morning. The driver had never been here before. And I hope he never, ever, comes again.'

Maxine was silent. What disaster was coming next?

'As you know, Maxine, we have security staff here day and night. But during Covid we have been short-staffed. To cut to the chase, someone was on duty that night who didn't know the complete procedure for fuel delivery. He found the access point for the fuel storage tanks, unlocked it, showed it to the driver and assumed he would know what to do.'

'Sounds alright,' admitted Maxine. 'So what went wrong?'

Martin made a strangling sound as he revisited the disaster in his mind. 'What went wrong, Maxine, was that this idiot, whom we'd paid to come from the back end of Wales, up to Bristol and back to Cornwall, had a complete tank full of petrol. Which he proceeded to add to a tank already half-full of heavy fuel oil. Thus, at a stroke, making most of our emergency fuel supply unusable.'

Maxine didn't know what to say. It was a complete calamity. Poor, poor Martin. But this couldn't be the end of the tale.

She smiled at him empathetically. It was important that he realised she was on his side.

'Martin, you must have a procedure here to drain a tank that contains a mixture of fuels? After all, the problem can happen easily enough with a car.'

'Oh, we have a procedure all right. Though it's one we've never had to use. Of course, it all had to be done at night. In total secret. It'd be a disaster for the Camp if any of this story ever reached the public domain.'

Martin drank more of his coffee, then continued. 'Mercifully the National Grid continued to perform well for the rest of that week, so we didn't need our own power generator.'

'So how was it resolved?'

'First of all, we had to hire two special tankers, to take away the contaminated fuel. That turned out to cost nearly as much as buying the stuff in the first place. Also a huge effort by our own engineers to access the emergency valve at the bottom of the tank, then connect a pipe to it that led back to the surface.

'After that we had to go round the whole loop again, to find a supplier of heavy fuel oil that could deliver to us in a hurry. But we were very lucky. The fuel crisis didn't last that long and one of our regular suppliers quickly became available.

'Finally we had to lay off the security man who'd allowed the whole problem to develop, pay him compensation so he wouldn't say anything to anyone and then hire someone new to replace him.'

Maxine nodded. 'So, in all, you had to pay firstly for an initial delivery at a premium, secondly for the tankers to take away the unusable mixture, and thirdly for the replacement fuel. No wonder the energy bill for the month trebled. And you had to keep the whole thing as secret as possible. I can see why you chose not to say anything in your monthly report to Bill Oakshot. It wasn't a matter of keeping it from him, it was who else might read it. It's a living nightmare.'

Even so, Maxine felt relieved that she now understood the

problem and its resolution. She'd have something to tell Bill Oakshot when she next saw him.

Later, after they'd finished their coffees, Martin led Maxine behind the scenes. They went down some long, unpainted corridors, a couple of stairwells and then an even longer tunnel, to see the generator and to meet the engineers who maintained it.

'Which came first, the well-below ground generator or these tunnels?' she asked. 'They all look pretty old to me.'

'There used to be a manor on this site,' Martin told her. 'You might see the site referenced on very old maps. Not recently, mind, it was knocked down years and years ago. I think these passageways might have led down to the manor's cellars.'

They continued their journey and eventually came to a large cavern with a big piece of machinery in the middle. 'This is the power generator.'

'It's much bigger than I expected. I assume there must be some sort of ventilation to get rid of the exhaust fumes?'

'That's this shaft over here,' Martin replied. 'It's been here for a long time, too. We had to enlarge the chamber to fit it all in. It's a large plant.'

'So where are your engineers?'

Martin looked puzzled. 'I'd expected to find them here, doing some sort of maintenance. Perhaps we'd better come back another time?'

Maxine didn't mind that much. It had been an interesting morning anyway. Now she was starting to look forward to her lunch.

CHAPTER 15   Wednesday Nov 10th

Notwithstanding her new job in management, Wednesday's highlight for Maxine was going to be lunch out with her new friend Sam at the Morwenstow Rectory Tea Room.

Maxine had been there often enough over the years with her husband, Peter, though it was always a treat. She was amazed to find that Sam had never been there at all.

'Where d'you live? It can't be that far from where we're going today,' she asked her companion, as they set out in Maxine's car on the three-mile journey to the famous tea room.

'I share a house with a couple of friends, on the south side of Bude. How about you?'

'I'm in Poughill. My husband's a police officer in Bude, so we've got a house midway between our two jobs. Mind, Peter often has to travel about on his cases. But he says that makes the work more interesting.'

'So in a way you're both covering aspects of security. That must be tricky. How d'you manage the potential conflicts?'

Maxine gave a rueful smile. 'We had a few misunderstandings and one blazing row early on. In the end we agreed it would be best to erect an imaginary Chinese wall between us – in other words, we wouldn't talk about our work to one another at all. That's a relief, most of the time. You and I had better be careful over lunch, by the way.'

Soon they were in Morwenstow and parked along from the Rectory. 'The local church is over there,' said Maxine. 'You can just see the tower. It's quite renowned. In the century before last it had a famous vicar called Robert Hawker.'

'What was he famous for?'

'He was a bit of an eccentric. For example, he once dressed up as a mermaid and sat on the quayside in Bude. He was also a poet and a writer. He used to encourage his congregation to care for the survivors of shipwrecks, which happened often enough on the nearby shores. He built himself a small wooden hut to watch for them.'

'A beach hut, you mean?'

Maxine frowned. 'Not exactly. It was a four-hundred-foot drop from his hut to the rocks below. He'd sit in it for hours, writing poetry as he watched out for potential shipwrecks. It's also claimed that he invented a Harvest Festival service, to use when the harvest had been gathered in. That's a legacy still widely celebrated over the whole country today.'

Maxine turned and led her colleague into the tea room. 'I rang to book a table for us earlier,' she remarked. 'Though I don't expect the place is busy at this time of year. I mainly wanted to check it was open.'

Soon they were seated out of earshot of the few other guests, with a view over the rectory garden. Orders were placed.

'Better to skip the alcohol,' Sam murmured. 'We don't want to get into trouble on our first exeat.' They each ordered a light lunch and a lime and soda.

Sam glanced round the dark-wood panelled walls and the Punch-Style cartoons hung to adorn them. 'You know, this is all a bit special,' she remarked. 'I'll have to bring my housemates here.'

'OK then,' she continued. 'Let's see some photos of your little one.'

Maxine got out her phone. The chatter over Rosanna and

her quirky ways continued until their lunches were brought. Then she put her phone away; she knew not to overdo it.

'I had a good meeting with Martin Jordan yesterday.'

'Well done. That's one leader down on meeting the team. He's a wise old owl, I think.'

'He was telling all about how they generated energy. Then he showed me the kit they use to produce it.'

'Wow. You have made a hit. I've never been offered the chance to see any machinery. Is it interesting? I mean, to anybody but an engineer?'

Maxine nodded. 'It's an impressive size and well looked after. There's a whole gang on the job. But what struck me most was that it was all located so deep underground. Martin had some sort of explanation. He said it had been put in "one of the cellars of Cleave Manor, that used to stand on the site". It was news to me that there'd ever been a manor there.'

Sam mused for a few seconds. 'It's news to me too. But it's not that surprising. If you look carefully on the Bude Explorer map you can see lots of remains of old manors – they're often named in an old font. A few are still inhabited: most of these have been revamped and turned into farmhouses. One or two are professionally unearthed ruins, managed by English Heritage. But there must be a few others like Cleave Manor, with no trace left at all.'

Maxine nodded. 'I'm surprised, though, that if there's no trace at all left on the surface there are still a wealth of cellars left down below. I mean, what else might be down there?'

They pondered as they munched their quiches. But the arrival of the waitress, to see if they wanted cream scones, closed off the topic.

'So I've still to meet the rest of the management team. Have you any advice on how I should handle them?'

Sam mused for a moment. 'You've started well.' Then she began to go through them. This time, off-site, she was less discreet than she'd been in Maxine's office. There was lots of sensible advice. Then she decided it was her turn to push the boat out.

'Did Bill give you any longer-term project? That's what he usually tries. It's his own form of personal assessment.'

Maxine nodded. 'He asked me to take a fresh look at Anglo-American relations at the site. How might they be handled better?'

'Wow. That sounds like one of those insoluble problems that tutors give their students to keep them off their backs.'

Maxine grimaced. 'Thanks for the encouragement. But there are issues, aren't there?'

'Bound to be. My ailing boss, Vanessa – the one who contracted long Covid – used to despair about it. She tried to make sense of the rows at national level, too. She could see that they all made running the Camp harder. For Vanessa it became an obsession.'

Was that another source emerging? 'Sam, maybe I could talk to her? Pick her brains. Is she visitable? Or is she infectious?'

'I don't think she's infectious any more. Her trouble is that she has so little energy. She tried coming back to work a year ago, but after a couple of hours tidying her desk, she was exhausted. It was a mess. We had to send her home in a taxi. Privately, afterwards, Bill was quite annoyed about the whole thing. Said she shouldn't come back till she could do a full day's work like the rest of us. But I think he was more annoyed with the medics than with Vanessa herself.'

'Covid's a brand-new disease, Sam,' protested Maxine. 'Doctors need time to process things like everyone else. Hey, d'you think she could cope with a visit from someone new to the team, like me?'

'She'd love it, Maxine, provided you didn't stay too long. You're easy to talk to anyway. I've got her home number; would you like it? She could handle a short call, at any rate.'

Maxine decided she wouldn't rush making the call; she'd reflect before barging in. Work out what she really wanted. She didn't want the recovering woman to feel pushed out even further.

It was as they were settling the bill that Sam noticed the cashier had leaflets for sale about the Revd Robert Hawker. She recalled their earlier conversation, decided she might as well learn a bit more about him. 'Can I have one of those, please?'

'Certainly. We've a few of the great man's books too. They're all out of print, so I'm afraid we've no copies to sell. But you could have a look at one while you ate, the next time you come.'

'I'd certainly like a return visit,' enthused Sam, as they headed back to the car. 'Could we come again next week?'

CHAPTER 16   Thursday Nov 11th

Maxine decided that she would ring Vanessa. Later she was extremely glad that she had done so.

'I'd love to see someone from Camp, Maxine. Anyone. New or old. It'd be better than daytime television, anyway. When can you come?'

In the end Maxine agreed she'd come early next week, in time for mid-morning coffee. Vanessa had declared this was generally her most awake period of the day.

'But I'll leave as soon as you've had enough,' Maxine promised. 'I certainly don't want to make you exhausted.'

When she got to the specified address, Maxine found that Vanessa lived in an charming thatched cottage, close to the centre of Stratton.

'I bought this nearly forty years ago,' Vanessa explained, as she welcomed Maxine in. 'That's when I started at Cleave Camp: 1984. Prices were far lower then, of course. I could just about afford it.' She smiled. 'I was very lucky, wouldn't have a cat in hell's chance of buying the place now.'

Maxine looked at her carefully. Vanessa was a tall, serious-looking woman with an oval face and long, grey hair, probably in her early sixties. She didn't look that ill, wasn't coughing or wheezing. But she didn't have much spark in her eyes and was moving very slowly.

'Shall I begin by making us coffee?' Vanessa asked.

'That'd be great, Vanessa. D'you want me to help make it?'

'That's kind of you, m'dear. But it's not hard, the way I do it. I wouldn't mind a hand reaching down the biscuits, though.'

Ten minutes later they were sat on soft chairs in the living room with a tray of coffees and a plate of chocolate biscuits between them.

'Do you get many visitors?' asked Maxine.

'Not many, these days. I have online delivery from the local Morrison's for my groceries. I don't suppose he's supposed to, but the delivery man comes right in and helps me put things away. That's a big help. A nurse comes to check on me from time to time. And one or two friends in Stratton drop in occasionally. But I haven't been outside by myself in the village for months.'

It sounded dire. No wonder she was looking forward to Maxine's visit.

The next twenty minutes was spent on Cleave Camp. Vanessa sounded pleased rather than jealous that Sam was covering for her and remembered the names of all the management team. There was nothing wrong with her brain, at any rate.

'Right, m'dear,' she said at last. 'Thank you so much for giving me some attention. You've made me feel part of things again. I'd love to keep the chat going. But I know there was a specific reason that you wanted to see me. Ought we give some attention to that before my energy goes?'

Maxine outlined the remit she'd been given by Bill Oakshot. 'He sensed that all was not as it should be. But he wasn't sure exactly what was wrong. One area that worried him was the links between the British team and the American staff in the Camp.'

'There've been worries around that, Maxine, for all the time I've worked here,' Vanessa responded. 'I've spent ages trying to make sense of it as well.'

'If you don't mind telling me, what were your best ideas?'

'My first degree was in Psychology. I wondered if there was a kink in the personalities of the Americans who were chosen to come here that clashed intrinsically, and repeatedly, with our own management team.'

Maxine thought for a moment. 'That's an interesting idea, Vanessa. It'll be true for some combinations of British and American leaders we've had at the Camp over the years. Like chalk and cheese. But haven't there always been problems?'

Vanessa laughed. 'That's more or less what Bill told me, when I tried to talk to him about it.'

'So what came next?'

'Well, I wondered if it wasn't the individuals, but if there was a clash between British and American cultures.'

'You mean, like the British always being more reserved, while the Americans are far more gung-ho?'

Vanessa shook her head. 'Not exactly. You see, we still have far more things in common than we have that's different. The variation isn't enough. No, I was more thinking about cultural differences peculiar to the secret services.'

Maxine wasn't sure she was following and said so.

'Well, are there huge, deep differences in what each nation is trying to achieve? Trouble is, that's hard to pin down.'

There was a moment of silence. Maxine wondered if Vanessa was a spent force, but no, she still looked quite animated. She was obviously a woman who relished the discussion of ideas.

'When I met Bill,' said Maxine, 'he was still frustrated about aspects of the visit by Princess Anne, even though that was five years ago. Were you around that day? Did that have any cross-cultural impact on our American friends?'

Vanessa smiled. 'It most certainly did. The American coordinator at the time was a strong supporter of Donald Trump.

He was apoplectic at the thought of a freestanding Royal, breezing through the whole place, seeing everything and asking whatever questions she liked. "You guys like to boast about the strength of British security," the coordinator said, "but you're the least secure place on the planet." It took Bill a long time to settle the poor bloke down again, once the Princess had gone.'

There was silence. That seemed like a bit of a one-off. Both women struggled to see where the conversation might be going.

'Suppose,' said Maxine, speaking slowly as she pulled ideas together, 'we keep to the notion of differences around Camp security. Might that be a recurring theme? Even a running sore? I mean, did it come up often over your time at the Camp?'

Vanessa nodded. 'Yes. I'd say it was a persistent undercurrent. But how much it mattered depended on events on the international stage.'

'How d'you mean?'

'Well, President Obama wanted to dial down US military effort. He wasn't pushing security too hard. In his time we didn't have much of a problem.'

'But what about George Bush? He had to contend with the horrors of Nine-Eleven. And after that the invasions of Afghanistan and then Iraq.'

Vanessa nodded again. 'Yes, Maxine. But on our side, whether you liked it or not, Tony Blair was Bush's biggest supporter. Which helped links here too.'

'Alright, then. When were things most tense?'

Vanessa paused as she thought back. 'I'd say the worst was soon after I arrived. Of course, I was only junior then, but Personnel had a hard job to keep both sides together. It was the final years of the Cold War.'

Maxine considered her hostess's reply.

'I hate to admit it, Vanessa, but in 1984 I was still at school.

I didn't follow politics at all. But in those days wasn't Margaret Thatcher our Prime Minister?'

Vanessa nodded. 'She was, yes.'

'And her soulmate, Ronald Reagan, ran the United States?'

Vanessa nodded again.

'So, if they were singing from the same hymn sheet, shouldn't that have made things easier here at the Camp?'

'It's a good question,' admitted the older woman. 'I don't know the full answer. You'd need to talk to the Security Director – that's Zak Howarth, I believe – and he might not be willing to tell you. But I recall there was a potential development on a new piece of eavesdropping kit in 1985 that was thought to threaten the Camp. It made everyone very twitchy – especially our American cousins.'

Maxine would love to take this further. But she could see that Vanessa was starting to look very tired. And she remembered her promise to leave when that happened.

'Vanessa, why don't we stop for now. I'll come back another time, assuming you'll still have me. As soon as I've seen the Security Director, if you like?'

Maxine felt she was making progress. But she could see it was going to be a long haul.

CHAPTER 17   Monday Nov 15th

Fortunately, on her planned schedule to meet every member of the management team, security supremo Zak Howarth happened to be the next person booked onto her list. Maxine was due to see him the following afternoon.

As she sat at her desk after the meeting with Vanessa, she recalled Sam's perceptive comments about Zak over lunch. 'He's very bright and well up with the latest technology. Trouble is, he knows it. And that makes him overwhelmingly self-confident. I've no direct proof, but I fear he's something of a misogynist. Good luck!'

But if that was true, how on earth was she going to get anything out of this security wizard? It didn't sound like he'd find it easy to cooperate.

It took half an hour before the answer came to her. Actually, it was obvious. She would break with domestic protocol and ask her husband for help. The police might not be up to date with the latest security issues but there would surely be someone on the police books – maybe a guru over in Bodmin – who would be something of an expert.

What made this a plausible idea was that she wasn't after the latest technology. She wanted to explore ideas which had threatened the Camp – or at least its top management – forty years ago. Maybe she was being too fussy, didn't need to understand them at all? But Maxine was an astute woman, didn't like to be ill-informed on anything she was studying. Or to appear any more ignorant than was strictly necessary.

Five minutes later she was on the phone to Bude police station. She was in luck: Peter Travers was in his office and could take a direct call from his wife. Though he sounded surprised to hear from her.

'Peter, I'm sorry to disturb you, but something has come up here where police expertise might be a great help.'

'Go on. This is supposed to be my lunch hour, darling, so it's not a bad time to chat.'

Briefly Maxine sketched out the nub of her problem. 'Is there anyone in the North Cornwall police who might be able to help me?'

The conversation continued until Peter Travers felt he understood what his wife was after. 'Let me check with our so-called experts. If I make any progress and find someone, I'll get them to ring you back straight away, on your mobile. You and I can perhaps talk more around this this evening.'

Maxine felt she'd done the best she could. Now all she could do was wait.

The call came later in the afternoon. It was the gruff voice of an older person – exactly what she needed. Moreover, he sounded friendly. 'Call me Walter,' he said. No doubt Peter had been at his most charming in seeking help; and she wouldn't need to say exactly where she was based.

'I've been told that there was some insiders' development in technology, Walter, that was being talked about in the early eighties. It caused consternation at security sites, though that's long since passed away. Have you any idea what it might have been?'

'Right. I'm with you. I'm guessing the precise context, but I presume you'd rather not tell me too much?'

Maxine agreed. There were a few seconds of silence.

'The nineteen eighties are a long time ago in security terms. I wasn't into security then myself. So I'm working from the old records here, which fortunately for us haven't been thrown away. Sometimes scruffy housekeeping has its advantages.'

'OK,' said Maxine cautiously.

'There are lots of things listed here which even I can hardly understand, let alone share. This was before the internet, you realise.'

'I understand some bits of my problem but I'm not a technical wizard,' Maxine said. 'It's a broad outline that I'm after.'

There was silence for a few moments. She could hear pages being turned in the background. Then came a prolonged scratching of a beard.

'Well,' said Walter, 'there's one idea here which is very intriguing.'

'Go on.' He must be teasing her now. She had to stay cool.

'Apparently, there was a point in time when it was realised that special lasers might be used to pick up conversations which were happening on the other side of a glass window.' A moment of panic seized him. 'You do know what I mean by a laser?'

Maxine smiled. 'I know the basics. Incredibly focussed beams of energy. My main degree is in pure mathematics, but we had one or two courses in physics. This was back in the early nineties. Tell me more.'

'Well, special kit was developed that showed the idea would work well on plain glass. But it turned out that it couldn't handle double glazing. So, if you wanted to avoid the risk, you'd just have to use double (or even treble) glazing on every key window. Which on modern buildings, where security mattered, wasn't that difficult. The idea quickly passed into distant legend. By now it's been almost totally forgotten.'

'Walter, thank you. Hang onto those records. They might

continue to be useful.'

Maxine moved away from her desk to one of her easy chairs. She needed to think outside the box.

She now had one possible idea – mad, but not just science fiction – that might have caused panic in security circles thirty-odd years ago. How would this help her interview tomorrow with Zak Howarth?

Zak was the one member of the management team that had arrived while she was on maternity leave. She'd seen him at a distance, passed him on the corridor, but never spoken with him directly. He was probably a decade younger than she was.

Walter's finding of laser-based listening was years before any courses that Zak might have been on. He'd probably dismiss it out of hand – especially if it came from a woman. Was there anything she could do to make herself sound more convincing?

Maxine pondered for some time. There was one thing she could do: traverse the outer boundary of Cleave Camp for herself. Try to imagine how a piece of advanced technical kit like a listening laser might be used to eavesdrop on key conversations inside camp buildings. Where might it be hidden and what might it pick up? How dangerous was it? What would happen if it rained?

But it would be unwise to take this step on her own. She didn't know exactly how the camp boundary was protected these days – it certainly wasn't armed guards in watch towers – but she didn't want to trip some deep-seated alert into action. Being tasered was not on her list of desirable experiences.

On the other hand, she was part of the management team. The general public were allowed to walk along the Coast path, not far from the Camp: why not her?

It was as she called at the security hut to check out on her way home that vague notion turned into a concrete action. If she handled it right, might one of the security staff be persuaded to come to reconnoitre with her?

There was a friendly man she had seen on duty every day so far who sported a magnificent black beard, making him look like a modern-day pirate. He was no youngster, must be around her own age. By chance there was no-one else in the hut when she went in.

'What happens to people like you in mid shift,' she asked, 'between checking us all in and checking us out again?'

The man laughed. 'We're supposed to be off duty. Which is daft, really. There's no point in me going home for a couple of hours. We have a security rest room and I've been doing plenty of reading. Why d'you ask?'

'I'm seeing the security supremo tomorrow afternoon. Zak Howarth. I'd like to be as well-informed as I can about the lie of the land before I meet him. In particular, I'd like to walk right around the camp perimeter – see the whole thing from the outside.'

'I probably know less about it than you do. I've only been here for a month.' (Was he the replacement brought in by Martin Jordan?)

But Maxine wasn't taking no for an answer. 'I need to make my survey look official. I don't want to be tasered, or whatever the default response is these days.'

The man considered. 'Two of us in security jackets will be safe enough. I'll tell my boss I'm taking management on a guided tour.' He glanced at the pass she'd just checked in. 'Why don't you come for me here, Mrs Travers, just after eleven?'

CHAPTER 18   Tuesday Nov 16th

Maxine made sure she was ready for an outdoor hike as she dressed next morning. Jeans and walking boots replaced her business skirt and shoes. The smarter items went into her backpack, as well as coffee to drink on the way round. She'd smarten herself up once she'd completed the survey. There was no point in alienating Zak by meeting him dressed as a hiker.

She was at the hut just on eleven. The jolly pirate was waiting for her. Was that a gleam of excitement in his eye?

'Still fine with this?' she asked.

'Looking forward to it,' he replied. 'Security's deadly dull. I like anything that's a change from routine. Though I'm not sure what we're going to find. Here's your security jacket. My name's Marcus, by the way.'

She smiled. 'Please call me Maxine. I've been here for a decade, but I was off on maternity leave till two weeks back. Right, I think we'll do this whole thing anticlockwise.'

They walked out to the road and headed north along the camp double fence for a short distance.

'What were you doing before you came here, Marcus?'

'Other security jobs, mostly in London. But my boss knew I'd jump at a job in Cornwall when there was a chance.'

'Are you from Cornwall? I can't hear the accent, I'm afraid.'

Marcus grinned. 'I'm hoping it will return if I stay here long enough. I was brought up in Padstow, actually.'

'And I'm a Helston lass, from the Lizard. I lost most of my accent at Cambridge. The posh girls talked me out of it. Then I worked at Cheltenham for years. That didn't help much either.'

There was a short pause. 'Are we looking for anything in particular?' asked Marcus as they tramped along.

Maxine had wondered how much she dare share. She guessed that, if he knew, Zak would be incandescent about her sharing anything with a lowly security man. But Marcus seemed a sensible guy; and at this stage she'd been told nothing officially at all.

By now they'd reached the corner of the Camp. If they wanted to stay close to its fence, they needed to turn off the road and tramp over rough ground instead. Not much of a path there.

'Can we agree, Marcus, that everything we say to one another this morning is background only, it's off the record?'

'That's fine by me.'

'I've been asked to look into reasons for recurring quarrels between Brits and Americans here at the Camp. Things got tense, I gather, in the 1980s. Someone else suggested to me that one security threat in those days might have been a device to allow you to eavesdrop on conversations from outside a building – maybe even from outside the surrounding fence.'

Marcus glanced at the array of structures inside the high fencing. Most were satellite dishes of varying sizes. 'You wouldn't be able to listen to them. All you'd hear would be the background hum and whirring.' He noted that there was just one brick building in the middle of the area.

'It wouldn't do much good these days though, Maxine. Practically everything that matters here churns away deep underground.'

'Yes. But remember, we're talking about the mid-eighties. Nearly forty years ago. My husband has an old Explorer map published in 1980. We were looking at it last night. There were more buildings in those days. They even had a first-floor restaurant so staff could enjoy coastal views. If you could regularly pick up lunchtime chatter, when staff were off their guard, you might learn something of value.'

They tramped on. The rough ground continued over the bracken, but there weren't any buildings around here where you might hide some sort of laser-based listener.

'This device would presumably be powered by electricity?' asked Marcus.

'Or batteries, I guess. It would need power of some sort.'

'But in either case you'd want to keep the instrument itself dry; and it'd need to be set in a fixed position.'

Maxine frowned. 'Might you use a tent?'

'If you hid it inside a tent, however well camouflaged, it would be easy for security to spot.' He shrugged. 'I'm sorry, Maxine, I'd say the whole thing is a non-starter.'

Maxine did not respond, though she feared he might be right.

They were still beside the fence, heading steadily towards the coast. Ten minutes later they'd reached the end of that stretch and could see the Coast Path, a hundred yards away, running along the cliff top and heading towards them.

Suddenly they saw it, just ahead. An odd, round structure, six feet high and ten feet across, with stone walls. It had grass growing on top of a corrugated metal roof.

'Whatever's that?' asked Maxine.

Her companion knew his history better than she did. 'It's a pillbox. Built in the Second World War to guard the coast from invasion. I guess there'd always be soldiers stationed inside it.'

'Can we get inside?'

They circled the structure slowly. There were slits on the side looking out to sea, presumably to watch for enemy vessels; and to protect the soldiers inside from enemy fire, if there was ever

110

a battle. Plus a closed door, facing inland. Which, to Maxine's frustration, was locked.

'It's only a simple lock,' declared Marcus, as he peered at it. 'You could break it open if you were determined enough. I could do it myself if I'd brought the right kit. It could have been here for decades.'

He glanced at her. 'Well, congratulations, Maxine. It's not impossible after all. Something like this pillbox might well have done the trick forty years ago.'

At long last Maxine started to feel relaxed. It would have been possible, after all, to eavesdrop on the Camp remotely in the 1980s. She had something to put to Zak Howarth that he would find hard to dismiss as total nonsense.

'We're about halfway round,' she observed. 'Would you like to share my coffee?' She pulled the flask out from her backpack, plus a couple of plastic beakers.

Marcus nodded. 'It'd help warm us up. Let's go down to the cliff edge to drink it.'

It was as they sat looking down that they saw them. Two older women on the beach far below. There was no obvious path, it was unclear how they'd got down to it. Incredibly, it looked like they were both going to go skinny dipping.

'They're brave souls,' said Marcus. 'I bet they don't stay in long. This wind is biting.'

Maxine was shivering in sympathy. 'Please don't use those binoculars, Marcus. It's not polite to watch. If they want to suffer, they can do it on their own. Come on, we'd better get going.'

They continued their circuit, passing a few more pillboxes as they walked. Several had a good view of the camp building. Half an hour later they were back at the entrance.

Just enough time, thought Maxine, to collect her thoughts and get changed, ready for her meeting with Zak Howarth.

111

CHAPTER 19   Wednesday Nov 17th

In the end, Maxine's efforts to learn about subtle eavesdropping methods forty years ago did not help much in her meeting with Zak Howarth. He was a man up with security trends and focussed on the future. He had little knowledge of past tensions at Cleave Camp and not much interest in them either.

Maxine took some comfort from the view that the Camp was more likely to be secure from this approach, maybe less vulnerable to fallouts with the Americans over security.

Meanwhile, her meetings with other members of the management team trundled on. She learned a lot about many other aspects of camp management, but no-one had been around for long enough to add much to her file of camp history. Her best hope of progress seemed to lie with Vanessa.

When she next drove to Stratton, Vanessa seemed more alert than before, keen to aid Maxine's project. Maybe knowing that at least someone found her of value was helping to combat the long Covid?

Once they'd got their coffees, Maxine couldn't help but start with her own findings. She was proud that she'd something practical to say; her contributions in the past had all been on subtleties of decoding. 'The notion of sophisticated eavesdropping, from just outside the camp boundary, wasn't daft at all.'

She described what she'd learned from the police specialist about the use of lasers for eavesdropping. That was new to Vanessa. Then she went on to her exploration of the camp perimeter and the discovery of the old pillboxes outside it.

'So I'd say that whichever nationality was most worried about the idea – whether it was the Brits or the Americans – was broadly correct,' she concluded.

'The Americans were right then,' Vanessa observed glumly.

There was a moment of silence.

'Looking back, d'you think that was generally the case? The Americans usually knew more?'

Vanessa nodded. 'It might well have been. Of course, we're proud in the UK of our security traditions – Bletchley Park and so on. But maybe that was the exception rather than the rule.'

'An out-of-the-box Prime Minister, allied to some outstanding, proactive mathematicians?'

Vanessa nodded. There was another pause for thought.

'Can we go any further back?' asked Maxine. 'I mean, there was a lot of tension between Britain and the United States in the 1960s, I'm told. Trouble is, that was long before I was born.'

'I was at school then,' said Vanessa. 'Not following politics at all. But I read it up later. There was huge pressure on our Prime Minister, Harold Wilson, from John Kennedy's successor, Lyndon Johnson. Wilson was asked, politely but repeatedly, to put a few troops into the Vietnam war. Even a token platoon from the Black Watch would do. But to his great credit he refused.'

Maxine was listening hard. 'And if our Prime Minister was having an ongoing row with the American President, that would probably feed down into the lesser mortals at Cleave Camp?'

'I believe so.'

'That's a long time ago, Vanessa. Do you have any hard data on this?'

Vanessa sipped more of her coffee before she replied. She reflected that this was the first time she had been asked this question directly. Was this the time to share?

Maxine noticed the silence, wondering if there was some secret she was about to be told.

'I've never seen anything written down,' Vanessa began.

'No?'

'When I first came here, in 1984, there was a Director of Personnel – though she didn't call herself that in those days – who'd been here since the 1960s. She was only a minion back then; but she was in Personnel, who talked to one another, so she knew most of what was going on. And what she knew worried her a great deal.'

'Go on, Vanessa.'

'So when this director retired, she took all her department off-site for a long afternoon, to a tea-room near Hartland – Docton Mill. It's in a streamed garden, way off the beaten track. No-one else around. There, in the stillness, she told us everything that she could remember.'

Vanessa paused, reflecting, but Maxine could see there was a lot more to come.

'How much of it can you remember?' she asked. 'This must have been a long time ago.'

Vanessa looked mildly embarrassed now. 'It was 1995. Thirty years after the events she was recalling. We knew this was what she was going to do. She was gung-ho for retirement, wanted to leave all her memories behind. And the nightmares. So, with her blessing, I took along a tape recorder to capture her memories for those she left behind.'

'But you'd have had to give the tape to the new department head?'

'Of course. Straightaway, next morning. I've no idea what happened to it. I mean, cassette tapes are obsolete these days. But I had the sense to take a copy for myself before I did so.

I've had it ever since and it's not leaving this cottage. But I could play it for you if you liked?'

Maxine nodded, trying to hide her excitement. 'Why don't we make some more coffee before we start?'

Vanessa pressed the "play" button and a warm, mature female voice started speaking.

'I'd say the trouble began in 1966. It came after Johnson first publicly pushed Wilson for some token British troops, to add to his own forces serving in Vietnam. That wasn't a popular war with young people even then – course, it got a lot worse as time went on. "It'll make us into a multi-national force," he pleaded, "show we're on the same side. Standing together against communism."

'But Wilson was a recently elected leader of a Labour party which had strong trade union links. He couldn't just be seen to cave in, least of all to American pressure. He refused. And made sure everyone knew it.

'That was when the Americans here at the camp started playing up.

'This place was a joint investment, you see. The United States had provided most of the funding needed to turn a rather ramshackle radio station, run by British intelligence for its own ends, into a collaborative, "best of breed" international tracking station. That was when the Americans became formally part of the management here.

'Of course, the senior commander was a British appointment and always would be: this is British soil. But now the Americans started exerting a stronger influence on the way the place was run. Especially, I would say, in the realm of security.

'There were lots of niggles behind the scenes. Britain had always been laid back, casual shall we say, on its procedures. As

115

we all know, Cleave Camp is miles off the beaten track - it's six miles off a main road for a start. It was hard to imagine it being subject to any serious threat. At least, that was the British view in 1966.

'But the Americans always went for overkill on security; and after all, they were the ones now at war. By and large we had to accept their new ways, whether we liked it or not.

'On issue after issue we gave way. Formal entry. Barbed wire fences. There were just one or two points where we dug in our heels. One was the Coast Path. The Americans were horrified that ordinary citizens - civilians, no less - could walk past the camp, within a hundred yards of the boundary fence, with no checks on them at all.

'The Americans wanted the camp boundary to be extended right to the cliff edge, with the Coast Path diverted well inland. It was a massive fight. Our commander knew it couldn't be done. Our military didn't have that much power. The Coast Path had been there long before the Camp was linked to security. The best thing to do, he said, was to strengthen the fence, move the sensitive work underground and otherwise say nothing at all. Those who walked the Coast Path were innocent hikers, not terrorists. Britain had fought two world wars to win them that freedom.'

'"So what happened?" asked another voice.

'In the end, the Americans backed down. They held total sway within the Camp. But that meant nothing outside. The Coast Path wasn't a military structure and not a subject for negotiation. Trouble was, the affair did nothing to enhance harmony and cooperation between our nations.

'"But surely such an issue would be forgotten inside a few months?" asked a listener. "After all, the Coast Path is still here."

116

There was a pause.

'Trouble was, ladies, the argument reminded one of the Americans – I never worked out who – about an even older controversy. Which for us Brits came completely out of the blue.

'"You British were always flaky at protecting the military," he alleged. "Even during the Second World War."

'A rustle of surprise could be heard in the background. "How dare they?" asked someone.

'"What was their evidence for this?" asked someone else.

'Finally, the main speaker responded.

'Well. The accuser said there'd been an experienced American pilot based here, who was shot down by British forces. And worst of all, the whole affair had been shoved under the carpet. No-one had ever been arrested or even charged. So how could they be expected to work in partnership with British forces now?

'It was a nasty accusation, one that could run and run. Of course, it was officially denied. Our commander asked for hard evidence – say the name of the airman killed, or the date when it happened – and nothing was ever produced. But that didn't mean the rumour was scotched – or that it was forgiven. I'd say it's been passed down from one American coordinator to another ever since. In my opinion it underpins everything that goes on here between our two nations in this Camp.'

There was a pause in the narrative. Vanessa sighed, reached behind and switched off the recorder.

'You're welcome to listen to more if you want, Maxine, but there's another hour of discussion on the tape. I've listened to it all in full several times, and never heard any more disclosures.'

Maxine pondered for several moments. 'An unresolved issue, like we've just heard described, could really feed ongoing conflict. Did this meeting in the teashop come to any firm conclusions about what could be done to clear it all up?'

'How d'you mean?'

'Well, on what we heard just now, it's not clear if this shooting down of an American airman happened at all, or if it was just a scurrilous rumour. Surely it's worth trying to nail which it is?'

Vanessa looked quizzical but slightly tired. 'Yes. But how could we do that?'

Maxine mused. She was perhaps more familiar with the latest technology.

'Well, for a start, it'd be worth trawling the internet. It might not have made the newspapers at the time – it was wartime, they might have been banned from publishing bad news from home – but if it was the scandal that was claimed, you'd have thought someone would have picked it up over the years. Would you like me to have a go and have a look?'

Vanessa looked relieved that she wasn't being asked to do more herself. 'Would you mind, Maxine? Actually, I think I'd better throw you out soon. It's been a great morning's sharing, thank you for listening so patiently. But now I'm starting to feel weary. Bloody Covid. I think I'd better stop soon. Please, though, do come again.'

CHAPTER 20

Maxine was now ready for her next meeting with Camp Commander Bill Oakshot.

As requested, she'd prepared a written explanation of the reason for the high energy bill which had been incurred last month and checked it with Martin Jordan. She hoped this would close off the issue.

She'd also got early findings on past rows between senior Brits and Americans at the Camp. The main question had been how much of her sources she could reveal. All being well, most of the meeting would be spent taking these ideas forwards.

Maxine's explanation of why the energy bill had been so high – the cost of recovering from a mistake by a hard-pressed supplier, during a national fuel crisis – caused no issue at all. Bill was mainly after an explanation. He wasn't out for blood. And he accepted that mistakes sometimes cost money to sort out.

On past conflicts, Bill was happy simply to be told her results so far. He wasn't wanting Maxine to account for every hour she had spent, or to know exactly whom she had talked to.

'Probably best if I don't know everything,' he said philosophically. 'You're meant to be of independent mind. I trust you. Let's just go through the ideas at this stage.'

'Right. Well, first of all, did you know that there used to be a manor on this site?'

Bill considered the idea, then nodded slowly. 'I didn't, but I guess the site land is flat enough. It'd be an obvious place to build, really. On a clear day the coast views are phenomenal. Mind, there are no trees. So you'd have little protection from that relentless wind. How might a manor make leaders more edgy? How might it add to conflict?'

'Well. Cleave Manor used to have a huge set of cellars and linking underground passages. The fuel tanks are in one and the generating plant is in another. Martin took me to see it.'

'Did he indeed. You are honoured, Maxine. No one else in the management team has been taken there. He certainly didn't offer to show it to Princess Anne.'

'The passages are twisted and winding. In some there are no lights, you'd need a torch. And they're not that high – you'd need a hard hat. The Princess might not have enjoyed it.'

'Royalty don't expect to "enjoy" anything, Maxine. The harder the better for Anne, I think. After all, she's a rugby fanatic. It's our fault for not offering. Might have given her more respect for us.' Bill mused for a moment. 'But I still don't see why it would set us all at loggerheads with one another?'

The fact that he hadn't resisted the idea completely gave Maxine heart.

'I'm still on the case, Bill. But suppose, for example, there was something horrible in one of those cellars. One we haven't visited. Instruments of torture, maybe; or a set of mutilated skeletons. Maybe from years and years ago. Right now I know nothing of the history of Cleave Manor. I don't even know how far back it goes. It could have seen a fight during the Civil War, for example, in the seventeenth century. Might a battle then have left an evil spirit, one that still breaks out from time to time?'

'You mean, if, more recently, one of our American cousins was into black magic and got it to talk? Sounds pretty far-fetched, I'd say. But worth a bit more research, perhaps.'

Maxine already had plans to explore the Cleave Manor

passages more thoroughly. Bill's words gave her cover for the attempt, anyway. This would be a good time to move on.

'You might find the other suggestion I picked up to be more of this world. Or at least this century.'

'Two completely fresh ideas in one meeting. Maxine, you have been working hard. Go on.

Maxine accepted the accolade with a wry smile and drank some of her tea before she began.

'I've been told one of the Americans here voiced a rumour in the 1960s. It concerned an American airman, based here, who was allegedly shot down by British forces during the Second World War. I've thought about it. If it were true, the idea might have a lot more traction for American forces based here today. It would explain why they didn't rush to volunteer for anything, at any rate.'

Bill drank more of his tea as he reflected in turn.

'Do you know if this idea – this accusation – is true?'

'All I've had time to do so far is to consult the internet for Americans killed by so called "friendly fire" during World War Two. So far I've found two cases that might cause us trouble.'

Bill was eager to know more. This was more surprising than his usual management meetings. 'Please, go on.'

Maxine smiled. 'Well, does the name Miller mean anything to you?'

Bill was a lifelong cricket enthusiast. 'Ah. You mean Keith Miller? The Australian cricketer.' He paused. 'No, it can't be him. He was still playing after the war. The Ian Botham of his day, in more ways than one. Anyway, he was no American.'

Bill pondered a little more, then had another thought. 'D'you mean Glenn Miller? The band leader? Master of the trombone, I believe. Did something odd happen to him?'

Maxine nodded. 'According to Wikipedia, he died over the

English Channel on his way to Paris, in December 1944. His body has never been found. Course, that might have been a carefully scripted distortion, put out at the time by the War Office. Especially if what really occurred was that he was killed in "friendly fire" at the airfield here.'

There was silence for a moment. This was a shocking suggestion. Was there any chance that it was true?

'If there was any truth in this, Maxine, I would have expected to have heard about it a long time ago. The media would have relished it, made it into a good film. Though I can see that, once you'd thought of it, it would also make a juicy rumour.'

He sighed. 'You said you had two cases?'

Maxine couldn't help giggling to herself at his discomfiture. 'Well, if it was true, the other one might be even more serious.'

'Hell's bells. Worse than the best band leader of the 1930s? I can't imagine. Unless you're thinking of someone from the Kennedy family?'

Bill smiled to show that he was trying to make a joke. Then froze as he saw that Maxine wasn't smiling at all.

'Joseph Kennedy, that's President Kennedy's older brother, was also killed in World War Two. His body has never been found, either.'

Bill swallowed hard. 'The official story being . . .'

'He volunteered to fly American bombers, B-17's, stuffed full of explosives, at German targets. The pilot was supposed to bail out before it crashed onto the target. But one time the explosives went off early. This was 1944 as well.'

This time Bill snorted. 'That could be another piece of War Office propaganda. Sounds a lot more heroic than being killed in a remote British airfield by your allies' troops. But the Kennedys always made themselves larger than life. Could this conceivably be true?'

Maxine had thought a lot about this and took a second to answer. 'I think it's conceivable, Bill. But it sounds more like the work of a scriptwriter. A better paid one than Glenn Miller's, anyway. In my opinion, there would need to be something that did happen at Cleave Airfield during the war to give the idea any substance whatsoever. Though that wouldn't need to be anyone as famous as the two men I found mentioned on the internet.'

Ten minutes later, Bill took delivery of another tray of tea. Now, though, he was firmly back in control.

'What you're saying, Maxine, is that, to check out this nasty rumour, we need the records of this place when it was an airfield in World War Two. That's eighty years ago. Sounds impossible, doesn't it?'

He took a breath. 'It would be. Except that this site was so remote from London its commanders kept their own personal logbooks of daily life here; and made sure they were secretly handed on to their successors.'

It had never occurred to Maxine that there might still be any hard copy records of life at the airfield. It was a salutary lesson: the internet contained an awful lot, but it didn't know everything.

She blinked. 'You mean, we might be able to check it out for ourselves?'

Bill smiled. 'I hope so. When I first came here, I was told there were two safes in my office. One of these, the larger one, controlled by a series of passwords, holds the records of the camp since it's been part of the UK intelligence network. The other one contains records from the war years, when the place was an operational airfield. To be honest, I've never needed to open that. But I'm going to have to now.'

Bill rose from his seat and turned to the large, black-and-white photograph of the site, looking down from the control tower in 1943, which hung on the wall behind him. A lasting reminder of past conflict. With a bit of a struggle, he removed it from the wall to reveal a heavy metal door. Then he produced a ring of keys from his inner pocket.

A moment later the door swung open. Maxine could see it hadn't been opened recently: there was a thin layer of dust.

There was a pause whilst Bill coughed. Then he reached inside and drew out a pile of blue covered, hard backed logbooks.

'I believe this is everything the commanders of the time thought worth recording about life here.'

But at this point there was a call from Bill's secretary. Their time was up. The meeting had already overrun by fifteen minutes.

Bill turned to Maxine. 'These are not so much confidential as priceless history. They must never go off site. But there's far too much material for me to wade through.'

He picked up the pile, scanned the books' titles and dates.

'I'll let you take away a year at a time, Maxine, to keep locked in your office. The rest will go back in the safe. When you've examined one year to your satisfaction, bring them back and I'll swap them for the next.'

'Right, Bill. I'm happy to do that. D'you have any other specific tasks for me over the next couple of weeks?'

Bill turned to her, smiling. 'These logbooks can either quash the "friendly fire" rumour for good; or they can tell you and me the real facts behind it. Either of those could help smooth out relations between us and our American colleagues, put everything here on a more even keel. I'd say that's much the most important task you could be doing right now. Please, Maxine, make this your top priority.'

PART THREE

GEORGE GILBERT STEPS IN

BUDE, MERRIFIELD AND BRIDGERULE
NOVEMBER 12th - 18th

St Winwaloe Church Poundstock, [Gildhouse nearby]

CHAPTER 21   Friday Nov 12th

George Gilbert stared at Edward Gabriel in rank disbelief.

'Are you joking? Because, if you are, it's not very funny.'

The pair were sitting once again in the restaurant of the Falcon Hotel in Bude. They'd placed their orders, but the service tonight was unusually slow. No doubt Covid had decimated staff numbers.

It was another Friday evening; their relationship was continuing, in a gentle manner. But for the time being it had seemed wise, given the circumstances, to meet on neutral territory, well away from Merrifield Manor.

Edward nodded. 'I agree, George. It's not funny at all. But I was with my father when the inspector called, two nights ago. Heard it all for myself.'

'Tell me again what he said.'

'First of all, he explained that they had now found my mother's bicycle, under one of the railway bridges. But it had a puncture.'

'Right. So they were hot on the trail, at least. That's good. And the puncture would slow her down.'

'Yes. Then he told us how he'd gone a couple of miles down the road and called in at the Community Shop in Marhamchurch. These days it's the nearest shop to the Manor and it stocks almost everything. It was there that the inspector had obtained the latest bus timetable.'

'Presumably he was thinking of ways that Daphne might have continued her journey, once her bike had suffered the puncture?'

Edward looked slightly deflated. 'He didn't actually say that, but then the police don't often explain their thought processes.'

'Right. And what did he glean from the timetable?'

'He'd found that there was a twice-weekly community bus from Bude to Launceston that came through Marhamchurch. After that it wandered through various villages along the Tamar valley and ended up, late morning, in Launceston.'

'And this bus ran, I take it, on Monday mornings?'

'That's what the inspector said. Hey, how did you know that?'

George smiled. 'Well, he'd only be interested in the Monday buses. I mean, buses are non-existent on Sundays, at least for country folk in Cornwall. And Tuesday would be too late. Dare I guess that this bus went close to the bridge where the bike had been abandoned?'

Edward looked at her in gob-smacked admiration. His opinion of management consultants rose a notch further. Then a possible reason struck him. 'Ah. Have you been talking to the inspector?'

'No. Not at all. Though I was rung up by his sidekick, Holly Berry, late on Sunday afternoon. She wanted to know what I'd made of your party. But when I told her that I'd never met Daphne Gabriel, had no idea what she looked like, had never even been inside the Manor, she seemed to lose interest.'

George continued, 'As you said earlier, the police don't usually give much away. But I've worked with them once or twice, I know something of their methods. Go on then. What else did the inspector tell you?'

'He said they had managed to obtain black and white CCTV images from when the bus reached Launceston.'

'And you mother was on the bus?'

'Well, probably. They couldn't be certain. But there was someone who looked a lot like my mum. The trouble was, she was wearing a beanie. That covered her hair and obscured a lot of her face. Given all the rest of what they'd found, the inspector reckoned that must be her.'

George reflected for a moment. There were no obvious holes in the declared logic. 'So what was the inspector's conclusion to all this?'

'He said that the police force's view, given all that they'd found, was that my mother was almost certainly acting on her own initiative. There was no criminal case to investigate. In any case, Launceston is on the main road to the rest of the country. Her mysterious caller could have picked her up, in an unknown car, and taken her anywhere. Even if she didn't get a lift, there were frequent bus routes to Exeter and Plymouth. And, of course, buses into the rest of Cornwall.'

'So what action would the police take?'

Edward wrinkled his face dismissively. 'He said they would add her to the "Missing Persons" register. Which meant their colleagues would keep an eye out for her. They'd alert hospitals and so on, in case she was brought in, but they wouldn't give it a high priority.'

George sighed in sympathy. 'A more cynical way of putting it, Edward, would be that there wasn't a hope in hell of tracing her out of Launceston, so they'd decided that they wouldn't bother looking.'

Edward nodded his agreement. 'That's about the nub of it, I reckon. My poor dad was left totally devastated. He'd pinned all his hopes on a vigilant local police force unpicking the mystery. Now he's got nothing and not even a wife to share it with. I fear this might be the end of him.'

Their meal arrived at that point, causing a break in the

conversation. Edward was treating himself to grilled steak and chips, with tomatoes and mushrooms; George had ordered roast duck with dauphinoise potatoes. Both meals looked delicious. And by this time in the day both of them were hungry.

The break also gave George a chance to think. She could see that Edward, like his dad, was very upset. He'd suffered a massive change in family circumstances over the past week. Completely out of the blue. Primitive self-preservation warned her it was dangerous to get too involved in someone else's problems; but her emotions left her itching to help in any way she could. And right now, for George, with her handsome new companion, emotion was stronger than reason.

For a few moments the conversation halted as they started eating. As she carved and then enjoyed her duck, George kept glancing at her new friend, saw distress and anguish etched in his long face. A week might be a long time in politics, but it was an age in this relationship.

She remembered she'd been happy enough, a week ago, to offer a few days help on Edward's long-term question: making better use of the Manor. Had even started to mug up on the old railway. How much more use could she be in resolving his latest crisis? Indeed, how could she hold back?

Eventually, George spoke. 'Whether the police are correct, and your mum has gone away for some private reason of her own; or whether there is more evil around in Merrifield than their team managed to uncover in two long days; there's still a question of what on earth she thought she was doing.'

Edward nodded. But she could see he was still focussed primarily on his steak.

'And there was that mysterious phone call to your mum. Half past nine on a Saturday evening, in the middle of a firework party. That's not been explained at all.'

This time there was a longer pause before Edward shook his head. But the steak still held most of his attention. He took another mouthful.

George tried one more time. 'How much attention did the police give directly to you, in trying to make sense of your mum's actions?'

This time Edward stopped eating and gave her his full attention. 'They talked to me on Sunday morning. Not for that long, maybe half an hour. To be honest, I didn't have too much to tell them. I was still in shock, I suppose.'

There was a pause then he continued. 'I think they had another session with my father in the afternoon, once they'd heard about the kitchen phone call to mother from Sheila. But I'd say their prime goal was to find out where mother might have gone, rather than what she was trying to do.'

George ate more of her dinner as she considered her friend's response, and the seeming shortcomings of the official investigation. But to be fair, she had no idea what other problems they might have on their plate. No doubt the police were as short-staffed as everyone else.

'The police didn't have any inside track on Bridgerule?'

'Not that they told us. I mean, they were from Bude. I'm not sure they'd ever been to the village before. They were sympathetic enough and tried their best. They did well to find mother's bicycle. But they were trying to break in to what is really a closed community.'

'And which is one you know fairly well?'

'Not as well as my parents, obviously. I've been away a lot. Spent many years in London. In recent times I've just been here for the odd weekend. But the villagers still know me. They wouldn't mind answering a few more questions – they all know my basic problem, anyway. That's if I knew what to ask.'

There was a short pause. George told herself this was the moment to offer her intervention.

'Maybe, if you wanted, I could help you?'

It was clear the thought of George offering practical assistance had never occurred to him. For he smiled, gave himself a shake, then smiled again.

'George. Might you be able to? Oh, my. That would be wonderful.'

'Well, let's not overreach ourselves, Edward. I'm no private investigator and I've plenty of other things to keep going. But I am self-employed. We could give it, say, a week: see how far we'd got. If we found nothing significant, then we'd stop. But if we did find anything, we could hand it over to the police, push for them to reopen their investigation. Right,' George said briskly. 'Our main courses are getting cold. Let's finish them, then make some initial plans over dessert.'

CHAPTER 22   Saturday Nov 13th

After breakfast on Saturday morning, George Gilbert set out from her cottage in Treknow, a small village next to Tintagel. She turned off the A39 at Marhamchurch, just before Bude, then picked her way over the rolling countryside and quiet roads to Merrifield Manor.

Her first challenge was to meet Sir Wilfred and to convince him that she could, and was, offering serious support to his son. Any further work she did on Daphne's disappearance could only be done with his approval. It wouldn't do just to have grudging acquiescence. In any case she was keen to meet Edward's father on her own account.

George had seen Sir Wilfred hosting the firework party a week ago. He'd looked cheerful enough, but he'd been busy managing the crowds and keeping an eye on the children, she hadn't spoken to him at any length. Now, though, it was important to make a good first impression.

This was the first time George had been to the Manor in daylight. Merrifield itself was a disappointment: a tiny hamlet, no shops of any sort apart from a do-it-yourself warehouse. But the traditional, stone-built Manor looked even more beautiful in daylight than it had been by night. She drove up the tree-lined drive and parked on the gravel outside. How ready would Sir Wilfred be to welcome her?

But Edward had done well. Before she had even got to the front door it swung open and Sir Wilfred stood there to welcome her. He held out his hand in greeting.

'Ms Gilbert, you are very welcome,' he smiled.

'Thank you, Sir Wilfred. Please, call me George.'

'Do come in. Can I offer you coffee or do you only drink tea?'

'Coffee would be fine, thank you. Is Edward up yet?'

Sir Wilfred shook his head as he led her through the hall and into the spacious lounge. She sat on the settee, awaiting coffee. There were oil paintings adorning the walls, many old and dark. She presumed that most were portraits of the Gabriel family's ancestors.

She'd had a potted history of the Manor from Edward when they first met, but the portraits seemed to make it all more substantial. Even so, she judged it best to wait patiently for her coffee, not to be found peering at them inquisitively when Sir Wilfred reappeared.

A few minutes later her host brought in a tray holding a coffee percolator and two elegantly engraved, bone-China mugs.

'Edward will be with us shortly,' he declared. 'I'm sure you've heard about our troubles here and we'll get onto them later. But why don't you start by telling me a bit about yourself?'

It was almost like an interview for the post of daughter-in-law. But it obviously wasn't intended that way. And George had had many years' experience of introducing herself to a wide range of people. Soon the two were chatting animatedly and George sensed she'd made a good opening impression.

Twenty minutes later Edward joined them, bringing his own mug with him. His father turned towards him.

'George and I are getting on famously,' he declared.

'Great,' replied Edward. 'I hoped you would.'

'Mind, we haven't started talking about Daphne yet. I thought it would be best to wait until you were with us.'

Edward nodded in acknowledgement. 'Thanks for waiting.

As I told you, Dad, I've given George all the details of events so far. And shared our disappointments. But she was offering to help us for a few days.'

George thought it was time to intervene. 'The part of the puzzle where I felt more might be done, Sir Wilfred, was to try and make sense of what drove Daphne to these extraordinary actions. It must have started with her. An explanation is needed whether she acted on her own or was egged on by someone else. The answer must lie somewhere in Bridgerule, and you two are the best people to find it.'

'That's what I felt, George,' said the owner. 'That's why the police did their best to prompt me. But maybe they tried too hard.'

'Or were in too much of a hurry. Well, you must still have been in shock. But you've had a few more days since then to reflect. Have you had any further ideas?'

Sir Wilfred was being far more open than George had dared to hope. Maybe, in some odd way, her presence as an interested newcomer was acting as a catalyst?

'It seemed to me, George, that there must be some big issue that had raised its head for Daphne. And it must be something that, for some reason, she didn't feel able to discuss directly with me.'

He sighed and then continued. 'I mean, if she had some desire to take on a new hobby, say, or visit a new location, we'd have discussed it. We did that lots of times over the years. When she decided to take up bell ringing, for example. That didn't grab me at all, seemed a waste of Tuesday evenings, but I didn't stand in her way. And before long it became a regular part of her life.'

He paused, then continued. 'Poor woman. There must have been something that really bothered her. Trouble is, I've no idea at all what it might be.'

'Nor do I,' added Edward. 'She was a very open woman. Not afraid to face her foes. So what on earth could have put her in such a spin?'

There was a resolute silence in the room as the problem was considered.

'I often work with managers who are troubled,' said George, after a while. 'Sometimes, if it's all been bottled up, the solution is simply letting them talk and being a good listener. Often they give you the answer themselves. But in this case, obviously, we can't do that.

'In other cases, though, it may be a matter of looking at the difficulty through a different pair of eyes. Giving it a fresh perspective. So what I was going to suggest is that Edward and I spend a few days talking to as many of Daphne's friends in Bridgerule as we can.'

George turned to face Sir Wilfred directly. 'But before we do, my first question for you, Sir Wilfred, is: can you give us a list of Daphne's closest friends to go and visit?'

Sir Wilfred considered and then nodded. 'That sounds easy enough. I take it we're talking about Daphne's close friends and not just casual acquaintances. People that might ask her a serious question, say about the Manor or her family, that she wasn't able to answer but felt that she should have been. Fine. I'll start to produce a list once we've finished talking. In most cases I can also give you their address or at least their phone number.'

But George hadn't finished. 'One other line of uncertainty that you might be able to narrow down, Sir Wilfred, is where Daphne actually went on these long walks. Were there any that she did regularly?'

'How would that help?' asked the owner. He wasn't trying to be awkward but wanted to be sure of the avenues they were pursuing.

'Well, if Daphne's issue didn't come from a close friend, then it might have come from someone that you don't know at all, but she met on one of her walks. A casual contact. But if there was someone that she came across regularly, they might have raised some issue that worried her. In fact, you not knowing this person might have been exactly why she didn't feel able to discuss the whole thing with you.'

To her surprise, George saw that Sir Wilfred was smiling.

'I can answer that better than you might expect. You see, I started to worry a while back that something might happen to Daphne on one of her walks; and if she didn't return, I wouldn't know where on earth she was. So I insisted that she jotted down beforehand an outline of each planned walk. In this notebook here.'

As he spoke, the Manor owner rose from his seat and strode over to the bookshelf by the door. There he extracted a rather smart, leather-bound notebook, brought it back and handed it to George.

'I believe this includes every walk that Daphne did on her own in the past three years. I leave it to you to work out which ones were most repeated, and which were the most remote. I hope you don't need to repeat them all yourself to find this potential troublemaker. I'm afraid, my dear, that would take you many, many weeks.'

CHAPTER 23   Sunday Nov 14th

Edward had wanted George to stay in Merrifield Manor while the pair embarked on their investigation, but she had declined the offer.

'That's kind of you, Edward, but it's really not far to Tintagel: half an hour at most. I can't be here all the time, anyway, I've various other things I need to do. And if I'm not here night and day, it'll keep me at a distance from the Gabriel family tensions – help me to stay detached, able to think outside the box. Don't worry, though, I'll be here early enough tomorrow.'

Edward accepted her words with some reluctance. But on Sunday she was back as promised by nine. The plan today was to go to the regular morning service at St Bridget's, the Bridgerule church that Daphne attended. That would give them a chance to meet some of Daphne's friends in a more informal setting; and maybe lead onto further conversations once the service was over.

They were into Bridgerule well ahead of time and heard bells sounding as they approached the church. The chimes reminded George of Sir Wilfred's words: Daphne had been a bellringer here.

They were hardly inside the building when Edward saw the vicar, already robed, standing at the front and making her service preparations; he headed towards her. No doubt he wanted to make sure she was fully informed of the latest situation, before she made any announcements.

George saw an opportunity for some research of her own

and slipped away to observe the bell ringing. This was happening behind some heavy-duty velvet curtains, in a room beneath the square tower. Slipping quietly in, she saw a small team of five bell ringers, carefully conducted by a smart, older man, dressed for the occasion in a suit and bow tie.

Glancing round, George spotted an old pew at one side. She slid onto it to watch their continuing efforts. The ringing activity was quite strenuous. One pull of the rope on its own wasn't particularly difficult, but the ringers had to keep going for some time – no chance of a break or a rest.

And for one of the team the effort was doubled. For she had two ropes to keep under control; and needed to keep track of which one to pull next.

Ten minutes went by. Then, with a flourish from the conducting bow tie, the ringing was over. As they let go of their ropes and relaxed, they started to share thoughts they'd had during the ringing. But not in anger: these were the cheerful sounds of a group that enjoyed working together.

After a few minutes of repartee, the bow tie turned to George.

'Good morning. I don't think we've met?'

'No. I hope you didn't mind me slipping in to listen. It was very melodic. My name is George . . . George Gilbert. I'm a friend of Edward Gabriel.'

'Pleased to meet you. I'm Thomas Vardy. I've conducted the bells here for the last ten years.' He turned towards his team. 'And these are the workhorses that bring all our ideas to fruition.'

The group were casually dressed and of varying ages, George guessed from mid-thirties to early seventies. Swiftly and with good grace they introduced themselves: 'Hi, I'm Jonny'; 'Morwenna'; 'Stella'; 'Tracey'; and finally, 'And I'm Henry'.

It was a good job, thought George, that there weren't more names to remember. She endeavoured to repeat each one as she shook their hand; she'd jot them down in her notebook once she had the chance.

'Pleased to meet you.' She nodded to the woman holding two ropes. 'You had a hard job, Stella.'

Stella nodded. 'One of these ropes is usually pulled by Daphne Gabriel. But as you'll know, she's disappeared. We do have one or two reserve bellringers, but we like to give them some rehearsal time before we drag them into active service.'

'I used to ring bells when I was at college,' admitted George. 'But that was a long time ago.'

'It's like riding a bike, George. Once you've done it, got the notion of pulling steadily but not too hard and then letting the rope run back, you never forget the basics. In some ways it's like country dancing: being part of a team that knows what they're doing makes your part a lot easier.'

'You could join us for a rehearsal if you liked,' said Thomas. 'They're on Tuesday evenings.'

'I'm not sure I'm up to your standard,' said George doubtfully.

'I bet two hours ringing under my tuition would bring you up to scratch, though.'

'In any case,' said Jonny, 'we don't know how long Daphne will be gone for. You might not be needed at all.'

George sighed. Secretly she was delighted – her preliminary visit couldn't have gone better. 'I must say, that's very kind of you all. OK then. What time do rehearsals start?'

'Seven thirty sharp,' said Thomas. 'But we never go on a minute later than nine. The residents of Bridgerule would complain like mad if we did. They like their early nights round here. After that we have a drink down the road, in the Bridge Inn.

Please, do join us, George. It'd do us all good to encounter someone completely new.'

By the time George got back to the nave there was a sizeable congregation, all of whom seemed to know one another, and plenty of chatter. But there was enough room that they didn't need to cluster too closely together; and everyone was wearing a mask.

Edward had taken a seat towards the back of the church and had a woman on either side, both a few years older. George decided she might as well join them.

'I'm Martha,' said the woman she was seated next to. 'That's my sister Mary on Ed's other side.'

'I'm George. I only met Edward recently.'

'But you've heard about his mother? Daphne? She disappeared like a wisp of smoke a week ago. It was all very peculiar.'

George nodded. 'Yes. So I heard. But I've not had the chance to meet her. Not yet, anyway.'

'Ed started to ask us about how recently we'd seen her. Mary thought she'd better invite him back for coffee after the service. She could see it might be a long conversation. You can join us if you like.'

'Oh, thank you.' But there was no time to say more. The service was about to begin.

As far as George could judge, it was a traditional Anglican service. The prayers were familiar and George knew most of the hymns from her childhood, though there was one new one, with fresh lyrics and a melodic tune, that the earnest-looking musician led from the piano rather than the organ.

George wondered if the Bible reading for the day had been chosen for the situation the village found itself in. For it was the well-known parable of the Prodigal Son.

The vicar made no explicit mention of Daphne; but she re-told the parable in a way that could easily apply to the missing woman. 'This family member left home without a proper fare-well,' she said. 'With a mad scheme to make their mark in a faraway venue where they knew no-one. One which failed so badly that they had to return home in disgrace.'

'But when they did,' she continued, 'they were given the warmest of welcomes by those whom they'd left behind. For-giveness and love can – should – overcome the greatest of dis-ruptions.'

The vicar did not apply the passage directly to Daphne Ga-briel but there was no doubt what she was trying to say. It was a call for the congregation to withhold judgement, if – when – Daphne reappeared.

George reflected that this was not the only possible interpre-tation of what had happened. Everyone was assuming that the woman had gone off of her own accord. But she had yet to be told a credible reason why Daphne might have done so.

There was plenty more greeting and chatter outside, standing among the gravestones, after the service. Edward seemed to know – or at least be known by – half the congregation. And they all had plenty to say to him.

Perhaps being a natural partner for Edward in his quest for information needed further thought. If she had been Edward's fiancée or longstanding girlfriend it might have been different, but she was a completely unknown quantity. Their weeks-old friendship brought an extra dimension to the problem that was already disturbing enough.

George wandered round the graveyard as she waited. She was intrigued by the gravestone of a former vicar: he'd lasted long enough; and been around in the 1950s. Had he kept a diary? He might have known Daphne, might have had face-to-face contact with the Gabriel family.

Then Martha spotted that George was being ignored and came to join her. 'Why don't you and I go on down to our cottage? Looks like Edward might be here for some time.' The two set off down towards Bridgerule.

'Have you lived here for long?' asked George.

'Most of my life,' replied Martha. 'Our mother was the District Nurse around here for most of her life. That was what started our link with Daphne.'

'I didn't realise Daphne had medical links.'

'Oh, it wasn't medical,' laughed Martha. 'Well, not really. Mum had been the midwife, you see, when Daphne was born at the Manor. Mary and I weren't that much younger. So it was more a matter for Mum of keeping a professional eye on her handiwork. The three of us girls grew up together. For one thing, we were all in the local Guide Company.'

'With Bude the centre of attraction?'

'Certainly. Remember, we could go there by train in the late 1950s. From Merrifield.'

George was surprised. 'Why on earth have a station there? Isn't it the middle of nowhere?'

'No. It's halfway between Bridgerule and Whetstone. Also midway between Bude and Holsworthy. It was never a fast line, there were too many twists and turns, but it was fun to ride. And ideal for us youngsters. Not that there was much to do in Bude.'

George decided she'd better make the most of this conversation while it was flowing. 'So have you any ideas about where Daphne might have gone? That's if she went of her own accord, of course.'

Martha was silent for a moment. But it was clear she was

thinking. She hadn't taken offence, anyway.

'Daphne and I often used to go walking along the Coast Path. Even recently. North of Bude, mostly. They're fine cliffs up there. With just the odd, unoccupied beach. My friend was always keen to reach the beaches and explore them.'

George frowned. 'Had she some goal in mind?'

Martha giggled. 'She was after long-lost smugglers' hauls. I think she reckoned that these might have been stored away in an inaccessible cave, somewhere along the coast.'

George was sceptical. 'That might have been true two hundred years ago. But surely anything like that would have been found long ago?'

'Well, the shoreline rocks are really treacherous. Even small boats hesitate to come close inshore. And most of the time there are no paths down anyway. So no-one would even try to access them. Unless they were very determined indeed.'

'Which, you say, Daphne was. Had she any solid reason?'

'She'd studied various accounts of smugglers in the nineteenth century that had connections with North Cornwall. Of course, they had limited historical basis, they were a mixture of rumours and anecdotes. I think it was an idle hobby that was in danger of becoming an obsession.'

'Well, that's always dangerous. Thank you for sharing that, Martha. It starts to bring Daphne to life – well, it does for me, anyway.

CHAPTER 24

It was nearly one o'clock before George and Edward managed to get away from Martha and Mary and arrive at the Bridge Inn. This was George's first visit to the Bridgerule hostelry, but for Edward it was familiar territory for meals out around Merrifield Manor. He was warmly greeted by the landlord and in turn introduced him to George.

George asked herself whether Edward would receive such a warm greeting in less stressful circumstances. What was the standing of the Merrifield household in normal times? Was it tolerance and mutual respect, something even warmer, or something far more distant?

At this time of year, with no tourists, the pub was not that crowded, even on Sunday lunchtime. It wasn't hard for Edward to find the pair a quiet table towards the rear. They each ordered a traditional roast dinner, along with pints of bitter.

'It's been a useful morning,' said Edward brightly.

'Martha and Mary certainly had plenty to say,' replied George. 'Trouble is, I'm not sure how much further it takes us.'

Over coffee the sisters had gushed remorselessly. Each had shared plenty of incidents with Daphne over the past couple of years, but to George's ears neither account contained much that was unexpected.

'There's nothing they said to suggest that my mother was depressed. And she seemed as alert as usual. Isn't it good to be able to rule out mental illness?' asked Edward.

'I suppose so. But they didn't give us any positive reasons for

Daphne to make such a hasty departure. If that's what happened.'

There was a pause. A waitress brought their drinks over and Edward took a swig. He was thirsty after his morning's talking.

'Did you learn any more during your walk down with Martha?' he asked.

George mused for a moment. She had hoped, bizarrely, not to pass on too much of her conversation to Edward until she had processed it for herself; but it wouldn't do to keep it completely hidden.

'I'd say the main thing that emerged was that Daphne had a hobby. That was looking for old smuggler material, in caves along the coast.'

Edward smiled. 'Ah. A reason emerges at last, perhaps, for those long walks. Couldn't that make her want to continue her search somewhere a bit further away – maybe on the south coast?'

George nodded, though not fully convinced. 'Yes, I guess it could. But why on earth would it make her leave home in such a secretive manner?'

It was a mystery with no clues at all. Their meals arrived at that point and gave them each a moment to ponder, as the condiments were organised and a mixture of winter vegetables added to each plate.

Once they'd started eating, George was the first to speak.

'This is terrific, Edward. As good as the Falcon in Bude.' She took another mouthful and then continued.

'Remember, Daphne didn't leave Merrifield totally unaided. There was someone else behind the move – that mysterious caller. Maybe he – or she – wanted to remain secret? Maybe that was the condition he imposed on their trip?'

For a few moments they concentrated on their food. But

145

George was still wrestling with the issues.

'So we've at least got to one of her obsessions. What did you pick up from all those people you were talking to at church?'

She noticed that Edward was in no hurry to reply. Maybe embarrassed at his lack of progress.

'They were all concerned about her and trying to help,' he began. 'There were lots of general comments. All kinds of incidental activities were mentioned. Her long membership of "Knitter and Natter", for instance. Her contributions to the Christmas pantomime in recent years. And, for some reason, her bell ringing. But I didn't pick up anything that could turn into a solid reason for moving away, whether secretly or otherwise.'

They continued eating. The meal was splendid. But George sensed they had less of a common mind than they'd had in Bude. As they ate, she silently reviewed all that she had been told and how it might be made to hold together.

There had been another visit from the waitress. After consulting the dessert menu, puddings had been ordered and shortly afterwards had been served: blackcurrant crumble and cream for George, Eton Mess for Edward.

It was as they started eating that George plunged into a radical alternative.

'You know, Daphne's unexplained disappearance would make far more sense if something had happened to her that was completely outside her control.'

Edward stopped eating and stared at her. 'But that's not possible. I told you all the evidence the police had discovered. There's a solid evidence trail, at least as far as Launceston.'

George finished her mouthful before replying. 'Well, I agree it's a well-laid trail. Easy enough to believe, I'll grant you. But not too hard to construct if someone was trying to fool us

146

all.'

'Whatever d'you mean?'

Dimly, George sensed there was a danger of Edward being upset and starting to become angry. It would be wise to be gentle here, take things slowly. But she was driven on by her latest ideas.

'Well, let's start with the bicycle found under the railway bridge. It was certainly your mother's. It could have been Daphne riding it until she had the puncture. But it could equally well have been put there by someone else.'

Edward was silent for a moment. 'You mean, my mother was absent-minded. The bike got left around in all sorts of places on the Merrifield estate. Generally speaking that wouldn't matter much. Mother wouldn't cycle a lot at this time of year. But someone else might have seen it and removed it. Are you saying it might have been left under the railway bridge beforehand?'

Caught up in her enthusiasm, taking no notice of emotional signals, George continued her critique. 'And Daphne's long blue dress, found by the police in the caravan park. That –'

To his horror, Edward saw where she was going. He swallowed and took over the narrative. 'That could have been left by anyone.'

Then his mind went on ahead. 'But only if they'd undressed my Mum first. But that would mean . . .' Then it hit him. His eyes clouded in tears.

Too late, George realised she had been grossly insensitive. This wasn't a random body they were talking about. They weren't solving a crime mystery. This was her friend's mother.

She reached across the table for his hand. 'Edward, I'm so sorry. I've been completely selfish. I was only voicing a logical possibility. I've no reason at all to think that's what happened.'

But the apology, though sincere, was far too late. The meal

was over, emotionally speaking. There was no way it could continue. Edward pushed aside his half-finished dessert and rose to his feet.

'I'm sorry, George. Right now I need some time on my own. Can you settle up, please, when you've finished. We'll divvy the bill next time we meet. For now I want to go on a long, long walk. And no thank you, I don't want your company.'

The River Tamar, flowing through Bridgerule.
A hundred metres from the Bridge Inn.

CHAPTER 25

George looked forlornly after Edward as he made his lonely way out of the Bridge Inn. Was their friendship all over, before it had hardly begun? She sensed there was no point right now in chasing after him. How could she have been so stupid? And so insensitive?

Absent-mindedly, out of habit, she continued eating her crumble. She'd never been walked out on before. What was supposed to happen now?

What happened next was that the alert waitress saw what had happened and came to check that her customer was alright.

'My friend didn't feel well,' she mumbled.

'That's all right, m'dear. Probably eating too quickly. To be safe you'd probably better have some coffee before you think of driving away. Americano? With or without milk?'

In this way her worst moment passed. There was no need for her to hurry off at all. Slow down! Take it easy. George took a deep breath and settled down for whatever life threw at her next. Starting with a fresh cafetière of strong coffee.

Twenty minutes later the landlord himself brought her the combined bill. 'I've put your coffee on the house,' he observed. 'It's an old Devon tradition, whenever the man flounces out.'

For the first time George gave a wan smile. 'Thank you.'

'It's not the first time he's done it, mind,' the landlord continued. 'That Merrifield lot, they're all too stuck up. Don't care about the rest of us. No wonder the mother upped and left. She's best out of it.'

It was a point of view. For the first time it occurred to George that she might do better continuing her enquiries without Edward at her side. If Daphne's exit had been driven by local resentment, she was more likely to find that out on her own than in Edward's company.

George shrugged. She decided that she had done enough research for one day. She'd walk back to the church and pick up her car, then drive straight back to her cottage in Treknow.

It was as she walked out of the Inn that George saw the notice on the doorway outside. "The only Devon pub west of the Tamar". George sensed an unspoken subtext: "Thriving despite the choking grip of Cornwall." And what would the pubs on Hartland Quay, or the Isle of Lundy, make of the claim?

Surely this whole saga couldn't be the result of some long-standing feud between Cornwall and its neighbouring county?

It was as she reached her car, parked close to St Bridget's, that it occurred to George that, while she was so close to Bude, she could perhaps drop in on her old friend Maxine. She could give her a ring, at least.

She could hear Maxine's phone ringing. It wasn't switched off. She must be busy. Then the penny dropped. Time at home with daughter Rosanna must be precious, now she was back at work. Maybe she'd gone out for a walk with her husband?

At that point another metaphorical cloud appeared on the horizon. How would Inspector Peter Travers view her attempt to make sense of the exit of Daphne Gabriel? Might he not be furious that any lay person, even his old friend George, was taking such a direct interest in the case?

George recalled an unfortunate incident not too long ago where her attempt to help, trapping a suspect, had misfired. Peter hadn't taken that well. Maybe it would be good if she didn't call on the Travers' right now? She left a brief voice message for Maxine, then went on her way.

The journey home gave George time to think. Should she now abandon any interest in Daphne's disappearance? Was that the right thing to do? Was there a real alternative?

In truth, she told herself, there was little she could do without Edward's active support. He was the one that knew the location and the locals. And had a life-long link to his mother. Similar, in one way, to his father.

On the other hand, she had been invited to a bell-ringing rehearsal next Tuesday evening; and Daphne had been an enthusiastic member of that group. She could still take up that invitation, talk to the group and see where it led. Even without Edward's approval. By pure chance she'd not had a chance to tell him about bellringing in their hurried lunchtime catch-up. Which meant he wasn't in a position to veto it now.

She looked sadly back on a wreck of a day. It had all begun so well. Were there any other strands left for her to pursue, even without Edward's support?

Then, as she reflected, she remembered the unusual gravestone. A previous vicar at St Bridget's had been in post for an amazing seventy years. And not back in the Middle Ages, it was from the 1880s to the late 1950s.

George considered. For a start, that would mean that he was the local vicar during both World Wars. He had even been there when the railway arrived. And over the period when Daphne Gabriel was born.

He might well have baptised her. He'd probably been to Merrifield Manor in the 1950s. Might even have been a regular visitor. The feudal habit of keeping on good terms with the local gentry was probably engrained in a man whose ministry started

151

in the nineteenth century.

She recalled the final comments of the landlord. It would be good to know if others had noticed anything. The vicar would surely have observed any major disconnect between life in the Manor and life in the village of Bridgerule, over such a long ministry. But had he written anything down?

The key question, then, was had he kept a private diary? And if so, had it been preserved? George resolved to look him up on the internet when she got home.

Now she was onto internet searches, George realised there were other things she might do. Things which she could try, whatever the views of Edward, or indeed of Inspector Peter Travers.

For a start she could look up Merrifield Manor itself. Was it famous enough to warrant a mention? Sir Wilfred Gabriel had been vague, almost dithery, about its history. Made no suggestion of archives hidden away. Edward, too, on that first train journey out of Exeter, had not claimed much knowledge of its past. It was surely worth a Google search to see what turned up.

More broadly, it occurred to George that if Daphne had left of her own accord or been kidnapped, either of these might come out of events that had happened around the Manor at some time in the past. It could also be useful if she had a deeper understanding of the history of other manors around North Cornwall. She'd noticed plenty of sites marked on the map. Some were now farms, but others were ruins.

If she'd had more time, George would love to have studied these. But right now, time was of the essence. She could do with a professional historian to help her. For a moment she pined over the memory of her special friend Harry Jennings. But he was in no position to help her now.

The thought led on to the Exeter Cornish History Outpost,

based at Truro. ECHO was still operating, and she knew one of the post-graduate students there fairly well. Emma Eastham had worked closely with her at the start of the Covid pandemic. She had been full of energy, wisdom and ideas. It would be worth contacting her, asking what she knew of Cornish manor histories; and whether she fancied a diversion for a day or two, to pass on some of that knowledge to George.

By now it was twilight and George was almost back to her cottage. She smiled. Her reflections had made much better use of the journey than if she'd merely been moping over Edward. She was no longer close to tears.

George was a very positive person. She'd had plenty of knocks in her life and had always, eventually, bounced back. There was no reason why this should not happen again. Of course, all these ideas might come to nothing. Even if they produced concrete, useful facts they might still be a waste of time if Edward refused to see her again.

But at least she had to try. And now she had a number of actions that she could take.

CHAPTER 26   Monday Nov 15th

On Monday morning George Gilbert set off up the A39 to Barnstaple. This followed a busy evening the night before, once she was back home from Bridgerule.

One immediately relevant finding had been about the long-lasting vicar of Bridgerule, Frank Hawker Kingdon. Careful internet search had revealed that this vicar had indeed kept a personal diary for many years; and this diary was now held in the North Devon Records Office in Barnstaple. For George, starting from Tintagel, that would be a round trip of well over a hundred miles.

An early-morning phone call to the Office had told George that the diary was indeed present in the archive, available to be studied by members of the general public; but that, regrettably, sections could not be photocopied or even photographed.

'It's a series of documents, you see, madam. Handwritten and mostly well over sixty years old. Fortunately for us, the vicar had many notebooks – a new one for each year. You can narrow the search down easily if you know which year you're after. But these are fragile documents and we've a duty to protect them. Visitors can only look at one book at a time, under glass, and they need special gloves to turn the pages.'

George started to appreciate the difficulties for historians in working before computers or the benefits of digitisation and cross reference. 'Can I at least make notes on what I read?'

'Of course. Though most visitors don't want that much, they just want to check some detail or other. When would you like to come?'

George decided she might as well go today. She'd no idea whether the source would prove unhelpful in just a few minutes; or would be worth interrogating for hours. But she didn't want to spend more than one day of her life in the Records Office if she could help it.

As she drove along, George attempted to focus her mind on what she hoped to find.

The vicar might have been cautious in what he recorded. Or he might have been wildly indiscreet, the Alan Clark of the clerical world. The diaries were never intended to be published, so he might have seen no reason to hide his own views of the events around him. They might have been his way of letting off steam.

But assuming he had things to say, which of these might be of interest to George?

The key thing was whether he had direct contact with Merrifield Manor. George reckoned this was the only manor in the parish still occupied, so it should have some status in the community. The estate farm must have employed local staff, at least until the Second World War. Might Kingdon have any notes on how employees were treated? Was this a source of the friction between Manor and village, of which the Bridge Inn landlord had spoken?

A related question was, had the vicar any dealings with Daphne? Was this the start of her long connection to St Bridget's? Was there anything useful to learn about her place in the Manor household?

Besides these specifics, the diary might reveal something about progress over the decades. For example, what had been the effect of the new railway, with its station at the bottom of the Manor garden? But this might be much harder to discern without reading many volumes.

She could only hope that Kingdon had legible handwriting.

An hour and a half later, George was inside the Records Office and introducing herself to the archivist. She recognised his voice; it was the man she'd talked to earlier. And he quickly recognised her.

'Ah, Ms Gilbert, sign in here please. Another reader for the Kingdon diaries. I've got them laid out downstairs.'

George followed him down a sweeping staircase into the basement. There were a series of rows of glass-topped desks, each with a different item beneath. Most were unattended.

The archivist pointed to the furthest row. 'Those are the latest ten diaries: 1945 to 1954. Kingdon didn't write any in his final years. Mind, he was well over ninety by then. And here are the gloves I'd like you to wear, as you turn the pages.'

He handed her a pair of thin white gloves, which fitted George perfectly. 'Now, when you want an earlier ten diaries, come upstairs and I'll change them over.' He smiled. 'We do have a café. You can have a drink of coffee or something while you wait.'

At that point he left her to it. George had a notebook and a laptop in her backpack but didn't remove them immediately. She first needed to know if there was likely to be anything worth recording.

She started with the diary for 1945. The opening page was for January 1ˢᵗ. George's first reaction was relief: at least Kingdon had beautiful, legible handwriting. He was also concise and masterful in his use of English. The page was almost poetic in its contrast of emotions: hope for the year ahead, now the war seemed to be in its final stages; but sadness for all those who would no longer be there when it was over.

George put her hand under the glass and carefully turned the page. There was less effort recording the next few days. But that was good as far as George was concerned. A vicar with an eye for interesting detail was ideal from her point of view.

She continued to turn the pages. Fortunately, her consultancy background gave her an ability to speed-read pages and pick out key words. "Daphne" and "Merrifield" were the ones she was after. They might not appear in 1945. But it wouldn't take long to find out.

Then she saw them – both words on the same page. April 13th. An infant baptism service in the chapel at Merrifield Manor. With Daphne Hamlyn the infant in focus.

For some reason Kingdon had been seized by the whole occasion. He appreciated the tiny chapel in the grounds of the estate. Then he mentioned that Daphne was the two-week-old daughter of Carolyn Hamlyn, the cook at the Manor. Oddly, she wasn't at the service. Maybe she was in the kitchen, preparing a meal for them all later? It sounded like the vicar was to be one of the guests. He was certainly looking forward to a feast – it would be a treat in the war years.

More or less as expected so far. Though George was interested in the chapel. Nothing had been said about that on her only visit. Maybe it was now in ruins? After all, this was a scene from seventy-six years ago.

Daphne was only two weeks old at her baptism. That was probably normal in wartime. In contrast, in these Covid days months would go by. George knew that: she was the godmother of Rosanna, the daughter of her friend Maxine. Rosanna's baptism had taken place when she was six months old.

Timings must have been different in wartime. There'd be pressure to have the service as quickly as possible, given the surrounding uncertainties. No-one would want a dead and unbaptised baby if that could be avoided.

George glanced back at the page. Who else was at the service? There was no guest list in the diary, but several people were mentioned in Kingdon's description. These included Francis and Matilda Gabriel, presumably the owners of the Manor at the time.

Then she spotted something unusual. There was a second child being baptised that day. Wilfred Gabriel, the child of Francis and Matilda. He was also said to be just two weeks old.

Quickly George swung the backpack off her back and grabbed her notebook. It was important to write this down, she could think harder about it later. She double checked her notes. Yes, they agreed completely with the words in the diary.

Maybe Kingdon had got confused? That would certainly be possible in his final years. But this was 1945. The man would only be in his eighties and was evidently capable of running a thriving church. He couldn't be suffering from dementia, surely?

George disciplined herself to press on with the diaries. She still wanted to find mentions of Daphne or Merrifield, but now she included Wilfred in her keyword short list.

Slowly, carefully, George scanned page after page. There was plenty of comment on church life in the days after the war was over, and on the many differences in attitudes from the days before. George sensed that, in his old age, the vicar was falling behind post-war fashions. But he was no outcast, even at ninety he seemed to be the life and soul of many a local festivity.

George found occasional mentions of her target children. Daphne joined the St Bridget's church choir in 1953. Wilfred, somehow, avoided this privilege. The older generation at Merrifield Manor made no further mark on church life. But there was nothing else in the remaining diaries on display as riveting as the infants' baptisms.

By now it was half past twelve. George wondered whether she had found all that Barnstaple had on offer. But she was a persistent searcher and had come some distance to look. She decided to go and find her archivist, ask for the earliest Kingdon diaries to be put on display; and to enjoy a leisurely coffee break in the Records Office café while they were being installed.

When she went back to the basement half an hour later, George found that the Kingdon diaries from 1945 onwards had been replaced by ones starting in 1891 and running up to the turn of the twentieth century.

There was a mass of material here that would be of interest to the social historian. George's studious friend, Emma Eastham, would have been ecstatic. These were the observations of a relatively inexperienced but alert vicar in his early thirties, observing late Victorian life in a rural community, as it came to terms with the challenges of progress.

George, though, was not a historian. She could resist the detail. What was she really looking for? Presumably some Gabriel or other was master of Merrifield Manor in the 1890s. Perhaps any mention of the hamlet itself would be worth further scrutiny.

Once again she scanned the first of these diaries, page by page. Then, without warning, she came across the name Merrifield. But it wasn't the Manor this time, it was the railway station. For the line from Okehampton was nearing its final destination in Bude. Merrifield was the last but one station and it opened in July 1891. With the Revd Frank Kingdon of Bridgerule one of the guests of honour.

The event obviously meant a lot to him for the account took several pages of his diary. He described the station itself and how the single line became double for a few hundred yards to allow trains to pass one another. One direction, now completed, looked back towards Holsworthy. The other led into a cutting that was the start of the planned continuation to Bude.

A symbolic train (with just two carriages) was due at eleven from Holsworthy; Kingdon was part of the welcoming party. The fact that it was nearly an hour late did not spoil the occasion. Time mattered less in those days – or perhaps it was measured in a different way.

Kingdon obviously made good use of the wait. For he was alerted, seemingly for the first time, that there was also a canal here: the Bude Canal, developed over half a century earlier and once intended to link Bude to the metropolis of Plymouth.

The fact that the Bude Canal came anywhere close to the Manor was also a surprise to George. She had seen no trace of it so far. So where did it run? She read on, intrigued.

Kingdon could do nothing until the train had arrived and been welcomed. Or till a light lunch had been enjoyed by all those present.

But once lunch was over, he insisted on seeing the Canal for himself. Over the meal he must have found the right person to show him round.

The Canal ran at right angles to the railway, he wrote. It tracked the River Tamar down towards Launceston. Of course, Kingdon would know the river: it flowed through Bridgerule, rampant in the winter and a tiny stream in the height of summer.

George could only wish that the vicar had used a map to illustrate his explorations. A sketch of the layout, the interaction of rail and canal, would have been helpful. She would need to revisit it all for herself one day – if there was anything left to be found.

She read on. To her amazement, the vicar was outlining an

160

incline of over a hundred feet, which raised the level of the canal. There was a chain to pull the small boats – wheeled tubs, he called them – up the incline. The chain went round massive wheels at top and bottom.

He didn't seem to have enquired what power made the wheels turn. But then, George reflected, he wasn't an engineer.

The incline started on the Manor side of the railway line and seemed (to the vicar) to be tunnelled almost underneath it.

The railway then bridged the lower canal. This then continued south, towards Launceston.

The way the vicar wrote about this suggested he was almost in raptures. He could see a great deal prefigured in the arrangement. For it seemed to go from the old to the new. This was a transformation from the old way of travel – by canal – to the new way, which would no doubt be by rail.

George had no doubt that the notion of "transformation" would be explored in many of the vicar's future sermons.

But had it any significance today?

CHAPTER 27   Tuesday Nov 16th

George spent the first part of Tuesday morning in her Treknow cottage, pursuing some of the ideas she'd hatched on her way home on Sunday. She'd be going over to Bridgerule later. There was the bellringing practice on this evening, which despite fraught relations with Edward she still hoped to attend. But first she needed to work out what she might learn about Daphne from the conversations that would ensure.

One of her ideas was to compare the exhaustive diary of Daphne's walks which Sir Wilfred had lent her with the anecdotes from Martha, which she'd heard on the way back from church. A good job he'd handed the book to her and not to Edward.

It was a well laid out notebook, in date order. A useful document for checking Daphne's location on any specific date but less well arranged if one wanted to categorise her walks.

Time for action: George grabbed a large sheet of paper. Then went through the notebook diary page by page, summarising the various walk locations on her sheet.

After a while she started to come across duplicate locations, from a repeated or similar walk. When this happened, she began to tally walks in that location. Gradually the list grew. Daphne had certainly covered a great deal of the Tamar valley.

It took half an hour to complete this primitive location index. George stopped to make herself a mug of coffee, then examined what she had found.

The locations on her list were well spread out. There were walks all round Merrifield Manor, especially if you allowed yourself to cycle to their starting points (as Daphne might). Or took a bus into Bude.

There was something odd, though. George had found not a single walk starting north of Sandy Mouth. Though there were a lot – almost too many – that looped out of Bude, along the coast and back via the Bude canal.

She went back to the notebook to check. Was she simply failing to recognise any of the ones further north? Was Daphne using some acronym, some nickname of her own, to describe them?

She flipped through the notebook carefully. But no. It wasn't just that Daphne had failed to record one or two of her walks along these cliffs. She hadn't recorded any at all. And these were exactly the walks which Martha had told her were their favourites, as they looked for isolated beaches.

It was certainly odd. Almost as though Daphne was keeping these particular walks private; or at least, private from Sir Wilfred.

Unless, of course, Martha had some reason of her own to distort her and Daphne's walking destinations?

But whoever had arranged it, it seemed like a deliberate distortion. George mused for a while but could find no satisfactory explanation. And this, potentially, was on a detail that might help explain the woman's disappearance.

George had noted Martha's phone number at the end of Sunday's coffee morning, so she could contact her. Glancing out, it looked to be a fine day. Would Martha be game for a walk with her today? Would she be willing to show her where she and Daphne had explored, along those northerly cliffs?

Nothing ventured, nothing gained. A moment later she had

made the call.

Martha was enthusiastic to go on a walk with George to show her where she'd explored with Daphne. 'Yes, today would be great. You have to make the most of every fine day in November, they're not exactly frequent.'

George arranged to pick her up in an hour's time.

'Thank you for being so flexible, Martha,' said the analyst as she picked up her new walking partner, turned the car and set off back towards the A39.

'It's a relief to be with someone who has their own car,' Martha admitted.

'How did you and Daphne get there, then?'

'Daily bus from Bude to Morwenstow. It leaves Bude at half past nine, returns at four. That got us to the area. Then we walked down to the cliffs. It made for a strenuous day.'

George nodded. 'Yes. It would. Did you ever cycle?'

'Sometimes Daphne did when she was on her own. I don't have a bike, you see. Other times Daphne would take the Merrifield car. But not too much; she didn't want to alert her husband.'

'Wow. That keen to keep the trips secret, eh? Did she ever say why?'

Martha shook her head. 'I think it all hung on this hidden treasure that she hoped to find. She didn't want anyone else getting there first.'

They had reached the junction between Bude and Stratton. George turned right, following the road up toward Kilkhampton.

'What gave her the idea in the first place?

Martha shrugged. 'Not sure. As I said before, she read lots of historical books about smugglers in North Cornwall.'

'Anything in particular?'

'She'd a biography by a vicar of Morwenstow she'd found in the Manor library that started her off. I just came for the walks.'

Silence for a moment.

'What's the best place for us to park? Morwenstow? Or somewhere closer? Anything to save us time. It's dark early at this time of year.'

Martha pulled her Hartland explorer map from her cagoule pocket and perused it.

'Head for Morwenstow, George, but take the Stanbury exit once we reach the hamlet of Shop,' she requested.

Twenty minutes later they had reached the end of the tarmac road and were parked at the top of a footpath leading down to the coast.

'Right. We'll go down this track here.' Martha was in charge now and George was happy to follow.

Going down towards the sea was easy enough. It would take longer to come back up again. But it was only just after noon. There was plenty of daylight left. Ten minutes later they had reached the Coast Path and could look down on the savage, rock-strewn coastline.

'You'll see plenty of walkers along here,' said George doubt-fully.

Martha pointed left. 'That calls itself Stanbury Beach. At low tide, anyway. Don't worry. We'll be off the beaten path soon enough.'

The Coast Path followed the cliffs down until they emerged barely a hundred feet above the rocky beach. The Coast Path continued up the other side; the slope below them looked almost vertical.

'Looks impossible, doesn't it?' asked Martha with a

mischievous grin.

'Impassable, you mean.'

'Watch me then. And follow carefully.' Martha headed for a boulder ten yards off to the side, nestling in the bracken. She stood on top; then skipped to one side. And disappeared completely.

George blinked. Looked away and blinked again. Was she going mad?

Slowly she followed her companion's route to the boulder and stood on it. Looked around. It was surrounded by bracken on every side. Where on earth had Martha gone?

Then she noticed a hollow in the bracken to her left. It didn't look large enough to take a human body, but she was small by normal standards. Martha had taken a skip, hadn't she?

Her body resistant but her mind determined, George took a deep breath and then skipped towards the bracken hollow; and disappeared inside it. The ferns came right over her head.

But she was alright: her feet had landed on something soft - moss of some sort. Then a hand – Martha's – grabbed her to stop her falling. 'Step inside the cave. There's a path right down to the beach.'

And there was. It even had stepping-stones at muddy spots. George looked up but they were tucked well into the cliff, invisible from above. It was the best hidden path she had ever been on.

The path didn't go to Stanbury beach itself, though. It hugged the cliff face, dropping steadily, until it reached an even smaller beach beyond.

'This is Rane beach.' George wondered why her companion was whispering. 'It really is almost unreachable. And it's pure white sand.'

There was no need to delay now. They clambered over more

rough rocks until they were standing on the beach proper.

'It took us ages to find this,' Martha continued. 'Daphne said it was just like the entrance she'd found described in her biography.'

Slowly, George stared around her. Very few people had ever been here and she wanted to make the most of it. It was wild enough. Though there was no inviting cave, full of smugglers' trove.

'The path is out of sight, but we're not,' she observed. 'Someone could see us from the Coast Path. What happens then?'

Martha smiled. 'Daphne and I talked about that. We did have a plan. In the last resort we'd both strip off and go for a dip. We're no spring chickens. We reckoned that two older women, both stark naked, would embarrass any watchers into moving on.'

George was shocked. Not by the notion of swimming naked, she'd done that from time to time on remote Cornish beaches. But by the thoroughness of her new friend's preparations.

She was about to congratulate her. Then, to her horror, she saw that right now there was someone on the Coast Path; it looked like the women had been seen.

'Martha, are you feeling brave? I'm afraid we're going to have to strip off. There's someone up there. They might even have got binoculars.'

In the years ahead George would wake up with nightmares from the next half hour. For to protect their secret passage from the watcher George could see no choice but to enact the plan.

It would have been a clever scheme in summertime. But in November the sea was cold and the wind biting, whistling along the beach. George was shivering almost uncontrollably as she removed the last of her clothes. But she saw Martha was naked as well. If the older woman could handle it, then so must she.

'I've a towel in my backpack,' Martha muttered. 'It's a fully worked out plan, you see. Come on. We might feel warmer once we're in the sea. We don't need to go out far.'

George had never swum in the sea at this time of year, not even in the Mediterranean. And she resolved she would never do it again.

There was a sudden shock as their feet came into contact with the first waves. That turned to incredible coldness as they stepped forward, the sea rising higher and higher up their un-protected bodies.

Once they were immersed it wasn't quite so bad. The women could lower themselves into the water and be protected from the worst of the wind. After that they kept moving. But the sea itself was astonishingly cold. They didn't stay in for long.

'You can have first go with the towel,' declared Martha as they came out and headed for the limited wind protection, close to the cliff face. George decided she wasn't going to argue. She was almost numb: there was no feeling left in her legs at all.

She seized the towel and rubbed herself dry. Then pulled on her clothes. It was hard work fixing the buttons with her icy fin-gers. She was thankful that she had layered up well before they set out. Once dressed she bounced up and down to restore lim-ited warmth. She saw that Martha, now she had the towel, was almost dressed, not far behind her.

She would never forget this. It was one way of turning a one-day companion into a lifelong friend. But one she hoped never to repeat.

George glanced up. There was no-one on the Coast path above them now. The plan seemed to have worked. But the tide was on the turn and the sea starting to come in.

'Did you ever find more secrets here, Martha?'

'Not yet. But Daphne reckoned it was all to do with the tide. With a low spring tide, she said, we might have been able to get round the next headland. I was excited enough to get this far.'

It occurred to George as they clambered back up the secret pathway, with life returning only slowly to her lower limbs, that climbing back over the boulder would be a challenge. But it must be possible: Martha had done it before.

'It's OK doing this with two of us,' explained Martha as they reached the boulder. 'Daphne was much taller than either of us. Mind, I couldn't do it on my own. You'd need to be terrifically tall.'

So saying, she gave George a heave up the boulder, enough for her to take hold on top. Once she'd pulled herself up, George in turn could haul up Martha. Once back onto the Coast Path they plodded their way slowly back to the car.

It had been an interesting afternoon. George felt grateful to Martha for allowing her to experience something of Daphne's hopes and dreams. But it was almost five o'clock and starting to get dark. They hadn't had much daylight to spare.

But the two had become much closer – an unexpected friendship, formed in adversity. As the car set off George had an idea and turned to Martha. 'I'm very grateful for your memories and guidance. To say thank you, would you let me buy you dinner on the way home?'

Martha smiled. As the car's heating began to function she was starting to feel less cold. 'That would be very nice. But . . . you're a fair distance from Tintagel.'

'I've been invited to join the bellringers tonight. I'll have to be in Bridgerule for most of the evening.'

'In that case,' said Martha, smiling more broadly, 'it's an invitation I'd love to accept.'

CHAPTER 28

The Falcon Hotel was starting to feel like her local, thought George, as she led Martha through the foyer and into the restaurant. It was only, what, four evenings since she'd been here with Edward. But at least she knew from the earlier visit that they would start serving meals early.

They were shown a discreet table on the far side. Fish and chips and glasses of house white wine were ordered (the waitress had advised this choice came fastest) and their evening began. A glow had returned to Martha's face and, presumably, to her own. Comfort and warmth were welcome after the rigours of the beach.

'I'm afraid you won't find the church very warm tonight,' warned Martha. 'These days they ration the heating to the main Sunday service. And it's not that warm then.'

George nodded. 'Thanks for the warning. I'll put all my layers back on. Have you had much to do with the bell ringers?'

'Daphne invited me along once, after one of our walks, but it didn't grab me. Though afterwards one of the ringers tried to.'

Surprising. Martha was a charming woman, but she was in her sixties. One of them must have felt desperate – presumably one of the men? 'Thanks for that warning, too, Martha. I met some of them briefly on Sunday. They all looked harmless enough then. And the conductor in his bow tie was very friendly. That's how I came to be invited.'

There was no need to admit that she had contrived the invitation herself, in the hope of learning more about Daphne. But the thought reminded George that there might be more still she could learn from Martha.

Their meal had not yet arrived. Now was as good a time as any. She turned to her new friend, who was looking very relaxed, and smiled mischievously.

'You know, Daphne might not have been completely paranoid. I mean, the idea of finding old smugglers' treasure trove is fanciful, but someone else might have found it interesting. Are you sure she didn't mention it to anyone else in Bridgerule?'

Martha seemed happy enough to continue the discussion around her friend. She wrinkled her nose as she pondered.

'I'm practically certain she wouldn't talk to anyone in Bridgerule. She made it clear to me that all this was a secret between us. And Merrifield folk generally kept their distance from the "Bridgerule dwellers".'

She continued to muse. 'The only person she might have talked to, I suppose, was someone in Bude that might help her search.'

'Someone in the Visitors' Centre, perhaps?'

'I doubt it. They've plenty of data there for short-term visitors but they wouldn't know more than Daphne. I mean, she's lived here all her life.'

'Right.' George thought for a moment. 'Was Daphne always interested in coves and beaches?'

'Oh no. For a long time we just went up there occasionally, for those special bits of cliff. I mean, some parts are really spectacular. Higher Sharpnose Point, for example. You can go right out over the sea on what's almost a knife edge.'

Their fish and chips were brought at that moment, giving George a moment for thought. Dare she keep going on this? Might Martha start to object?

But once they were eating, Martha herself continued the

topic.

'In fact, it was from Higher Sharpnose Point that we saw Stanbury Beach, where we were today. It must have been low tide, I suppose; there's no sand when the tide's in. "That's very remote. I wonder if you can get down there," Daphne asked. So next time we were out that way we went for a look.'

'Ah. And you found the secret route?'

Martha shook her head. 'Not at once. Not for ages, actually. It was one of the lifeguards that seemed to know how to find it.'

Martha didn't seem to realise that she had given George an answer to her earlier question. Maybe in her mind lifeguards were like servants: you didn't notice them, simply took them for granted? Perhaps it would be as well to change the subject.

George took a long sip of her wine. An interesting taste. If she wasn't driving, she'd have enjoyed a second glass. Then she remembered her findings in Barnstaple the day before; and that Martha was a daughter of the midwife that had delivered Daphne.

But, she recalled, Martha was also a churchgoer. Perhaps she'd also known the long-life vicar?

'Did you ever know the Revd Frank Hawker Kingdon?'

Martha giggled. 'I think the continuity girl must have gone for a break. Try again.'

George realised she'd made a disconnect. 'I'm sorry, Martha. I was thinking of my own struggles, actually. Kingdon was a former vicar at St Bridget's. I saw his name on a gravestone. It said he was there for seventy years. So -'

'Oh, him. The vicar when I was a small child. But he was very old. He didn't move very fast; or have much to do with the children. Why d'you ask?'

George ate a few chips as she wondered how much to reveal. Normally she kept all her research secret. But Martha had been a close friend of the woman she was investigating; maybe sharing would help them both?

'This'll take a minute or two.'

'I'm not going anywhere. The floor is yours.'

George smiled. 'OK. It turns out this Kingdon chap kept a personal diary for most of his life; it's now in the Record Office in Barnstaple. I spent most of yesterday reading it.'

Martha stared at her, gobsmacked. 'Gosh. That must have made coming out with me an attractive alternative.'

George grinned. 'It's an interesting read, actually. Better than you might think. A social history of England – or at least Bridgerule. And it had a few memories that touched on Daphne and Merrifield Manor.'

Martha was no longer so dismissive. She didn't have many contacts who featured in a Records Office. 'Go on.'

'The Revd Kingdon records that he baptised Daphne at Merrifield Manor in the last year of the war. She was just two weeks old. He records that she was the daughter of the Manor cook. Did you know that?'

Martha's mouth had dropped open. 'Well, I never. All I knew from my mum was that she'd been Daphne's midwife. Didn't know it was in the war. So Daphne was a bit older than she admitted. And was part of the Merrifield household long before she married into it.'

It was time to take the investigation further. 'I assume your mum is no longer with us?'

Martha's head shook. 'No. She died a long time ago.'

'And she never spoke about this case? Even at home, off the record?'

'I'm afraid not. Why? Was there something odd about it?'

'Well. Kingdon's diary also showed he did a second baptism at Merrifield that day. That was Wilfred Gabriel. And he was the same age as Daphne. Both babies were two weeks old. So Kingdon implied that they were born on the same day.'

Martha blinked. She was silent for a moment.

'But George, if that's true it's an amazing coincidence. Two children born to different mothers, in the same house on the same day. Wow. I suppose it is true?'

'That's what I've been wondering. Perhaps it was what Daphne was wondering too.' There was another silence, this one longer.

They had both finished their meals by this point and the wait-ress was eyeing them from the far side of the room. Now she came over to take their plates and show them the dessert menu.

Both women ordered blackcurrant crumble and cream. It wasn't the day for anything cold. By mutual consent conversa-tion stopped until this had been served and they had started to eat it.

'Trouble is, Martha, I doubt we'll find any witnesses of those days who are still alive today. Apart from a pair of two-week-old babies, of course. I don't suppose your mum left any profes-sional records?'

George held her breath. This was her last hope.

Martha took a few seconds to respond. 'Mum kept them, of course. All her life. Even after she'd stopped work. But Mary and I ditched them after she died. Couldn't see that anyone would want them, now she'd gone.'

George grimaced but it was only too easy to be wise after the event. 'The thing I would be interested in, Martha, is her mid-wife diary for Merrifield Manor in 1945. Crucially, did she de-liver babies to two separate mothers on the same day? Or did she, in fact, deliver a pair of twins?'

174

CHAPTER 29

By half past seven George had driven back from Bude, dropped a well-satisfied but tired Martha at her home in Bridgerule and then driven on up to St Bridget's church, ready for bellringing practice. But she found it hard to set aside issues raised during their meal at the Falcon.

There were big questions like alternative ways to collect birth records from over seventy years ago (if these existed). Maybe these were best left to authorities such as the police? Also more parochial issues, like trying to identify which lifeguards Daphne had talked to regarding isolated beaches. Presumably the guides would all be based in Bude?

George told herself sternly that such issues could be taken further once the practice was over. Now she must focus on bells.

The same team of ringers were present as George had met on Sunday, and they all remembered her. She touched elbows with each in turn, voicing their names out loud. There was Jonny; Morwenna; Stella; Tracey; and Henry. Secretly she was pleased that she could match them all up.

But there were no reserve ringers and, of course, Daphne was still missing. Unless Stella wanted to pull two ropes for the whole evening, George expected she'd be taking an active role. She combed her long-term memory for almost-forgotten details of how to ring. As a carefree student that had felt like fun. Now she was much older, ringing bells with farms and other dwellings all around them seemed a lot more serious.

Conductor Thomas Vardy was there too, though no longer wearing his bow tie (this was, after all, only a rehearsal). The six bell ropes could all be seen, dangling down through three-inch holes in the floor above. Each one had a thick cloth collar near the bottom, softer material to protect the ringer's hands from the rigours of holding a rough rope. What was that called? Her mind went blank. Then it came back to her: it was a "sally".

But the key thing to get clear in her mind, George remembered from thirty years before, was to identify which rope rang which bell. For there was no guarantee the ropes hung down in a natural note order. It would all depend on the layout of the belfry high above. But she couldn't worry about that for the moment.

'So, George, you've rung before?' Thomas was busy assigning bodies to bells for the evening. 'High or low: any preference?'

'Some are harder work than others. But I can't recall which ones I preferred. I'll leave it to you.'

Five minutes later George found herself in the middle of a semicircle of bellringers, next to Stella. She would have the nearest rope.

Once they were all in position Thomas addressed them. 'Tonight, my friends, we are going to keep it simple. I'm going to assign a number to each bell, which won't change. Since you won't be changing bells, you'll just have one number to remember. And I'll call the numbers in the order which will generate an interesting peal.'

One hour of steady, repetitive exercise later it was over. George had found the basics of ringing coming back to her. Her initial timing had been poor, always a fraction behind the regular beat, making the overall effect sound almost syncopated. Thomas had frowned at her once or twice. She had concentrated hard and gradually speeded up. But then, with all her urgent efforts, her bell was sounding too loud.

Gradually, with encouragement from all sides, she found herself fitting into the collective effort; she took great pride in doing so. Maybe this was a hobby she should indulge more often? She wondered if there were any bellringers in Tintagel or Boscastle. There were plenty of square-towered church buildings in the latter.

Afterwards, she was happy to join the team down in the Bridge Inn. Thomas didn't join them but then, she was told, he hardly ever did. This allowed the rest to relax and the discussion to range more widely, though George noticed they didn't speak out of turn. Mr Bow Tie was obviously held in high regard for his musical wisdom.

'They keep the snug clear for us on Tuesdays,' explained Morwenna as she led George through the pub's saloon bar to the smaller room beyond. 'It's a good night to come, they're never busy on Tuesdays. Means we needn't bother with masks: not much point really, since we've already spent an hour breathing hard over each other.'

George found herself directed to a comfortable long settee, with Morwenna perched on one side and Stella on the other. The other three seized the chairs opposite.

'Right. I'll get the drinks,' said Henry. 'We'll do the usual tab, shall we? Beers all round?'

'Just a half for me,' said George. 'I've got to drive home afterwards.'

There was a momentary pause after Henry disappeared.

'So Daphne Gabriel is normally part of your group?' asked George. She wouldn't normally have been the first to speak, but she was conscious this might be the best chance she'd have.

'Yes. She's a regular; been with us for about five years,' said Tracey.

'She started coming after she and Wilfred came back from Australia,' added Stella. 'I think meeting her sister-in-law inspired her to be more active in her later years.'

'When you first meet her, you think she's a fairly unobtrusive woman. Quiet, even shy, perhaps. But we soon thawed her out. Or at least Thomas did. But then, those two are of a similar age.'

'Morwenna, that's your youthful imagination,' rebuked Jonny. 'You don't know that at all. Or even which one's the older.'

That started a wide-ranging discussion. George was happy to sit back and listen. Fresh views on Daphne were really what she'd come for.

Five minutes later Henry appeared as the argument went back and forth, holding a tray of glasses and some packets of crisps; he set them all on the coffee table between them. George was glad to see she was not the only one who was restricting herself to just half a pint.

Henry quickly picked up the topic under discussion and added his opinion.

'Daphne might not have had much formal education, but she took a great interest in a lot of things,' he declared. 'For example, she badgered me to take her up the bell tower. Not just to the bells but right to the top.'

'Wasn't it a bit hairy on those narrow steps?' asked Jonny. 'They're pretty steep, I recall.'

Henry nodded. 'To be honest, that's what I feared. But she's jolly fit, you know. Nothing wrong with her balance. But then, she goes walking twice a week, up and down the coastline. There are plenty of ups and downs there.'

'Or else she explores the Tamar Valley,' added Morwenna. 'I tried to get her to write a guidebook about her walks there. There isn't one, as far as I know. But she was far too busy for that.'

George thought it was time to steer the discussion. 'Did she always walk on her own? Or had she special walking companions?'

'Most of the time she was on her own,' asserted Stella. 'She was a self-sufficient woman.'

'Her friend Martha went with her sometimes,' added Tracey. 'But I can't think of anyone else.'

'Did she say anything to any of you about long-term worries? Anything that might propel her away?'

There was a pause as beer was swigged and memories consulted.

'We'd meet up for coffee from time to time in Bude, but I never picked up anything serious,' said Stella. 'Until six months ago I'd say she was a contented woman. Hardly worried about anything. Recently, mind, she was wrestling with some sort of puzzle.' She shrugged. 'I'm afraid I've no idea what it might be.'

'At least the Gabriels are financially viable,' said Jonny. 'With that estate. And not many extravagant hobbies.'

George thought she'd pressed them enough. 'Anyway, that's enough talk about Daphne. Tell me a bit more about what the rest of you do. Hey, d'you link up with bellringers anywhere else?'

'There's a federation of ringers for North Cornwall. There are over half a dozen churches near here with regular ringers. Up as far as Kilkhampton and Morwenstow and down to Week St Mary's. We even have an annual social gathering.'

'That's in Poundstock,' added Morwenna. 'In a couple of weeks' time. There's a Tudor gildhouse next to the church. It's

179

not used very much for weddings in late November. Come and join us if you like, George. There's plenty to eat and drink and we also do lots of country dancing.'

George noted the invitation and said she'd check her diary. It was a sign she was accepted. The conversation continued for some time but drew to a close soon after ten. As the group made their way out, George found herself next to Henry.

She gave him her most enticing smile. 'You say you took Daphne for a trip up the bell tower. Is there any chance you could take me?'

'Sure. The main problem's getting into the church itself. Thomas has the key for the bellringer group, he's the tower captain. But St Bridget's is locked most of the time.'

Morwenna overheard their conversation and butted in. 'The church is cleaned on Thursday mornings, Henry, between eleven and twelve thirty. You'd be able to get in then.'

George agreed the time at once. At least she'd follow the footsteps of the missing woman. Though she doubted she'd learn a great deal more.

CHAPTER 30   Thursday Nov 18th

George heard not a thing from Edward over Wednesday, nor even by early Thursday morning. She could no longer claim an official remit to help in the search from his family. Even so, she wanted to go up the bell tower for herself – though it was hard to say exactly why.

It was certainly one of the more surprising things Daphne had done that she knew about. It was now well over a week since the woman had disappeared. Whatever trail there might have been, whether she was now dead or alive, was growing ever colder.

There was less traffic than she'd expected on the A39; George reached St Bridget's twenty minutes ahead of schedule. She parked and walked through the churchyard, up to the main doorway, but it was locked: the cleaners must still be on their way.

George stood back and looked up at the square church tower where the bells were located. The top was perhaps fifty feet above her. Out of curiosity, and because she'd always enjoyed numbers, she decided to pace the dimensions of the tower.

Each side was almost exactly six paces. As far as she could judge the tower was exactly square.

At that point a couple of cleaners arrived, older church ladies dressed today for cleansing action. George introduced herself and found they were called Sheila and Janet. Then she recalled Edward mentioning a Sheila when he was first outlining events at Merrifield.

'Are you by any chance a friend of Daphne Gabriel, Sheila?'

'I am, dear. She and I normally do this duty together but for the moment she's not with us. You must be Edward's friend?'

George didn't want to lie but nor did she want to elaborate on their recent mix-up; that had to be kept private. She just smiled and nodded.

'One of the bellringers – Henry – agreed to give me a guided tour of the tower. He knew the church was always cleaned on Thursdays. Is he right: does one of you have a key?'

Sheila nodded and drew a large iron key from her pocket. 'It's a big thing to carry about. We'd make copies but it's too large to duplicate. Come on, we might as well go in. Henry will be here in a few minutes, I expect.'

George followed them inside. The church was no warmer than it had been the night before last, but it was at least out of the wind. Clearly the leadership here was frugal with their resources.

'Right. We'd better get on with our dusting and hoovering.' Sheila glanced at George in a friendly manner. 'Janet and I will be going for lunch at the Bridge Inn afterwards. You can join us if you like.'

'That's very kind. Thank you.'

At that moment there was the creaking of a door behind them and Henry appeared.

'Morning ladies. Sorry I'm late, George,' he smiled. 'Are you game to start the magical mystery tour?'

They left the cleaners to their duties and headed for the room below the bell tower. It looked exactly as it had when they left it on Tuesday.

'From a safety point of view, shouldn't this be locked?' asked George.

'The cleaners always do that when they leave. But it doesn't matter much. There's no-one here most of the time. Right.'

To George's surprise, Henry clambered onto the pew she'd sat on a few days ago and walked to the far end. Then he looked up, reached over his head to the ceiling.

What on earth was he doing?

There must be some sort of catch up there. For there was a click. Then a small, rectangular section of ceiling folded down. Behind it George could see some sort of metal contraption. But for the moment her eyes boggled; she was speechless.

Henry glanced down at her and smiled. 'Daphne was amazed by this too.'

He reached up to the contraption and pulled. In fact it was just a simple two-tier ladder, similar to the one she had in her own loft.

George had to admit to herself that safety wasn't a problem. All this was well out of the reach of children. It didn't need locking at all.

There was nothing stopping them now.

'D'you want to go first or second, George?'

George was wearing a skirt, so the choice was easy. 'I'll follow you.'

'OK.' Henry stood down from the pew and started to climb the ladder. 'Now you can see what the other ringers were on about.' He disappeared through the hole in the ceiling into pitch darkness beyond.

No reason to panic, George told herself sternly as she slowly mounted the ladder. Handsome Henry is here to help me. She was into the blackness now and felt for the top of the ladder. It must be time to step sideways. This was scary.

A moment later she was standing on the floor above where they'd pulled the bell ropes. A faint light from below gave a glimmer of illumination. George, you're an idiot, she told herself.

You didn't even think to bring a torch.

But Henry had one. He shone it around and she saw they were in a largely empty room, with the bell ropes running through from above to below. There was something slightly odd about it, but she couldn't make out what it was.

'We're halfway,' her guide murmured. Once more he walked to a corner of the room and reached up. Another click and a small door dropped down. She could see another ladder, ready to be pulled down. But this time the space above wasn't pitch dark. There was some sort of lighting up there.

'That's the belfry,' Henry explained. 'All the bells are up there, each one mounted on a large wheel. D'you want to see?'

It was a rhetorical question and they both knew it. Once more Henry pulled down the ladder and started to climb. Once he had disappeared, George started to follow. Two minutes later she was up to the floor above, standing on a narrow ledge which ran right around, inside the belfry.

Now the subdued lighting made sense. For there were slatted windows on every side, presumably to allow the sound of the rung bells to be heard in the nearby village. Each was covered in wire netting, she guessed to prevent an invasion of birds.

The bells were in the well and the ledge ran round the edge. Each bell was staunchly attached to its own large, wooden wheel. The axle for each wheel was held in a separate metal harness, laid out at different angles to make full use of the limited space. No wonder the ropes below hung down in a strange pattern.

'Are these bells very old?' asked George.

Henry pointed. 'These four are. Cast around 1770 in Plymouth and been here ever since.' He turned to the other two, on the far side. 'These two were added a century later.'

'Is the metal frame that holds them equally old?'

Henry smiled. 'Fortunately it isn't. That was updated in the

1930s. 'Course, it's the frame which carries the weight of the bells. That's checked by structural engineers every few years.' He grinned. 'Even Thomas Vardy takes some bits of health and safety seriously.'

George took a few minutes to peer at the bells and their fittings.

'What are those wooden stays?'

'They're to stop the wheels continuously rotating. Our bell ropes can only pull each wheel through a restricted swing, no more than 360°. That's why it's an art to pull them.'

She finished her inspection and looked across to her guide. 'Is there anything else to see, Henry?'

'If you like we can go onto the roof. It'll be cold, mind.'

George nodded. Henry once more positioned himself in the corner and fiddled with a catch over his head. This time the doorway opened upwards; George could see dark clouds in the sky beyond. Then he reached up and hauled down a ladder.

'The final viewpoint,' he murmured and led the way out onto the roof of the tower. Gingerly, George followed.

She was relieved to see a waist-high wall around the edge. It was safe enough, anyway. She stepped towards it and looked across the valley, trying to make sense of the view.

'Did you bring an old lady like Daphne right up here?'

'She insisted. Mind, that was early September. It wasn't nearly as breezy then. I think basically she wanted to see how far it was to Merrifield Manor.'

George oriented herself. Bridgerule was below them, with the river Tamar meandering through. So that direction must be south. Half a minute later she spotted the Manor, a stone building up on the hill beyond.

'So the Bude Canal used to run along there?' She pointed to the hillside high above the twisting Tamar.

Henry looked at her curiously. 'I have not the faintest idea what you're talking about.'

'Well, you can't see it now.' She shivered. 'It's really cold up here, Henry. I think I've seen enough. Can we go down, please?'

George went down first. Henry came after her, stopping to close and bolt each door, but she hastened on ahead.

Down past the belfry and into the middle room of the tower below. There must be something awkward about fixing the roof catch. Whatever it was, Henry was lagging behind.

The mid-tower room was dark but there was a little light from above and from below. George glanced round again. There was nothing on the floor. So what was odd?

Then something occurred to her. She stood with her back to one wall and walked, deliberately, across the room, counting her paces. Then she did the same with the other two walls.

She was right. There was something peculiar. For this room, unlike the one above and the one below, was not exactly square. She made it five and half paces one way and four and a half the other.

George heard Henry starting to come down from the belfry. The obvious thing was to ask him, but for some reason she couldn't. Instead, she headed for the ladder to the ground floor. She needed to think harder about what she'd found before she told anyone at all.

PART FOUR

MAXINE DIGS DEEPER

NOVEMBER NOV 17th – 19th

The cliffs close to Cleave Camp:
Stanbury Beach with Higher Sharpnose Point beyond.
Lundy is the island on the far horizon.

187

CHAPTER 31   Wednesday Nov 17th

It was a good job that Maxine had learned, over many years of relentless decoding, to keep her head down and plough resolutely on. For the task of working through the diaries of the leaders of Cleave Airfield page by page, looking for anomalies that might have led on to nasty rumours, was tedious.

Maxine had been handed two volumes that started in 1940. The airfield wasn't operational before then. Cleave was the wrong end of Cornwall to launch RAF planes far out into the Atlantic in search for enemy U-boats. But it was a natural airfield: an almost flat, grassy field, right on the edge of high cliffs. What could be done with it?

In the end, she learned, it had been decided to turn the land into an airfield to train anti-aircraft gunners on the art of hitting aerial targets. Those weren't the RAF planes themselves, of course: they were far too valuable. But a scheme was devised whereby the planes would tow what they termed "drapes", each one painted with the full-scale outline of an enemy aircraft. Of course, there was quite a distance between the tow-er and the towed. But Maxine could imagine it was still a nerve-racking job to be one of the pulling pilots. The risk of being hit by an inaccurate gunner from the cliffs below was always present. And just a single hit by an anti-aircraft shell was likely to prove fatal.

Maxine adjusted her expectations. She'd started the morning thinking that "friendly fire incidents" at a British airfield would be almost non-existent. Now she was surprised when, according to the diary, they weren't more frequent.

There was continual debate on the best length for the towing rope. All the pilots wanted it as long as was feasible, to keep the target as far from them as possible. But when it became too long the drape was no longer in the air at a similar height to the plane but lagged well below. Maxine gathered that the planes being used for towing were not that highly powered. It would be easy enough, with an over-long rope, for the drape to drift down towards the sea. Which, if it went in, would also be fatal for the plane doing the towing.

In the end a length of around two hundred and fifty feet for the tow rope became the accepted norm.

Not that long, mused Maxine. These airmen must be very brave indeed. Mind, there was no evidence that they were volunteers. Probably none had chosen to come here.

As she ploughed on, taking more notice now of dates, Maxine realised that one reason why there were not more accidents was that aerial "target days" did not happen that often. For one thing, wind direction would determine whether towing a big drape, as they flew along parallel to the cliffs, was even possible. And there were many days which were too stormy, or (occasionally) too calm.

There seemed to be plenty of days, too, when the gunners practised on land-based targets, positioned further up or down the coast.

There were also days when the pilots took out their aircraft to practise releasing and pulling the target drape, without any expectation of shooting at all. As she read on, Maxine came to realise that the pilots were not stationed here for the whole war, fresh teams would be brought in regularly. Perhaps it was accepted that it was too hard on the nerves for anyone to be a target-puller for very long.

But still there was no evidence of accidental fatalities.

Maxine browsed solidly. Eventually she got into a regular pattern of working. By lunch time she'd read the record for 1940. After lunch she'd swap these diaries for the ones covering 1941; or perhaps, now she was working faster, she'd get as far as 1942.

From time to time the diaries had a change of author as a new commander was brought in. Presumably they, too, became worn down over time, fatigued by the relentless strain. But each followed the writing style of their predecessor. The information was much the same. Though later ones included some details of base discipline and the occupants of the "sin bin" – as the solitary confinement cell was called.

Maxine started to wonder what she was really after. These were British troops, both the pilots and the gunners. There was no reason for American infiltrators, they'd all have trained at home. So how on earth could anything that happened here, at this airfield, possibly lead to American anxieties?

As she read, she also tried to make more sense of the airfield layout. There didn't seem to be many buildings in the war years and there was no mention of cellars. It didn't seem as though Cleave Manor was still standing. It must have fallen into decay well before the war.

That made her wonder where all these troops were billeted. It was hard to estimate numbers, but from the bits and pieces mentioned there could easily be a hundred in total. One or two might fit into local cottages around Cleave, but there weren't many of those. For the time being it was just another unknown.

By the end of the afternoon, Maxine had completed her examination of the diaries for 1941 and 1942. With a bit of luck she'd get through the rest by the end of tomorrow.

Next morning, she collected the next two years' diaries from Bill's office and started on 1943.

The middle year of the war. Action around the world was intense, even training gunners seemed harder than before – or perhaps the goals were more ambitious. But all the routines were now in place; it should be safer than ever.

Then there was a change. Previously all target flights had taken place in daytime. Now some took place at night. This was more realistic; it was when enemy bombers came. But it was also more dangerous.

Maxine presumed that only the more skilled gunners, perhaps ones here for a refresher course, would fire their weapons at night. But there would be extra complications, for example on nights which were intermittently cloudy. She doubted they would use searchlights.

Even so, there were no recordings of accidents from "friendly fire". By lunch time she had reached 1944.

Her later readings revealed that the latest airfield commander was more verbose than his predecessors. He seemed to appreciate the valour of the pilots and mentioned one or two by name.

He was also more open about near mishaps. For everyone was more on edge, tired and irritable, as the war went on. The decade-old planes still being used – which were the majority – felt even older. And maintenance was tricky: spare parts were not always available.

One flight had been aborted before it got anywhere near the target area and the crew had to be "rescued from the drink". Maxine took that to be shorthand for the Atlantic, not a reference to spirits.

Then, in July 1944, the commander admitted not just to one fatality but to two: the crew of a Hawker Henley on a night flight.

The night sky was cloudy, visibility intermittent. But several recent flights had been delayed and he had decided they mustn't postpone again.

The gunners were on an advanced course and apparently, he was told, "all proper routines had been followed". He had asked for a report but nothing untoward had been discovered. Except that, tragically, one of the shells had hit the Henley instead of the drape. The crew had had no chance at all. There weren't even bodies to be buried.

Then came the words that Maxine had been half-expecting for nearly two days. One of the crew, Bert Pearce, came from nearby, a family in Bridgerule. But the other, Chuck Colson, was an American.

So the rumour was correct. There had been a "friendly fire" incident at the airfield. And one of the victims was an American.

Maxine was tempted to tell Bill straight away. But she forced herself to read to the end of 1944. There had been no more incidents.

Then she realised she had to read 1945 as well. Bill was bound to ask her if the 1944 event was the only one they needed to worry about. She needed to have an answer.

So once more she went along to Bill's office for the remaining diary. She also booked a session with the Camp Commander for Thursday afternoon. A strategy was needed on what they should do next.

the perimeter of Cleave Camp. That's Stanbury Beach. I've no idea how you'd get down there, but it must be possible. I saw two women down there, when the officer and I stopped for coffee. Both skinny dipping.'

Sam blinked. 'Rather them than me, Maxine. In November, at least. OK, I concede there is some logic to your idea. It's not totally impossible. But you'd need some hard evidence to push the idea any further.'

That was a fair conclusion on what they knew so far. But Maxine had the first glimmerings of an idea on how to take it further.

CHAPTER 33

There was no good reason, thought Maxine, why the exploration she envisaged should not happen at night. You didn't need daylight at all in an underground tunnel, simply one good torch. Or perhaps two.

For the truth was that she didn't fancy going deep into the cellars beneath the old Cleave Manor on her own. It wouldn't be safe. The best ally she could have, from the limited selection of those she had reason to trust in action, would be security man Marcus.

It was fortunate that she still had his card and mobile number from their exploration of the camp perimeter.

The time was just after four o'clock. Close to dusk. Probably, by now, he would be back on duty, maybe checking staff out in the security hut. But he might not be that busy. One or two staff had permission to leave early, but not many. She keyed in his number.

'Marcus?'

'That's me. Is that. . . is that Maxine?'

He'd recognised her voice, at least. That was a good start.

'Are you busy?'

'I'm in the hut. No-one else here at the moment. Best not to talk for long, though.'

'When do you come off duty? And have you any plans for this evening?'

'Seven o'clock. Then I'm as free as a bird. Open to offers.'

'Good man. I'll join you then.'

As a senior manager, Maxine was on the loosest of flexi-hours. All she needed to do now was to check that her husband could, for once, get home early. Rosanna was the one person around her who was not flexible at all.

Maxine made good use of the next two hours, continuing her forensic reading from the airfield logbooks.

She then spent the remaining time on her desktop computer, reviewing old Ordnance Survey maps of the area around Cleave Camp. One thing she'd picked up during maternity leave was that the National Museum of Scotland gave open access to copies of everything. Maps could even be overlaid on top of one another.

The ruin of Cleave Manor didn't appear at all on recent maps but was there in the map for 1930; and also for 1920. But only the ruin. The Manor itself must have collapsed at least a century ago – sometime in the 1800s?

She also confirmed the proximity of the camp boundary to Stanbury Beach. That was something her expedition with Marcus might be about to explore.

At five to seven Maxine slipped on her scarf and cagoule and presented herself at the security hut. Marcus was just tidying up, there was no-one else around.

He smiled broadly as he saw her.

'Where are we off to this time?'

'There are some old tunnels under the camp. I've been shown the generating plant in one of them and been told there are fuel tanks in another. But there are plenty more.'

Marcus looked at her questioningly but didn't speak.

'I reckon,' she went on, 'they might have something or other to do with Cleave Manor. That's shown on this site, on older maps. It can't always have been a ruin. I'd like to see if there is anything else that's been stored inside them. Can security provide us with a pair of torches?'

'We'd best both have security jackets as well, then. And helmets. I've got my security keys. I don't think I'll need binoculars.'

'I don't suppose we'll find any skinny-dippers tonight,' Maxine agreed. 'Mind, it'll still be cold, even inside the tunnels.'

Maxine had asked Martin Jordan to loan her the keys to the generating tunnel for the evening. He'd looked hard at her then shrugged his shoulders, choosing not to ask awkward questions. That was real teamwork, she thought. Trusting one another, without the need to know everything.

Maxine and Marcus went into the main building and down the stairs, then down many more steps and turns to the power generator itself. Marcus hadn't seen the plant before and was suitably impressed.

Maxine used one of her keys to open another door. From this point on there were no lights at all. Good job they both had torches. But the passageways were high enough, anyway.

One of the benefits of coming to explore with someone new, Maxine realised, was that they wouldn't try to block you from things they'd already seen (and maybe were off limits). An open mind was certainly useful when searching like this.

Soon after they'd left the generator tunnel, they came to a three-way junction.

'It's a pity we don't have a map of the full tunnel layout,' murmured the security man, no doubt conscious of the risks of getting lost.

'I don't think such a thing exists. That's why I wanted to look for myself.' Maxine shone her torch down each passageway in turn, trying to pick out the main one – the spine of the network. They were all similar. In the end she went for the route that seemed to be heading downwards. 'Let's go for this one.'

'Wait a tick, Maxine. I'll note the time. It'll give us some sense of how far we've gone. Right, it's currently 7:23.'

The passage went steadily down and down. Marcus reminded her that they needed to keep an eye open for further junctions, especially any passages coming in from a trailing angle.

'One of these might not give us an obvious choice on the way down, Maxine. But it could lead to a huge headache on the way back.'

His comment made her glad that there was someone so capable with her. Marcus was wasted as a lowly security man.

Steadily, carefully, they went down and down. The walls of the passage were rougher now, looked like they'd been hewn out of the rock. The cross-section became less rectangular, closer to a cylindrical tunnel. It was relatively straight. But they'd both lost any sense of its direction.

Suddenly they became conscious that they were no longer alone.

There was a peculiar rustling noise ahead. Then something light brushed against her face and Maxine gave a scream.

'Help! Marcus, I think it's a bat. It flew straight into me. Aren't they infectious?'

Two steps behind her, Marcus stopped and cast his torch from side to side.

'It's not a bat, Maxine, it's a bird. Some sort of gull, I think.'

Now they'd stopped completely they could feel a slight draught coming towards them.

'Hey, there's something else.'

Carefully they shuffled forwards, Marcus now in front. The

faint breeze came more strongly now. When they stopped again and listened hard, there was a noise in the distance. It was the faint but distinctive sound of waves lapping on the shore.

Maxine gave a gasp. 'Marcus, that's the sea. We must be coming out onto the cliff. We can't be that far from where we saw those skinny-dippers.'

'Let's go very slowly. We don't want to fall over the edge.'

A few minutes later they found themselves peering through a jagged gap in the cliff-face.

The security guard was shaken. 'Wow. This is potentially a secret route into the camp cellars. We need to get it blocked off before any terrorists find it.'

Maxine was less stressed. 'This isn't a recent development, Marcus. It's hardly new. To me it looks much more like a secret route that was once used by smugglers.'

They took turns to peer through the gap. There was certainly sea down below. But it was too dark to make out how far above the water they were. It was high enough, though, to make the opening hard to spot from below.

It was on the way back that they lost their way. There had probably been a trailing junction, around the point where Maxine had come face to face with the bird.

The trouble was, they didn't realise they had gone wrong for a while. The passage looked much the same, but it wasn't ascending in the way it should, given they had earlier come steadily downwards.

They had just realised the problem, and that they needed to turn back, when they came to something else.

'What on earth . . .?' For the tunnel had widened out. Now they were in a cave, one that stretched out in several directions.

'Could this be the storage cellar for the old Manor?' asked

Marcus.

For it wasn't just a random sea-cave, strewn with rocks and boulders. There was a certain order in the way it was laid out.

Both searchers stared, silent and wide-eyed, for a moment.

'If we find wine bottles, I'd say the place must once have belonged to the Manor.'

'The trouble is, Maxine, these are wooden kegs. They might be kegs of spirit.' He shone his torch around. 'Wow, there are dozens. It's anyone's guess how old this lot is. If it's not gone off, this lot could be priceless.'

Marcus started to head towards the nearest kegs to explore further, but Maxine grabbed his arm. 'Marcus, it'd be very easy to get lost in here. There might be other ways in and out, which come out goodness knows where. We don't want to get confused again; I think we should go back now. We've found plenty to think about. At least, here, we're in a passage that we know is linked to the top.'

Marcus was wise enough to accept the dangers of going further. An odd-shaped cave was harder to explore than a narrow tunnel. If they intended to explore it properly, perhaps they needed a large ball of string to attach to their starting point.

He nodded in agreement. They turned and retraced their route back towards the cliff face.

Then, as they could faintly hear waves in the distance, Maxine recognised where she was. This was a trailing junction; it was the place she'd met the bat that was really a gull. It was easy to see how they'd got muddled.

This time they headed purposefully uphill.

Now they kept looking carefully for more trailing junctions but encountered nothing at all.

Twenty minutes later they were back at the three-way

junction where Marcus had first noted the time. They had been gone for just under an hour.

'Hey, it's only 8:20,' Marcus announced. 'Not that late. Whilst we're here, can't we take a quick look at these other passages – say, fifteen minutes on each?'

Maxine didn't want to block Marcus. After all, they needed to learn all they could.

'Go on, then. It'd be good to know what else is down here.'

They set off down one of the other passageways.

This one was fairly level. It took only five minutes to reach what was obviously some sort of wine cellar. A rectangle shape with whitened walls. Bottles of wine stacked everywhere.

'We've more chance of making sense of this, Maxine,' observed Marcus. 'Look. Most of these bottles are labelled. That'll surely tell us something about their age.'

They each seized a bottle from different racks and examined them carefully in the torchlight.

'Mine's from France,' said Maxine. 'But no clue on the date.'

'So's mine. But the label's old-fashioned. I'd say it's early last century if not older. It's probably undrinkable.'

They spent a few minutes wandering round. Then it was time to go.

'Right,' Maxine declared. 'One tunnel left.'

Marcus could tell from her tone that Maxine had had enough of the Cleave Camp tunnels.

Once more they walked the passageway. If anything, this one was heading slightly up hill.

They'd gone some distance when Maxine stumbled and nearly fell. 'What on earth's that?'

Marcus shone the torch at her feet. 'Well, well. It's a heavy-duty rope.' He shone the torch ahead of them. 'Goes on for a long way.'

Making sure they kept away from the rope, they continued along the passage, climbing steadily all the while. They came to its end. Not much further on was a rusty spiral staircase. Maxine pointed her torch up it, but they could see the top was closed.

'I wonder if you can see that cover from anywhere in the Camp? Mind, I'm not going up it. That staircase doesn't look safe to me.'

Marcus agreed. 'It's had its day. OK then. We'll pace ourselves back to the generator room. That'll tell us roughly where to look.'

Slowly they paced back. They'd gone eighty yards when they reached the far end of the rope. Then another hundred yards to the three-way junction where they'd started.

From there it was easy to find their way back past the generator room and up to the surface: these passages were part of the Camp, there were lights on the walls.

By the time they were back at the security hut it was well after nine. Maxine looked worn out and Marcus not much better. But it couldn't all end like this.

'Please don't say anything to anyone,' she instructed. 'But what are you doing tomorrow evening?'

He smiled. 'I'm as free as usual. I haven't much of a social life.'

'I'd love to bounce ideas around on what we've seen. I'll need to check with my husband, but if he doesn't mind, can I take you for a meal somewhere? I reckon we've earned it.'

CHAPTER 34   Thursday Nov 18th

Next afternoon was the time Maxine had booked with Bill Oakshot to report back on her search of the wartime diaries.

Now, though, she had a few additional facts to tell him.

'I've read through every word of the war-years logbooks,' she began. 'Learned a huge amount about what they were doing here in those days. It turns out, this airfield was basically a training ground for anti-aircraft gunners. The most crucial work for the aircraft crews was towing huge drape-based images of enemy bombers well behind them, which the gunners had to try and hit.

'I'd say it was inevitable that, sooner or later, there'd be a case of death by "friendly fire". The miracle was that, on what was told in those diaries, it only happened once in all the years of war. That was in the summer of 1944. The extra tragedy, from our point of view, was that one of the people killed was an American airman. But he wasn't Joe Kennedy or Glenn Miller. He went by the name of Chuck Colson.'

Bill Oakshot took a second to absorb her findings. Then he gave a blink of surprise.

'Well done, Maxine, for finding that out. And in such a short time, too. Well. The best thing, I think, would be for you and me to have an extended, off-the-record briefing with our American chief coordinator. Tell her all that we know – the full story – and see if between the three of us we can put this nasty rumour to bed.'

Maxine let him bask in the glow of a problem solved for a

moment. Then she voiced the "but".

'That'd be fine, Bill, if it was only a terrible accident. But suppose the whole thing was much, much worse.'

'How d'you mean?'

'Well, the coordinator might ask, was it just a coincidence that the only plane shot down here, in the entire war, had an American pilot? Was it possible that, in the extremes of war, he had antagonised the men in the base so much that someone decided to take a shot at him? Maybe they didn't intend to kill him, just to teach him a lesson, give him a huge fright? But whatever the intention, it all went horribly wrong.'

One of Bill's strengths, thought Maxine, was that he was not beset by the usual stubborn male pride. He would readily revise a view once it was shown to be problematic. As happened now.

'Hm. Perhaps the story you've told me so far doesn't end the rumour as neatly as I'd hoped. Tell me, was there any doubt expressed in the diaries about the nature of the accident?'

'None at all, Bill. It was a night-time flight, alternating bright moonlight and dark cloud. I gather that always makes for a difficult target practice. A report by the chief artillery officer was produced, but it found nothing untoward. This was 1944, they'd had several years to iron out their procedures and reduce the risks. And the trainees on this occasion were advanced gunners, not raw recruits.'

Bill looked relieved. 'So we've an answer to America's fears? It was a pure accident. No-one to blame. Just one of the hardships of war?'

'That's what I was thinking, Bill. Till last night. Then I found out something else.'

Bill could see this was getting more complicated. But he remembered his new resolution: Maxine needed support and empathy. 'Please, have some coffee before you start. Sounds like this might take some time.'

Maxine noted his concern. She had a drink then took a deep breath.

'There was much discussion, early in the diaries, about the best length of rope between the towing aircraft and the target. But gradually they agreed: this should be about two hundred and fifty feet.'

Bill nodded, though he had no idea where she was going.

'Well, you know I mentioned the other day, there was a need to explore the tunnels under the base, see what else was hidden down there.'

'Yes.'

'I went down yesterday evening. After I'd finished work, with one of the security guards.'

Bill almost exploded at this admission but managed to contain himself. Maxine, he recalled, was a capable, independent-minded woman. In any case, she was here now, hadn't been injured at all. 'Go on.'

'Well, we explored several tunnels. The one that's relevant to this conversation came last. This seemed to lead under the airfield itself. But the crucial thing was what we found lying inside it.'

This was turning from an account into an enigma. 'Which was . . .?'

'A strong, well-used rope, almost exactly two hundred and fifty feet long.'

Bill frowned. It wasn't the answer he'd been expecting. 'Am I missing something here? Why is that significant?'

Maxine paused before she answered. 'Well. Suppose someone on the airfield had fallen out with Chuck Colson. Wanted him dead. The most certain way to do that, I'd say, would be to shorten the tow rope between plane and target, so the two flew much closer – far too close – together.'

There was another pause. Cogs were clicking as Bill started to tune in. 'Ah. You mean, swap the standard tow rope kept in the cockpit for one, say, just half as long. Making Colson far more likely to be killed. And once the plane was hit, it would explode. Down into the sea. With nothing at all left to examine. Least of all any reduction in the length of tow rope.'

There was silence as the sequence was examined.

'A surplus, 250-foot tow rope is hard to get rid of, you see, Bill. It's a massive weight. Far too big to leave in a rubbish bin.'

'Not easy to burn, either.'

'Too big to be smuggled past the guards on security.'

'But if you'd previously found a really old tunnel with out-door access . . . you'd just need to prise the cover open and hide the original tow rope down there. Hope it'd never be found. As it wasn't, for nearly eighty years. Gosh.' Bill seemed staggered.

'Let's have some more coffee,' he said. 'This is a two-mug problem.'

Bill ordered more coffee and mused silently until it had been delivered.

'So it seems possible, at least, that Chuck Colson wasn't just killed, he was deliberately murdered. By someone working here on the airfield. That's awful. I don't suppose there's any chance of finding out who?'

Maxine was ahead of him. She grimaced. 'Someone in their mid-twenties, say, in 1944 would have been born around 1920. They'd probably have died years ago. Or else they'd now be a much-feted centurion and way beyond reproach. And we've no witnesses either.'

Silence.

Then, 'Your husband's a policeman, isn't he?'

'He's an Inspector in Bude. Fairly senior.'

'Don't the police tackle cold cases, these days?'

Maxine shook her head. 'This case isn't just cold, Bill, it's arctic. For a start, it happened on a military establishment. My husband has no jurisdiction here. And even if you could pull some strings and get him in, and he managed to take fingerprints off the rope - which must be highly doubtful after eighty years – how would you match them to the villain? No-one has records from that far back.'

There was a long, thoughtful silence as coffees were consumed.

'I can only see one chance of taking this any further,' said Maxine. 'And it's pretty remote,' she added.

Bill looked at her. She'd already stretched his credulity beyond its usual boundary. 'Whatever's that?'

'It might just be possible to get some hint on the motive. Whatever had Chuck done that was so offensive? If it was that bad, it might not have been that much of a secret. Either on the base itself, or in the local community.

'If we had some idea what it was, we'd have something we could share with the American coordinator. Balance the rumour books in some way. We both know that we can never re-write the past. But it sometimes helps if we can explain it.'

CHAPTER 35

Peter Travers had raised no complaint when his wife had suggested she might be out for the second evening in a row. 'You've had a lot less meals out than I have, darling. My work takes me out often enough. I'll be glad of the chance to read Rosanna more stories.'

He hadn't even quibbled when he heard that she was planning to eat out with a bearded security man, 'to say thank you for him going with me last night.'

'My only piece of advice, my love, is "Don't talk shop". The poor bloke can't possibly be as interested in Cleave Camp as you are.'

It turned out that Marcus had taken a holiday flat, out of season, in Stratton. Maxine was able to go home at her usual time and spend time with Rosanna, give the little one her tea. Once Peter came home, she changed into a dark green winter dress, before going out to meet him in the Kings Arms, one of the Stratton locals.

Marcus was already present and had found them a quiet table in a secluded alcove. The place wasn't that crowded anyway.

'If I'm allowed to say so, that dress really suits you,' he observed.

Maxine laughed. 'Better than my business suit, anyway. Thank you for joining me. This meal's on me, by the way. Appreciation for your support yesterday evening.'

'It was good to do something different,' he replied.

'Come on, your social life can't be that bleak.'

'It's totally empty. But I don't suppose I'll be here for long. I mean, I've only got a short-term contract with the Camp.'

'But you've a long-term employer in London?'

'Oh, yes.'

'Been with them long?'

'Several years, actually.'

'What were you doing before that?'

Marcus hesitated. 'I'm afraid that's rather a long story.'

Maxine didn't mind. 'We've got the evening ahead of us. We can review lessons from last night later on.' Then it occurred to her he might be covering up something shameful, like a spell in prison. 'But if it's some secret you'd rather not share, Marcus, I don't want to pry.'

There was a pause while Marcus decided what to do. He hadn't talked to anyone about his former life for ages. But Maxine was a friendly soul, he felt safe and comfortable in her company.

'A long while ago I was married. To a wonderful woman. She was gorgeous and caring. Also very bright. She'd done maths at Cambridge.'

Maxine laughed. 'That doesn't prove anything, Marcus. I did maths at Cambridge, and a PhD, and look at me now – helping to manage a remote security camp.' Then a thought came to her. 'What was her name? I might have known her once, a long time ago.'

'George . . . George Goode. That was her maiden name. Once we were married, she became George Gilbert.'

The name came completely out of the blue. It was a heart-stopping moment. Maxine hadn't been around when George had lost her husband, had never met him, but she had heard the dismal tale from George when they had reconnected. How ought she to respond?

Suddenly, Maxine remembered she was talking to someone known at the Camp as Marcus Tredwell. She blinked; he must have changed his name as well. This was indeed turning into a long and tangled tale. It would be better not to say too much until she knew more.

'There was someone of that name,' she responded. 'But it was a long time ago. We lost touch after university.' Best not to reveal that they had rediscovered one another more recently. 'Anyway, what happened to you two?'

'We were very happy. George was a hard-working consultant; I was successful in business. That was until the plane crash.'

Maxine recalled talking earlier today about a deadly plane crash. Two men shot down by fellow soldiers. But this one couldn't have been fatal: Marcus was here, still talking.

'Go on. Please.'

Her companion swallowed hard. 'I was on a business trip. Then my plane crashed, on the edge of Iran. I was thrown out, badly burned, lots of bones broken, the sole survivor. And worst of all, I'd lost my memory.'

'You poor man. But surely someone knew who you were?'

He gave a sad smile. 'My misfortune was, they thought they did. I was found beside a phone. That belonged to the man I'd been sitting next to: Marcus Tredwell. Trouble was, he was in the British security services: and was badly wanted by Iran. As a result, I was interrogated for month after month. In the end, after they'd found I could tell them nothing, I was swapped with an Iranian terrorist who'd been caught by the British. That was how I got back to the UK. And how I came to have my current lowly job in the security services.'

The waitress had been hovering close to reception but seen they were in deep conversation. Now she saw her chance and approached them, holding a pair of menus. Both chose grilled steak and chips with the usual trimmings, also a bottle of Merlot. Maxine planned to drink just a single glass. If it wasn't all finished, Marcus could walk home afterwards with anything left in the bottle.

'So you're not really Marcus Tredwell at all? Have you recovered your memory, then? Who on earth are you?'

The man smiled. 'I was born Mark Gilbert. But I only got my memory back eighteen months ago. Through a doctor that I used to know, who helped me.'

'Right.' Maxine frowned. This tale wasn't as tidy as she would have liked. 'So . . . why haven't you got back with George?'

This time it was his turn to sigh. 'It's been over ten years since the plane crash. It was what I hoped for, once I could recall my old life and all its joys. The trouble is, George has found someone else. I saw her walking down the road with him, hand in hand.

'Then the penny dropped. Ten years is a long time for both of us. She's not the same woman. Maybe she's forgotten me altogether. She thinks I'm dead, even attended my funeral. And if she's got herself a new life, is it really fair for me to burst back in and muck it up? So, in the end I decided I had to stick with security. Which is why I've kept the beard. It'll probably be best for now if you keep calling me Marcus. It's a pure fluke, but very fortunate, that both names happen to be almost the same.'

At that moment their meals arrived, both piping hot on heated iron platters. Marcus seized the bottle of Merlot and poured them each a generous glassful. Then they settled to eat.

Maxine was quite glad of the conversational pause. This wasn't so much a long story as a multi-episode epic. It didn't sound as though it was quite over. But she would need to reflect carefully before taking any action. As far as she knew, George hadn't got anyone else in her life at this moment. But she was an independent woman. It would be best for her to check.

Once their main meals had been consumed and desserts ordered, Maxine decided it was time to review last night's findings.

'So, Marcus, what are your first reflections from what we saw last night?'

There was a short pause. 'I'd say it looked like the legacy from some long-ago smuggling gang. Those tunnels were very old, but they were definitely man-made, not just the result of some ancient river overflow.'

'What makes you so certain?'

'It was that opening in the cliff. Completely unexpected. But you'd only need that if you were hauling things up from the beach. And the only reason why you might do that, I'd say, would be if you were a smuggler, with items to stash away.'

'Right. And what d'you think was being smuggled?'

'Those kegs. Containing either wine or some sort of alcoholic spirit.'

'Would it still be drinkable?'

'It might be. I've read that high-quality, well-corked spirit, kept in a dry, cool location, will last a long time – perhaps even a century. So the answer to that will depend on how long the stuff's been there.'

Another pause, then Maxine spoke. 'The most puzzling thing to me was why there was so much stored below ground – the kegs and the wine – when there's no trace left of the manor above it. That doesn't quite hang together.'

Marcus responded. 'Are you sure? It suggests to me that whoever was living in the manor didn't leave in a leisurely manner, they left in a tearing hurry. No time to take anything with them. I mean, those kegs might be valuable. They're medium sized, each one probably holds fifty litres. I looked it up when I got home. Top-quality spirit costs £50 a bottle at today's prices. Which makes each keg worth several thousand pounds. But they wouldn't be easy to move. Not in a hurry, anyway.'

These comments reinforced Maxine's ideas. 'Maybe, if it was smugglers living here, they were betrayed. Had to flee from the coastguards and the Revenue. But those authorities didn't know about anything below the surface. Maybe the entrance from inside the manor was well hidden? So once the smugglers had left, the Revenue simply flattened the manor itself, but left alone everything stored below.'

There was a short intermission as the waitress brought their desserts: gooseberry crumble and cream for Marcus, fruit salad for Maxine. Two coffees were also ordered. 'I won't bring these straight away. You can take them into the snug if you like.'

'This is a cosy establishment,' said Maxine, as the waitress walked away. 'I'll certainly bring my husband here when our little one's a bit older.'

Marcus smiled. 'How old is she at the moment?'

'Rosanna? She's just over a year. Did you have any children with George?' Maxine asked the question without thought, not even thinking how hard it might be for Marcus to answer. But he responded readily enough.

'We had just the one daughter, Polly. Who has long grown up. As far as I know she's now living in New Zealand. Which means . . . I may never see her again.'

Maxine daren't look him in the face. His voice had turned into a sob and there were tears in his eyes. Tragic. She'd start crying too if she wasn't careful. It would be best to keep away from family chatter and to stick to last night's finds.

'I can make some sense of that long rope we found in the third tunnel,' she said, between spoonfuls of the fruit salad.

Marcus seemed relieved to move away from family matters. 'Go on, Maxine. I don't have a clue.'

So, gradually, Maxine told him edited highlights of her search for victims of the target practice which had taken place during wartime. She didn't mention the reason why she'd started looking: Marcus didn't need to know that. But she did tell him about the one fatal flight that she'd discovered, with its American pilot. And how their rope discovery last night – whose length matched the standard tow rope - made it likely that this was no accident but murder.

'So now,' she concluded, 'I've been tasked with trying to find a motive.'

Marcus ate more of his crumble, cogitating, before he replied.

'I presume that planes at Cleave always flew with a two-man crew?'

'That's true. Hey, Marcus, how did you know that?'

'In those days they hadn't invented the autopilot. So the pilot wouldn't be able to throw a target out from the cockpit on his own, he'd be too busy flying. He'd need someone else with him to do that.'

'Right, you're very wise. So where's this heading?'

'Well. You said the pilot was an American. But what about his companion?'

Maxine struggled to remember. Shamefully, she'd not given him any consideration at all. 'I'm pretty sure he was local.'

Marcus's eyes gleamed. 'And if he was, there's a good chance that his family still live around here. If there was any hint of evil motive behind the crash, beyond a tragic accident, surely they'd have picked it up. It would be worth trying to track them down, wouldn't it?'

PART FIVE

GEORGE CALLS FOR HELP

NOVEMBER 19th

St Bridget's Church, Bridgerule

218

CHAPTER 36   Friday Nov 19th

George Gilbert had not heard a squeak from Edward Gabriel since he'd walked out of their Sunday lunch at the Bridge Inn. And she didn't feel inclined to ring him. Given his conduct, it was surely his place to ring her.

In some ways it had been easier to conduct enquiries on her own. She could be objective, both on where she'd headed and what she'd found. But then, it wasn't her mother that had disappeared.

On the other hand, it was hard work and stressful, carrying out an investigation in isolation. She had done such projects before, but it had always worked best in partnership. If she couldn't work with Edward any more, then who else might she continue with?

She had hoped that her studious, historical friend Emma would join her, if she'd been able to come over, to throw fresh light on manor houses. But Emma had told her that, though she would give the problem some attention, her two best sources were the Cornwall Records Office and the Royal Cornwall Museum. Both were based in her home town of Truro; hence she preferred to remain there for the time being.

Which left her old friend Maxine Travers. The two had been good friends for many years, indeed George had been chief bridesmaid at her wedding to Peter Travers on Land's End a few years ago. But Maxine now had a baby of her own and George wasn't inclined to overburden her. She was busy, working at Cleave Camp four days a week while managing her daughter on her days off.

In addition, Maxine's husband Peter had headed up the original inquiry on Daphne's disappearance. He might be extremely cross if he found that George was doing her best, on her own, to take that inquiry any further. It was hardly a vote of confidence in his own force, or in his judgement.

Perhaps she could contact Maxine over the coming weekend? At least her husband might be off shift then, could take his share of the parental burden.

In the meantime George thought back over the last week and made a list of possible contacts who might help in the search for Daphne – people whom she had not yet visited or needed to visit again. Which ones were the most urgent? And which were the least dangerous?

The most harmless person was probably the canal expert whose name she had been given by postmaster Mike Smith: James Gibbon. There was obviously something unusual about the layout of the canal around Merrifield. She needed to know what it was. After all, that was more or less where Daphne Gabriel had last been seen. Some sort of "incline", the long-life vicar of Bridgerule had reported: described in his diary, on his first visit to Merrifield railway station, in 1891.

If she'd felt welcome at Merrifield Manor, George would have gone to examine any remains of the canal there for herself. But until she heard from Edward a visit seemed out of the question.

James Gibbon was meant to be the chief authority on the Bude Canal. If anyone could help her it would be him.

She glanced at her kitchen clock. Half past eight. It wasn't too late to phone him, try to arrange a meeting. Ten minutes later she sat back satisfied. James had sounded only too pleased to meet anyone who wanted to learn about the Canal: it was his passion. A meeting had been arranged for the following morning: eleven o'clock at the Olive Tree. They could sit looking out across the lowest reach.

She smiled. The infrastructure experts of Bude, whether for rail or canal, seemed to agree on the best place to share their wisdom. She could only hope that James' knowledge would match his passion.

Next morning George set off in good time for her meeting. Traffic on the A39 was light and there were no holdups. These days she noticed the signposts off to the villages she'd been exploring: Bridgerule and then Marhamchurch. Once in Bude, she parked in the car park beside the Canal and ambled along towards the Olive Tree café.

It was a fine day and there were plenty of tables outside: it was a wide towpath. She grabbed an empty table and sat to await her expert.

A group of lifeguards, their jobs blazoned on their red tee shirts, were sitting at a nearby table. They wouldn't be on beach duty at this time of year, it was the off season for conventional tourists. They were off duty, obviously just relaxing.

George remembered Martha mentioning: Daphne had consulted one of them about the beaches north of Sandy Mouth. If they were still around when her consultation with James was over, it would be worth talking to them herself. There was just a chance they might remember something.

Then James appeared. George hadn't arranged any special signal but there were plenty of clues to identify him. He was older than she'd expected, obviously retired, dressed for an outdoor meeting in late autumn – less "smart" and more "casual".

And on his own. But clearly a man in search of coffee.

Or, in fact, hot chocolate, she found, once the two had made contact, introduced themselves and sat amicably facing one another on an Olive Tree picnic bench. Soon hot drinks had been ordered and brought out.

There was no problem getting James to talk. If anything, the challenge was to persuade him to pause long enough to take note of her specific questions. She guessed, though, that much of his general background on the Canal would be useful, if she ever resumed her quest for data to help Edward develop Merrifield.

'The Canal was the vision of Cornishman John Edyvean in 1784.' James, himself a Bude local, was keen to underline its Cornish provenance. 'John saw a need to link the village of Bude, as it then was, to the major city of the south, Plymouth, by what was then the only means of long-distance transport: travel by water.'

'Of course, this was years before the railways,' interleaved George.

'There were several false starts,' James continued, ignoring her comment. 'These were turbulent times. The Napoleonic Wars, after the French Revolution of 1789, hadn't helped. Finally, the Bude Canal Company was launched in 1819. An enabling Act of Parliament was passed. Then the Canal was dug, over the next four years, mostly along the upper Tamar Valley. In the end it reached almost as far as Launceston.'

James drew breath. 'A special feature of this Canal was the way it handled variations in height, arising from the rolling hillsides of North Cornwall.'

'Locks?' asked George, seeing a chance to squeeze a word in edgeways.

'Oh, no. This Canal couldn't use the traditional system of

locks: those required far too much water. Think how much you'd waste, every time the gates opened and a boat went up or down. And despite it being Cornwall, where rain was aplenty, water for the Canal was in short supply.'

'So where did it come from?' asked George, desperate to turn his impassioned monologue into a two-way discussion.

'Ah. The water came from a header pool, the Lower Tamar Lake. That was specially constructed – manually dug out – near Kilkhampton. Of course, that had to be linked to the Canal itself. Meant there was a canal junction, close to the road to Holsworthy.'

It was important to keep her expert on track. 'Anyway, how were the height adjustments achieved?'

'It was a unique system of what they called "inclines". Almost the only ones in Britain.'

At last, thought George, he'd reached a topic she cared about.

'Please, go on,' she urged.

'The key thing you need to know, George, to make sense of this, is that the boats specially built for the Canal – tubs, they were called – each had small wheels fitted underneath. They were amphibious. Which meant the inclines could help the tubs to be pulled up from one canal height to another.'

'Wow. How many inclines were there?'

'In the end there were six. Spread along the Tamar Valley. One's at Merrifield, that's where the Canal would one day meet the railway.'

George was thinking hard about this now. 'But these tubs weren't motorised. They didn't have internal combustion engines in 1820. So how were they pulled up the inclines?'

'Ah. They 'ad massive chains, made of cast iron, that ran round huge horizontal wheels, set at the top and bottom of each incline. Half a dozen tubs would come along the canal hitched together, pulled by a dray horse or two. Then they'd be separated. Each tub in turn would be attached to the chain and pulled up the incline until it reached the top. Then it'd be detached, left waiting for the rest beside the next canal reach. It wasn't the fastest means of travel.'

The expert was speaking more slowly now. He was being asked a level of detail beyond what was normally expected, was having to work out some of it as he went along.

But George was persistent. 'OK. I'm with you so far. But what power drove the chain wheels?'

James sipped his hot chocolate before he answered. 'That varied. In one case, at Hobbacott Down, it was steam-power. Don't be surprised. Steam was harnessed in mines and factories for decades before it pulled trains on railways.'

Dialogue at last, thought George. 'How high were these inclines?'

'Well. The biggest one, at Hobbacott, gained a height of 230 feet over a length of 1000 feet. That's a slope of one in four. The steam engine there had some work to do.'

'How heavy were the tubs? Or perhaps I should say, what kind of loads were they carrying?'

James blinked. 'Each of 'em carried four or five tons. Five feet wide and twenty feet long. Couldn't be wider or they wouldn't fit the canal, see. They mostly carried lime-absorbed sand, up from the beach to farmers inland. That was very important to agriculture in its day.'

'So what drove the other inclines, if it wasn't steam?'

'Water power, you could say. Each of 'em had deep wells, located at the top. Huge buckets of water would be lowered down with a rope attached. That was used to make the chain wheel turn.'

George wasn't completely convinced. That would mean a mega-bucket of water lost for each tub pulled up. But she wouldn't push that for now. There was plenty to think about later.

'So was this system reliable?'

James gave a hollow laugh. 'Well, it didn't do too well in a drought or a frost – or even a flood. The cast iron chains weren't that strong. They were pulling a huge load. If one of the links broke, the chain would sheer and whip back at huge speed. If it caught you, you were a goner. It could split a man clean in two, they said.' James shook his head. 'Dangerous times, they were. No health and safety in those days.'

George wanted to show some empathy. 'I guess what finally finished the Canal was the coming of the railway?'

James nodded, looking disconsolate. 'Trains did for the Canal alright. The two hardly even overlapped. But in truth, the Canal was never a great financial success. And these days you can't see much of it at all.'

'Apart from what's in front of us,' said George, nodding at the reach ten feet in front of them. 'That goes as far as Marhamchurch, doesn't it?'

James looked a bit brighter. 'That's true. And that's where you can see the first of the inclines. That's well worth a trip, I'd say.'

George could see that James had finished his introductory talk. He was starting to look weary as they swapped business cards. She thanked him and he wandered on his way.

As she gathered her notebook and stood up to head back to her car, one of the lifeguards drinking coffee on the next table called over.

'You had an interesting chat there, miss. All the ins and outs of this canal.'

George was happy to keep talking. 'Yes. James is the Bude expert. He knows a lot, doesn't he? My name's George, by the way.'

A second lifeguard joined in. 'We couldn't help listening, George. James was talking about inclines, but we couldn't quite understand. What were they supposed to do?'

George was happy enough to pass on what she'd learned. 'They were long ramps. Used to pull the boats up or down as the canal elevation varied. It had to go up and down quite a lot because of all the surrounding hills.'

'Amazing,' said one of the others. 'And all this was done in the nineteenth century.'

His friend shrugged. 'And now the whole lot's sunk without trace.'

'Sounds a bit like that woman from Bridgerule.'

George pricked up her ears. Clearly the sad tale of Daphne had reached as far as Bude. Perhaps this was her opportunity?

'D'you mean Daphne Gabriel?' she asked. 'I've been looking into her disappearance. Did any of you ever meet her?'

The group looked around, one of them answered.

'Just once, George. She was having coffee here with a friend. She wanted to know about the beaches further up the coast. All the ones past Sandy Mouth.'

George nodded. 'So what did you tell her?'

'I'm afraid we couldn't really help her. As I told her, the trouble is, there are too many rocks. You can't swim safely at many of 'em.'

'Except possibly at low tide,' added his neighbour.

'So, in fact, we couldn't really help her at all.'

That seemed to be that. It hadn't been a significant meeting after all. But she might as well learn what she could about the group.

'Are you all from round here, then?'

'Mostly.'

'I'm not,' said the one who'd started the exchange. 'I've come halfway round the world to be here. I admit, Cornish scenery is great. Just such a pity about the weather.'

The oldest lifeguard, who looked to be the leader, decided to take a wider responsibility.

'George, we're about to order lunch from the Olive Tree. Would you like to join us?'

'That's very kind of you. I'd love to,' George replied.

Then she glanced at her watch. 'Trouble is, my parking's about to run out. I'd love to chat some more. Perhaps I can join you another time?'

CHAPTER 37

George was almost tempted to buy a new parking ticket and re-join the lifeguards for lunch, but she doubted she'd learn much more – about Daphne, anyway. She'd had a summary of their chat which sounded convincing. And she didn't want to cramp the lifeguards' style. Nor to talk about swimming: she was done with that for the winter.

She wasn't far from Bridgerule, though. Maybe today was her chance to re-examine the St Bridget's bell tower? It would be good to do something more energetic than sitting on a canal bench. After that she could go back home and try to make more sense of inclines.

While she was in Bridgerule, George decided that she might as well have lunch at the Bridge Inn. She had a moment of panic as she got to the door: would Edward be inside? She didn't want a confrontation. But once through the door she saw that he wasn't present. In fact, there was no-one she recognised at all.

Apart from the landlord of course, he knew who she was. And was still empathetic. She ordered minestrone soup and a roll and resolved to eat this on a high stool at the bar; there was just a chance she'd learn something new.

The saloon was fairly empty, the landlord wasn't too busy with other customers.

'Have you seen Edward since Sunday?' asked George, when he was next free to chat.

'He's not been here,' the landlord replied. 'So you haven't seen him either?'

George shook her head. 'I've heard nothing about Daphne either. I assume that's the same for you?'

More agreement. In this case, though, no news was bad news. George decided the fraternising was a waste of her time. She'd just enjoy her lunch, then move on to the church tower.

But she needed Sheila's address if she was to borrow the church key. Once again the knowledgeable landlord obliged.

George had warned Sheila yesterday that she might need to borrow the key, so she wasn't embarrassed, a few minutes later, when she visited Daphne's friend for that purpose.

'There was something I saw in the tower that I'd like to go back and check,' she explained. 'I'll bring it back later.'

'That's alright, my love,' said the woman. 'Daphne borrowed it more than once herself over the last few months.'

Another insight into the woman's behaviour. How badly she needed a foil, to help her sift what she now knew. She hoped Maxine might have time for her over the weekend.

A few minutes later George had driven to St Bridget's and parked on the road nearby. This time she didn't leave her emergency torch in her glove box but put it in her backpack. Plus her all-purpose screwdriver. She didn't know why she might need it, but it was as well to be prepared.

It was as she walked up the church path that the reality hit: there were two distinct benefits from a working partner. One was to have someone to bounce ideas off and to focus her thinking. The other was a physical companion in case of danger.

Right now the second of these seemed the more urgent.

But she had the church key. No-one else should be in there before her; and no-one could get in without it. In any case, she wasn't expecting to be up the tower for long.

But she found the key awkward to turn, probably because

she hadn't acquired the knack. The door did open eventually. But it put George off locking herself in. Unlocking it again might be even harder from the inside.

Once inside, George made sure the door was closed before heading for the base of the tower. The building seemed even colder than yesterday. No doubt that was the result of being alone. Mind, it was quiet enough, she couldn't even hear the birds singing outside.

The first step was to loosen the ladder to the mid-floor room. She wasn't as tall as Henry: did that make it more difficult? It did, but the problem was surmountable. There were a host of hassocks – prayer cushions – at the back of the church nave. She went back and found one, a foot wide and six inches deep; returned and set it on the pew below the catch.

Problem solved. She could just reach the catch on the ceiling above. It opened and a doorway folded down.

Now all she needed to do was to reach the access ladder above. But this, too, was just out of reach: she would need a second hassock.

And once she'd got that, to balance one on top of the other.

George stared at it, hoped she wouldn't need a third. Even this arrangement looked wobbly. Slowly, she clambered up and reached over her head. It was just enough. She reached the ladder and started to ease it down. A moment later she had access to the floor above.

Now she climbed carefully. Her torch made the top few steps less frightening than her last visit. A moment later she had stepped out onto the mysterious, misshapen middle floor.

Why wasn't it square, like the floors below and above?

Was there a light? She shone her torch over the ceiling. There was certainly a socket, but no bulb. Was that deliberate or simply an accident? Carefully she paced the room in both directions: which two walls were the closest? After that she used her torch to see what was peculiar about them.

A moment later she knew which wall was different. They all looked the same, had been painted in the same shade of dingy cream. The odd wall, though, was made of wood, whereas the other three were plastered stone. The same paint led to different textures on the two surfaces.

It was a false wall. What was behind it?

George was excited. She'd found something tangible. How could she see whatever was behind it? Think, woman, think.

There must be some sort of catch. You wouldn't want it to swing open by accident.

It was probably near the ceiling. Once again George found her height limiting.

There was one ready solution. A moment later she'd climbed back down the ladder, grabbed the two prayer cushions and brought them up with her. But she still had no idea where the catch was located.

She had to balance the cushions, climb up, then peer at the join of wall and ceiling by tochlight. Nothing. She moved along, tried again. Still nothing. She had traversed almost the whole wall before she found the secret catch. A coat-hanger thickness of wire, next to the ceiling, painted white so it wasn't obvious to anyone standing below. Especially if they had no torch.

George gulped. This was the moment of truth. Then she had a horrible thought: might the wire give her a shock? Surely, she told herself, no-one would be that malicious. But she was a cautious woman and slipped on her gloves. Then mounted the hassocks one more time, reached up and pushed it sideways.

At which point one end of the false wall started to move.

CHAPTER 38

George was desperate to see what was behind the wall. But before she could do so something else caught her attention. It was the noise of the main church door, on the ground floor, being eased slowly open.

She had no idea who it might be. Was it the ladies charged with arranging the flower displays at the front, making the place welcoming ready for Sunday morning?

Or was it someone more sinister?

Whoever it was, she didn't want to be found up here. Certainly not with the false wall open.

When she'd come in at half past two, she hadn't needed a light; and she was still wearing her scarf and cagoule. And, mercifully, she had brought up the prayer cushions. The only evidence left down below was the access ladder that she had let down from the middle floor.

Quickly, quietly, she crossed back to the hanging doorway and pulled on the ladder. It was well-designed: light, balanced and well-oiled. A few seconds later she had managed to pull it up, seize it and restore it to a horizontal position on the floor beside her.

Now George listened hard. Which way were the newcomers moving? She frowned: it didn't sound like they were moving at all.

Then she realised that there was something else that would give her away: the folding door itself. She eased herself onto her stomach and put her head through the hatch. In the gloom she could just see a handle. She reached down and grabbed it, pulled as hard as she could. The folding door came up and then there was a click. The door had fastened itself shut. Phew. For the time being she was safe.

Suddenly George realised, she wasn't safe at all. For although she'd closed the door, there were still six small holes in the floor of the room, where the ropes for ringing passed down from the bells above to the ringing chamber below. Anyone standing below and looking up might see her moving.

And they would certainly see her torch.

Quickly, she turned it off and perched herself with her back to a wall, in silence, waiting until the coast was clear. This was a lot more frightening than she had anticipated.

There was someone in the chamber down below. But George was not completely cut off. She might be able to see something down one of the rope holes.

She crawled forward to the nearest one. It turned out she could see something, but not much. For the bell rope itself was still hanging in the hole and took up most of the space. She had a very limited view indeed. It wasn't possible to make out who it was.

Then the intruder went out of view altogether. But they were still down there. George listened hard. Then, to her horror, it sounded like the person was reaching for the catch that closed the ceiling doorway.

A moment of panic seized her. They were coming up. She was going to be caught! For there was no escape from the tower, except through the room below.

But, to her relief, the doorway didn't open. Maybe the person below was small like her, couldn't quite reach the catch? Would they think of bringing in prayer cushions to help them? Or would they just give up and go away? She held her breath, listened hard in the total silence.

A few minutes later George heard the main church door being opened and then banged shut. For the time being she was safe.

George was silent for ten minutes. There might have been more than one church visitor; there could easily be someone else still down there.

But she could hear nothing at all. She must be alone.

Now, at last, she could take a quick look: what was behind the false wall? She turned her torch towards it.

It was obviously some sort of storage cupboard. For she could see three wooden shelves, running behind the partly open wall.

On the bottom shelf were a few kegs. She did a quick calculation. If each was two foot wide and the shelf was full, there'd be eight kegs in all. Only one end of the wall had opened so she couldn't see; there might be fewer.

On the second shelf were many dark wine or spirit bottles, mostly empty. On the top shelf were various bits of equipment, including a length of rope, some plastic tubing and some corks. Presumably the rest of the wall could be opened, but she couldn't see how – without spending more time searching.

It wasn't certain what each keg contained but she assumed it would be some sort of wine – or perhaps spirit?

Whatever it was, it would be expensive stuff. These kegs could be worth a lot of money.

What an odd item to be found inside a vibrant church. Was this what Daphne had also found?

For now, there was nothing else George could do. The kegs were unlabelled. There was no way to get at the contents for a sip, she was no spirit expert, anyway. It would be best to close the false wall and get out as quickly as she could. Reflect once she was home.

She gave the false wall a shove and it swung gently shut. It was a well-oiled mechanism, like the ladder. It all suggested this was some sort of ongoing activity.

George turned back to the folding door down to the ground floor below. And suddenly realised that she had an even bigger problem.

For the catch to open this doorway was fastened on the ceiling below. There was no access to it from the floor she was now on.

For a moment, George assumed that there must be a way out. But she gritted her teeth and forced herself to think hard. In normal times, there'd be no good reason for someone inside the tower to close off their own way out.

In her earlier panic, pulling shut the doorway, she must have locked herself in.

Take it easy, she told herself. No-one else knows what you found behind that wall, or even that you found it. All you need to do is to call someone, ask them to come to the church and let you out.

George reached in her cagoule pocket for her phone. There was a moment of relief, at least she'd brought it with her. Thankfully, she was in the habit of keeping it well-charged.

But who should she ring? It was only four in the afternoon, hardly the middle of the night.

But who did she know well enough to ask for help?

She ran through the people that she'd met in Bridgerule. Although they were all good people, she didn't really know any of them well enough to ask for help. It was a big ask: it would soon be dark. They'd have to find their way into a darkened church, then open the critical hatch catch from below. This was really the task for a close friend.

Which brought her to Maxine. George couldn't remember which day her friend had off. But even if she was at work, it was almost time to come home. Maxine was her number one choice, anyway.

George seized her phone, called Maxine's number and waited. Nothing happened. The network struggled in this part of the world. Then she remembered: she was inside the tower, surrounded by thick, stone walls. No wonder her phone wasn't working.

For a second George came close to despair. Would she have to spend forty-eight hours alone in the tower, before the bell-ringers arrived on Sunday morning? She'd brought nothing to eat or drink; there wasn't even a toilet.

Then she gave herself a shake. The phone might still work from the roof of the tower. She just had to find her way up there.

No need to panic, she told herself. You've seen this done before. Just take it steady. At least, this time, you've got your torch to hand.

Carefully, she stacked her two cushions below the belfry catch. She could just reach it and it opened easily. The end of the access ladder was visible in the opening. Tantalisingly, it was just out of reach.

George was desperate now. Once more she stood on the cushions; this time she jumped up and, with the extra height, managed to grab the rung on display. Her weight was enough to start it moving. But soon it was moving too fast. It continued faster and faster. She let go, landed in a heap on the floor and twisted sideways to keep out of its way.

The ladder swung down just beside her. It was a mercy that she wasn't hit very hard on the head.

Five minutes later she was into the belfry itself. Be careful here, she intoned to herself, it's only a narrow ledge. Whatever happens, don't fall into the bells.

But the roof was now within reach. Once more she completed her manoeuvres with the cushions. Opening the doorway was easy, but once again she had to jump for the final ladder. Taking extra care, this time, where she fell.

At last, she had access to the roof of the tower. She gave an exclamation of joy.

There was only one question left bothering her: was there a signal? Would her phone work, once she was in the open air?

The tangled arrangement of a church belfry

237

PART SIX

COLLABORATION

MERRIFIELD AND STRATTON
NOVEMBER 19th – 22nd

St Andrew's Church, Stratton

CHAPTER 39   Friday Nov 19ᵗʰ

Maxine Travers was surprised to receive the phone call. She'd just been thinking that she needed someone fresh to help her make sense of the Cleave Airfield mystery.

She wasn't at the Camp today, it was one of her days at home with Rosanna. The two of them had such fun together. The little girl was learning new things every day at her nursery and wanted to share them with her mummy. But now the toddler was worn out with individual attention and Maxine had just started to give her an early tea.

Her husband had indicated he might be home on time this evening. Perhaps they could treat themselves to a Morrison's Chinese banquet and catch up? He had tried not to sound demanding as he spoke the words, but he sensed there were more intriguing things going on in his wife's work-life than in his own. Though he'd just had a tough week at the station.

At first Maxine had been inclined to ignore the call. Whoever (except perhaps grandma) rings the mother of a toddler just after five? But Rosanna seemed happy enough, spooning most of her spaghetti over the table and occasionally taking a bite from the rest. Perhaps best to see who it was.

'George! Hi, it's nice to hear from you. Can I ring you back in a few minutes? You see, I'm rather busy . . .'

But this wasn't a casual call. Her friend cut in. 'Maxine, I need some help. As soon as possible. I'm stuck –'

At that very second, Peter Travers walked through the door. He took in the whole situation at a glance. 'I'll handle

Rosanna, darling. She likes tea with her daddy. You deal with the call.'

Maxine mouthed the word 'thanks' and headed for the lounge.

'Right. I can listen to you properly now. Peter's just come in and is supervising Rosanna's tea. Where are you, for a start?'

She listened. Blinked. Asked her friend to repeat. 'On the roof of a church tower? OK. And . . .'

Listened again. 'You can't get down. It's a high tower. Right.'

Pause. 'On your own?'

Pause. 'Locked from below? You do get into these scrapes, George.'

Pause. 'Of course I'll come. Peter can put Rosanna to bed . . .'

Pause. 'You say I'll need to bring someone taller than me to reach up for the catch? And a torch. Right . . .'

Pause. 'St Bridget's in Bridgerule. Don't worry, I'll find it, I do work for GCHQ. Right, George. See you in half an hour. You might not need to jump off the roof after all.'

Ten minutes later Maxine had given her husband a brief summary of the call and then rung Marcus. The security man had just got back home to Stratton, a place she would pass on the way to Bridgerule; and he assured her that once again he'd be happy to help.

Maxine shook her head as she headed for the car. George had always had a knack for surprises, of one sort or another. It wasn't the first time she'd helped her friend out of a jam.

When she called to pick him up, Marcus seemed surprisingly calm. "Adventure before routine security" seemed to be his slogan – or perhaps his motto?

'I presume we'll find out more, once we've let your friend out?' he asked. 'What's her name, by the way?'

'George.' She felt her passenger flinch, but the name wasn't that rare. George's surname – Gilbert – was unlikely to be mentioned. Of course, Marcus might recognise her; but there was no reason for George to recognise him. His beard was intimidating. 'We go back a long way,' she added. 'She's always been the one to take a few risks. It'll be interesting to hear how she managed to lock herself in, halfway up a church tower.'

Satnav soon found them Bridgerule and then St Bridget's: over the Tamar and up a gentle hill. The church was in darkness; its tower looked brooding. Maxine felt glad she had someone with her, it would have been a bit ominous on her own.

'Won't the place be locked?' asked Marcus.

'It shouldn't be. George had been lent a key, she told me, but she didn't relock the church door once she was inside. At the worst we can ask her to chuck hers down from the tower.'

But this extremity wasn't necessary. When the two walked up the church path they found the door unlocked.

'There'll be light switches in the church somewhere, goodness knows where. All we need tonight is the ground floor below the tower. That'll be this way.' Maxine shone her flashlight and they stepped into the ringing chamber. Even with her torch and a companion the semi-darkness was unnerving.

'George,' she shouted, 'Your rescue team has arrived.'

They heard a movement above them. Someone was standing up. Then a tiny voice called down.

'Maxine?'

'That's me. I've a friend with me from the camp. He's called Marcus. Where do we find the catch to let you out?'

'It's above the pew,' said the voice. 'At the far end, in the corner.'

Marcus saw at once what she meant. He clambered on to the pew and walked to the far end.

'I can see the catch alright, George. Trouble is, looks like it's jammed.'

'Well then, get a bloody hammer and unjam it. It opened easily enough when I got here.'

Maxine hadn't told him to, but Marcus had brought his own security kit with him. That included a small hammer.

A moment later he had jumped down, retrieved the hammer and climbed back onto the pew. 'Stand clear,' he instructed.

There was a splintering sound. Then the catch sprung open and the ceiling door swung down.

'Is that contraption the access ladder?' he asked.

'Yes,' said the tiny voice.

'Good. Stand clear, I'm pulling it down now.' A moment later there was a ladder in place, leading up to the floor above.

Marcus shouted up, 'Are you able to move, George, or do you want me to come up and fetch you?'

What a kind man. 'I'm a bit stiff, Marcus, but I'll be OK if I come down slowly.'

And so it was, feet first and legs second, that the casually dressed body of George Gilbert began to appear in the torchlit room. Gradually, step by step, she came down to ground level.

Both rescuers looked at her carefully. George was pale and wan after four stressful hours in the gloom. But there were no signs of bleeding. It looked as though she hadn't sustained any broken bones.

'Are there more ladders further up?' asked Marcus.

'Two more. One's to reach the belfry and the other is to get onto the roof.' She gave a brave smile. 'But I've been here a long time. I managed to push them both back up while I was waiting. And I shut the flaps. There's just this one to shut here and then we can go.'

'Great,' said Marcus. He stepped over to the ladder and started to push it back up. Then he reached for the ceiling flap and closed it. Whatever he had done to the catch, it still seemed to be working.

The cold and darkened church was no place for celebration. Maxine was conscious that she had walked out on her husband when he'd been expecting a Chinese banquet. And this was the third night in a row she had been away.

'Right,' she said. 'I need to get back for that special meal I promised my husband. Is there anything else or can we go?'

For Marcus the adventure was far from over. For even in the torchlight gloom he had seen that George was his long-lost wife. But he couldn't spring that on her without a proper build up. Least of all in a darkened church.

'Would you like to join me for a meal, George?' he asked. 'I haven't eaten yet this evening, either. I know a good pub in Stratton. I'm living near it at the moment.'

George had no sense of the emotional turmoil shaking her rescuer. But she was suddenly mindful of how much these two had put themselves out to set her free. She had to show her appreciation.

'Marcus, that's very kind of you, I'd really love to. But right now I'm completely bushed. I just want to go home, have a snack, several mugs of tea and a long hot bath, then go to bed.

'But I'm free tomorrow if you like? You too, Maxine, if Peter and Rosanna can spare you. Mind, I insist the meals are on me. I need to say thanks to both of you properly. What time shall we go for?'

CHAPTER 40   Saturday Nov 20th

George drank the whole flask of water that she kept in her car as a stand-by – her first drink of the afternoon – and then travelled slowly back to Tintagel. It had been a busy day and she felt very tired.

But in real time it wasn't that late. At half past seven Peck'ish, the renowned fish and chip shop in Camelford, was still open. It wasn't even out of her way to call in, on the way back to her cottage, and pick up one of their famous take-home meals.

George unwrapped the meal onto a plate, gave it a final boost in her own cooker and took a bottle of Sauvignon out of her fridge. At long last, she could start to relax.

Ten minutes later, as she started her super-hot meal, George felt herself beginning to revive. She drank more of the wine than she'd intended but that was alright, she wasn't planning to go anywhere. Then she found a portion of Monday's home-made plum crumble that she'd left in her fridge and microwaved it to make her dessert.

She would gladly leave the small quantity of washing up till the morning.

It was at that point George received a phone call. She was tempted to ignore it, then saw it was her studious friend Emma, ringing from Truro. She'd be relaxing to talk to, anyway.

There followed ten minutes of inconsequential chatter. Then Emma said, 'I've made some progress on Cornish manors, George.'

'Wait a minute, Emma, I'll get my notebook. . . Right. What have you found?'

Emma launched forth. There were several manor houses close to Truro and she'd started with them. She went through each of their histories in some detail; skirmishes in the Civil War seemed to come up quite often. 'So, you see, they can be very different in all sorts of ways. The ones which are best preserved are often left to the National Trust. Like, for example, Lanhydrock, near to Bodmin.'

'I've been there quite often,' broke in George. She needed to say something, to show she was awake and keeping up.

'On the other hand,' Emma continued, 'the ones which are in ruins are sometimes taken over by English Heritage. They are less interesting to most people, unless you're an architect interested in ground layouts. Or an archaeologist who can glean something from fragments of artefacts and bits of pottery.'

'What about the ones where there's a ruin marked on the map but nothing to see at all?'

'Ah. You mean like Cleave Manor? That's not even mentioned at all on the latest Explorer map.'

'Go on, then, Emma. I've a friend that works there. Give me something new to tell her.'

'Well, I'd say that's a special case. Doesn't fit any standard pattern at all. There's some evidence that there was a small manor there in the eighteenth century. But the whole building was wiped out in the 1800s. Completely, deliberately flattened. My best guess is that it was the subject of a massive, punitive raid. Maybe the authorities had found there was someone illegal living there? Perhaps a pirate? There was one called Cruel Coppinger in North Cornwall around that time. Was it him?'

'There's a question,' said George. 'I'm seeing my friend tomorrow, actually. We're having a meal together. I'll bounce that one off her. Right, can you tell me anything else about manors in North Cornwall?'

There was a pause as Emma racked her brains. 'Well. You know that, in the Civil War, Cornwall was on the side of the Royalists and Devon was with the Roundheads?'

George thought of the sign outside the Bridge Inn. 'I know there's plenty of rivalry between them. How would that affect the manors?'

'Ones which are near the boundary – that's the River Tamar, of course – might be the scene of skirmishes or even battles. There was a famous battle at Stratton, for example, in 1643.'

'Ah. You mean manors might have battlements and moats?'

'A few might. Large ones. What other owners might do is to build themselves a priest hole, deep inside the structure. Or rather, they might add another wing and hide a tiny extra room inside as it was built. Hidden from all sides. Which in some cases might still be present.'

This was a radical new idea which George needed to think about. Her call with Emma ended soon afterwards. But sleep would be hard with her mind still whirring.

Was it remotely possible that Daphne had rediscovered the secret of a priest hole in Merrifield Manor? Had that phone call to her, late in the firework party, caused her to creep in there one more time?

And if something had happened, might she still be lying, trapped, inside it? George checked her calendar: yes, the party had only been two weeks ago. The old lady might still be alive – just.

George continued to ponder the notion as she prepared her breakfast. Saturday morning, when she didn't have to rush out, was one day of the week when she could treat herself to a cooked breakfast. Two slices of bacon and one fried egg, on a hot plate with plenty of toast and a mug of coffee. Scrumptious.

The whole idea was fanciful. Wild. But not totally impossible. George had certainly found evidence that Daphne was searching for something. That remote beach up near Morwenstow, for instance. And the church tower in Bridgerule, with its false wall.

So what if, during that wide-ranging search, she had come across mention of a priest hole in Merrifield Manor?

She had gleaned that Daphne was a curious woman. She wouldn't just note the possibility. It was surely something she would want to check out for herself.

But everything George had found indicated she was searching in secret. Not taking her husband into her confidence, anyway. He'd almost certainly have never heard of a priest hole, even if it was inside his own dwelling. Though might it be as well to ask him?

She ate more and thought harder.

After breakfast George decided she needed some exercise. A walk down to the beach at Trebarwith Strand would do her good. Even if there was a biting wind. It was as she was slipping on her cagoule that she made an embarrassing discovery.

The St Bridget's church key, that she'd borrowed from Sheila yesterday afternoon, was still in her pocket. In last night's tiredness, once she'd escaped from the tower, she had forgotten to return it.

Shame. And remorse. Quickly George seized her phone. She needed to apologise to Sheila as soon as possible. And get the key back to her. It was a community church. Goodness knows who else might be expecting to borrow it.

Sheila didn't sound too cross, anyway. 'I would have rung

you to remind you, dear, but I didn't have your number. Don't worry. Can you bring it back, say, sometime this morning?'

So there was no choice but to make another trip over to Bridgerule. But that wasn't too much of a problem. She was going to be in Stratton for a meal with Maxine and Marcus this evening anyway.

As she drove once more along the A39, it occurred to George that there was no reason why Sheila should know where she lived – didn't realise she was asking George to make a forty-mile round trip to return the key. Perhaps assumed she was staying in Merrifield Manor?

When she got to Sheila's cottage to return the key, George was invited in for coffee. And no doubt to provide some sort of update.

But in fact, information flowed the other way. Somehow or other (via the landlord of the Bridge?) Sheila knew about her row with Edward last Sunday. And was entirely on her side.

'I'm afraid he's too temperamental by half,' Sheila commented. 'This isn't the first time he's publicly fallen out with a female friend. Not even the first time it's happened at the Bridge. He takes himself far too seriously. You're much better off without him.'

'Is he still staying at the Manor?' asked George politely, though secretly she had to agree with Sheila's comment. She saw the woman shake her head. It didn't really matter. Her own interest in Edward had already faded.

Right now she was more exercised by her ideas on Daphne. Then she wondered what Sheila would make of them. After all, she was supposed to be Daphne's closest friend.

'Sheila, can I run a wild idea past you about Daphne?'

'Go on, dear. She was sometimes a wild woman too.'

'Well, I have a friend who's a social historian. I asked her about manors in North Cornwall, near the Devon border: did they have any special features?'

'Apart from mad owners, you mean?'

George smiled at the gentle joke. 'Yes. And she mentioned that some of them might have a "priest hole" – that's a special tiny room, used to hide rebel priests during the Civil War. Did Daphne ever mention a hidey-hole like that at Merrifield Manor?'

Sheila frowned but she didn't dismiss the notion out of hand. 'Are these priest hole places always high up in a building?'

George smiled. 'I guess they'd be anywhere that made them well hidden. It would depend on the building's architecture.'

'If there was a secret room in one of the stables, could you call that a priest hole? Even if it's not inside the main Manor building?'

'It doesn't really matter what you or I call it. The key thing is, was there somewhere really well hidden at the Manor, which Daphne knew about, or maybe had just found out about?'

Sheila was silent. Reflecting, perhaps, on limits to confidentiality and on circumstances when they might be broken.

'Daphne only spoke once to me about this. Then asked me never to divulge it. So I've done my best to forget it. Never told anyone, not even the police. But one time Daphne was excited, she claimed that she'd found a tiny room within the stable block, somewhere you'd never suspect was there at all.'

Quietly, George gave a sigh. So her mad idea wasn't completely stupid after all.

'You see, the reason I thought of this, Sheila, was, might that be where Daphne disappeared to during the fireworks?'

She could see that Sheila had never thought of this at all. For she gave a cry, put her hand to her face and looked horrified.

'You mean . . . she might not have run away after all? Never made it to Launceston and beyond. She might still be on the Manor premises? Might even be still alive?'

Shaken now, she turned to her visitor. 'George, we must go and look for ourselves. Are you free to go right away?'

Ten minutes later they were both in Sheila's car, heading for the Manor. But Sheila's mind was thinking more shrewdly now.

'If we can avoid it, George, I'd much prefer not to tell Sir Wilfred what we're doing.'

'Why ever not?'

'I keep remembering how Daphne was keeping so much from her husband in recent times. As though she didn't altogether trust him. She didn't tell me why. So if we could avoid meeting him, explaining what we were up to, that would be useful. And it wouldn't be fair, surely, to raise his hopes – not at least till we knew there was something to hope for.'

George hesitated. 'But it's his house, Sheila. We can't just tramp in there unannounced. His front door will be locked for a start.'

'But the stables are hidden away round the back. He wouldn't notice if we slipped in there. I'll leave the car in the road, though. He might recognise it on his drive.'

This was only George's third visit to Merrifield Manor. She wouldn't have minded looking for traces of the Canal, but this was not the time.

The task in hand was to infiltrate the Manor's stables and try to find any trace of the alleged priest hole and its contents. Would there be any sign that Daphne had been in there?

Or was even in there still?

CHAPTER 41

'So when did Daphne mention the stables?' asked George as the two women walked quietly up the path beside the drive, using the trees as cover. Access to the stables was round the side of the Manor, so they'd only be spotted if someone was looking out of the window on the stairs. The other windows were either frosted, had fitted blinds or were covered by net curtains.

'For some reason we'd come back late from a walk, and it was getting dark. Daphne kindly offered to run me home. It was as we were driving the car out of the stable that Daphne glanced behind us and said, "the way to the promised land is under there." Then I think she realised what she'd just said, instructed me to wipe it from my mind. It wasn't that long ago, actually.'

George didn't respond, conscious that she was here on private ground without permission from the owner. The words felt tantalising. The first question, though, was, could they get inside the stable? Or would it be locked?

It was locked. But Sheila knew local customs. She reached to a ledge over the top of the door and found a key. A moment later they were inside the stable, with the door firmly closed again behind them.

They'd decided beforehand that they wouldn't risk turning on the electric light. Sheila had brought her torch and shone the beam around. For the moment George left hers in her backpack.

The Gabriel's estate car was parked against one wall. On the wall opposite hung an organised tool rack. Sir Wilfred must

251

have been an active do-it-yourself enthusiast in his younger days. On the far wall was all the paraphernalia for a family on a hot sunny day: several deck chairs, a parasol, a small folding table, a rug. And a full set of croquet mallets.

'Priest holes were built centuries ago,' murmured George. 'The entrance has to be really well hidden. Everything here is far too recent.'

'But what's below us?' asked Sheila.

They peered carefully around the floor but there was nothing unusual. They even shone the torch under the car but could see nothing irregular there either.

That only left one piece of furniture in the stable that they'd not examined. Right in the corner, tight against the wall, stood a very old chest of drawers, made of heavy oak. A wooden box for croquet equipment was standing untidily on top.

'That's the only thing here that's conceivably old enough,' muttered George. Impatient now, she strode over and started pulling out the drawers one by one. Each one came easily: again, there was nothing to see.

She frowned: what else could she try?

'The entrance has to be something you can shut again, Sheila, once you're behind it. The priest needed to be well-hidden, once he was inside his hole.' Absent-mindedly, she let her hands run over the top of the chest.

'They had croquet in Victorian times,' observed Sheila, noticing the wooden box. 'It features in Alice in Wonderland. The game probably goes back even further.'

'But if all the mallets are over there, what's in here?' A moment later George had lifted the box off the chest and onto the floor. It wasn't heavy, hoops on their own didn't weigh much. But what movement had it been suppressing?

George felt the top of the chest again, but this time more

carefully. No. It was firm. Certainly couldn't be lifted from the front.

But what about the back?

George ran her hand along the side and then gave the back an experimental heave. This time there was movement. The top would rotate horizontally: there must be an axis at a front corner. And now, as she peered down, George could see that the top drawer didn't run right to the back. There was a foot of space available behind it. And a matching hollow, carved out of the wall itself.

An overweight friar would never get down there. The priest would have to be small and thin. Even then it wouldn't be easy, he'd have to squeeze and wriggle. But George could see there was a way through, down and behind the chest of drawers. Though there was no clue as to how far the passage went.

'Was your friend Daphne a plump woman?' asked George, as the pair stared at the opening before them.

'We were much the same build, but she was several inches taller. It'd be a struggle, but I reckon I could get through that gap. I guess Daphne could have done so, too.'

'What should we do now then, Sheila? Call Sir Wilfred?'

Sheila shook her head. 'We ought not to raise the poor man's hopes too early. Hadn't we better go down there ourselves? It might only run for ten yards. Could be just a dead end.'

It was an unfortunate phrase in the circumstances, but George decided to let it pass. 'Well, I'm game if you are. Two's always better than one. It's a dirty passageway, mind. I'm in my walking gear. But what about you?'

Sheila glanced down at her trousers. 'These'll wash easily enough if I have to. Remember, if Daphne did come this way, she did so wearing her smart long dress.'

The die was cast. 'OK. Shall I go first?' Sheila nodded and George hauled herself onto the chest of drawers, lowered her legs down the opening. Gradually, wiggle by wiggle, she disappeared.

A moment later a subdued voice came from below. 'It's tight but a bit bigger once you're through the entrance, Sheila. I'll stay here till you've joined me. Take your time, there's no need to panic.'

Five minutes later they were both in a narrow, pitch-black tunnel, less than three feet wide. Glad of their torches. It was sloping downwards for at least ten yards.

'Still OK to carry on?'

'George, we have to see if Daphne is down here. I'll only give up if it gets so narrow that I feel squashed. It's alright so far.'

'I'll go first. But I'll call out if I find a rock or something sticking out. We ought to have helmets, really. It's a pity there were none in the stable. Good job neither of us is very tall.'

They moved forwards slowly. The tunnel kept going, down and down. The walls were uneven but there was no threat to their heads. George was glad her walking gear included a beanie hat. That was some protection if the roof got lower. It was hard to judge, but she thought they'd probably gone a couple of hundred yards when she came to a wooden doorway.

George let her torch wander over it. 'Two strong looking bolts here. Both of 'em closed. Also a Yale key. We can get in alright, anyway.'

Sheila was looking more anxious now. Perhaps anticipating what (or whom) they might find behind the door. Was this Daphne's final resting place? But they couldn't stop here. Once again George went ahead.

Both bolts were well oiled. Another sign of a flourishing

operation. They opened easily, as did the lock. Slowly, George pushed the door open and stepped through.

It was another black space. But, unlike the passage, this one was huge. And, distantly, George could hear the lapping of water. It couldn't be an underground stream, surely?

Then she saw something crawling about, twenty yards away. It was some sort of being, covered in a black robe – it didn't look like Daphne, anyway, it was too tall. As it saw her the figure gave a grotesque howl of anger and pain. Then started to stumble towards her.

For a few seconds George was so shocked that she did not dare move. Then she remembered that Sheila wasn't yet in the cave, and might yet escape. She shouted out an instruction: 'Shut the door.' Sheila had the door closed and bolted while George was still standing on the other side.

That left her with no choice but to face this fearful being on her own. Remonstrating with Sheila, if she survived at all, could come later.

Much later, when George tried to account for her tactics to Maxine, as she struggled to escape from the frightening being, the event was still only a blur.

Even so, she managed not to panic. She had two things in her favour: she had her torch; and she could move faster. But she had no idea of the shape or the size of the cavern she was trapped in.

Her first move was to pace backwards, directly away from the being. But she'd only backed a few steps when she came up against a rock wall. She half-turned, saw the problem and veered sideways; this time she walked herself into a corner.

Then she inched along the next side, until she found herself next to the source of the watery noise. George shone her torch.

255

There was a pool of dark, still water ahead of her.

As she saw it, she remembered the talk from the Canal expert in Bude and had a flash of insight. Was she in the wharf built for offloading items shipped along the Canal to Merrifield? If so, might the water in front of her be part of the old Canal itself? And if it was, did that mean there was an incline somewhere nearby, a steep slope that might allow her to clamber down and escape to a lower level?

The figure was hobbling a little way behind her now. George took the chance to shine her torch around more widely. Could she make sense of the cavern? What was its shape; how far did it stretch?

That was when she had another shock. By the light of her torch she could make out a set of shelves, fastened to a wall she'd not yet reached, containing a row of small barrels – kegs. They looked similar to the ones she'd come across in the church tower, just the day before.

But before she could even begin to weave these ideas together, the figure gave an angry howl and leapt towards her. Instinctively, she backed away.

Which was how she tripped and fell into the dark, sluggish water that had once been part of the Bude Canal.

CHAPTER 42

Maxine Travers was also having a busy Saturday. She'd been woken early by her daughter, Rosanna, who wanted more time with her mummy. Her daddy was still fast asleep, but as he'd put her to bed no less than three nights in a row, he was a spent force for the time being. But the little girl was learning all kinds of exciting things in her days at nursery; some of these would surely interest her mother?

Maxine, though, was learning about motherhood from the other end. She'd gradually learned to give attention to her little one while also devoting a different part of her brain to thinking for herself. This morning her thoughts were focussed on the family of Bert Pearce – the second airman killed in the "friendly fire" incident at Cleave Airfield, so many years ago.

She recalled that the Pearce family had been relatively local; and might still be. If they were around today, would not Saturday be a good chance for catching up with Bert's descendants for a chat?

Rosanna was pressing for breakfast now. The little girl was used to multiple breakfasts; unknown to her parents, she would have a second one at nursery on the days she attended. In the days before Rosanna came along, Maxine and Peter had often treated themselves to pancakes on Saturdays, when they were both at home. Did this treat need reinstating? Maybe Rosanna would like to help with the process?

As the two mixed happily away, Maxine forced herself to grapple with the mechanics of the search. GCHQ was part of national security, so they were used to keeping track of suspected terrorists – though, these days, there were so many that they had to restrict which ones they kept a close eye on. But finding Bert Pearce's family wasn't that sort of search.

Nor, as far as she knew, was it a police matter. Tracing of potential witnesses was a routine task. It was conceivable a crime had been committed on Cleave Airfield, but that was a very long time ago. In any case, whatever might have been true of a wartime airfield, the police had no jurisdiction on Cleave Camp, now it was part of GCHQ. Her husband couldn't legitimately divert scarce police resources to his wife's inquiry. She wouldn't tempt him to do so.

But Maxine had no personal experience of tracking friends or relatives at all, let alone over a span of eighty years. Perhaps George could help her? Then she remembered how exhausted her friend was when she went home yesterday evening after her time "in the tower". It wasn't fair to phone her this early. Like her own husband, George needed the chance to catch up on her sleep.

So that left the security man from the Camp, Marcus. The man who was rapidly becoming her go-to companion and ally. He'd said he liked variety. And he had no social life. It was worth asking him, anyway. He might have no expertise in this area, but on the other hand . . .

For the next hour she had to concentrate on cooking and subsequently on eating. Rosanna needed close attention or the whole pancake mixture would flow across the kitchen floor. This wasn't some new form of gooey playdough. But the little girl didn't yet see the bigger picture.

Which was true for her too, in a way. She was looking forward to that meal George had promised her this evening, and to hear what else was going on. It couldn't all be crime from the last century but one.

When, finally, she rang Marcus at ten o'clock, he was awake, breakfasted and ready for a new challenge. It was clear that he was wasted in routine security.

She told him the little that she'd gleaned from the wartime logbook about Bert Pearce and his family, then left him to it. Marcus promised her he'd ring back as soon as he had anything to report. In the meantime, he said, she should give time to her husband and daughter.

It was half past twelve before Marcus rang her back. He didn't tell her all the details of his search, though she gathered he'd got quite a long way with the Census for 1921, in which Bert was a small boy living in Bridgerule, and other records for 1951, when he was no longer living at all. But the records had given him the address of Bert's family; and the name of Bert's younger sister: Amelia. She wasn't in the 1921 Census, so must have arrived a year or two later. No doubt an older brother who signed up to the Armed Forces would be a hero figure.

So what had happened to her? If her much-admired big brother had been shot down by his own troops, while still living close to home, that could easily have devastated Amelia enough to make her move away from the area completely.

But for some reason she hadn't. Maybe she couldn't afford to? The Census didn't give much detail on the property occupied, but he'd noted the address, they could see if it was still there.

Marcus had managed to use various sources, including local diocesan marriage records, to follow the next stage in the life of Amelia Pearce. She'd married another long-time resident of Bridgerule and changed her surname to Phillips. She was still living in Bridgerule (as a young bride) in 1951 and, at a different address in the village, in 1961. By which time she also had two young children.

Then Marcus had made a devastating discovery. Amelia Phillips had passed away in 2015.

'How sad,' said Maxine, once Marcus had told her the sequence. 'And how frustrating for us. Bert Pearce's only sibling. If anyone could have told us what really happened in that airfield all those years ago it would have been her.'

'It's not completely hopeless.' Marcus was certainly a glass-half-full character. 'Amelia lived in Bridgerule more or less all her life. We've got several of her addresses. Her own children might still be living nearby. It would be worth a fishing expedition, see if we could find the names of any friends, or even talk to them. We could try this afternoon if you liked.'

CHAPTER 43

The canal water was cold enough. Though not as cold as the open sea at Stanbury beach, with its crashing waves and biting wind. And this time, at least, she wasn't completely naked.

Although she found it wasn't easy to swim in her walking gear, especially now all of it was soaking wet. It was dragging her down.

For a second, George thought that, despite all this, she had found a safe haven. But then, to her horror, she realised that the figure that had been shuffling around after her could also swim. She had no idea how fast. At this point, still chuntering away, it was clambering slowly over the side and into the water.

Her torch was still in her hand and, miraculously, still working. She swung the beam round over her head one more time, desperate for somewhere else where she might take refuge. That was when she saw the brick wall. It reached right up to the roof of the cavern and completely blocked one end of the channel. She had fallen in close beside it. It made this section of canal isolated (assuming it was a canal in the first place). Which meant there was no escape at all.

Then it occurred to her that her torch might be the one thing that was giving her away. Should she ditch it; or at least turn it off? Then she had an even better idea. There was an alternative: could she use it to give the creature a false lead?

George was treading water to stay afloat. The channel was deep: she couldn't feel the bottom below her. She managed to pull the damp beanie off her head. Then to snuggle her torch

261

inside it. It still gave a faint glow. There might just be a chance.

After that she raised her arm and threw the torch-lit beanie as far as she could, towards the far end of the pool. There was a splash – was it going to sink without trace? Mercifully it floated and stayed alight, giving a subdued glow at the far end of the canal segment.

At least she had confused her pursuer. For she could just see its outline in the gloom. It was in the water now but heading slowly away from her, towards the torch. At least she'd gained a few seconds.

But what good was that? What earthly use to her was a few extra seconds?

Then, unbidden, a question came into her mind: how far down did the brick wall go? It might only be a few feet. There might be a gap between the wall bottom and the floor of the canal. A gap she could wiggle through, to whatever lay beyond.

There was no obvious alternative. The figure was still moving slowly away from her, heading towards the torch. But there was no telling what it might do, once it found it had been tricked. She had to disappear while it wasn't looking.

George decided it would be best to slide out of her jacket and scarf. They wouldn't help her swim under water.

Now there was no reason for delay. She took a deep breath. And lowering her head and kicking her legs, she started to force herself steadily downwards, keeping as close as she could to the brick wall.

Despite her desk-based job, writing reports and computer models, George kept herself reasonably fit. She had been a member of the university caving club in her student days. That had occasionally meant swimming under rock barriers encountered within a cave, to reach a dry continuation further along.

In those days she had been able to stay under water for a

minute and a half. Even today, she reckoned she could hold her breath for the best part of a minute. Was that enough to reach the bottom?

She swam down and down. It was far too dark to see anything, she was relying on the feel of the brick wall beside her. Would it ever end?

She remembered lessons from her caving days. Rule One: stay calm. She'd exhaust her breath more rapidly if she panicked. She must have come down ten feet by now. But the questions persisted. How deep was this canal? What had this wall been built for? How deep did it go? Would it be best to go back to the top, refill her lungs and try again?

Then, suddenly, the bricks ended. What was below? An old rusty girder? Or even worse, a set of spikes, installed to prevent access to the wharf from the other side?

There was only one way to find out. George clung to the bottom of the wall and pulled herself steadily underneath it. This was the most dangerous point in the whole endeavour: if she got stuck here, with the breath in her lungs almost depleted, she was a goner.

She could only assume – or hope and pray – that there would be no more complications on the far side.

A moment later she was through. Past the bottom of the wall and heading for the surface.

But would that be air; or would it be solid rock?

It was air of a sort: stale air, far from fresh. But it was breathable. Once at the surface she panted repeatedly, gradually recovering her normal breathing rhythm. The "continuity canal", as she was starting to think of it, was still running inside a tunnel, but this time one that was much narrower.

It was pitch dark so she couldn't be sure, but this didn't feel like a huge cavern. It wasn't a wharf either. Perhaps she was in an underground reach, close to the top of the incline?

It was hard to be sure of direction. Then she heard a tiny tweet: somewhere nearby, a bird was singing. It must be outside. Hugely relieved, she started swimming towards it.

Then, as she came round a bend, a semi-circular opening came into view. Light at the end of a tunnel. She had escaped!

Gradually, slowly, George swam towards the opening. She was physically exhausted and emotionally drained. There was less light here than she had expected: either there were dark clouds, or it was later than she had thought – heading for dusk.

She'd lost all track of time in the previous chase; and it was too gloomy to make out the time on her watch.

What she needed now was to get out of the water and into a change of clothes. She was cold but she knew she'd be even colder, standing in wet clothes in the open air.

The trouble was that the walls of this reach were vertical and rose several feet above the water level. She hadn't the energy to get out. There was no choice but to swim on.

Finally she was out in the open. There was a huge, horizontal rusty wheel ahead. Recalling James Gibbon's talk from the day before, George realised she must be at the top of the incline, built two hundred years ago to drop the canal elevation by a hundred feet. Here the side was only a couple of feet above the water level and now, at last, she could scramble out. She felt exhausted and freezing. Her teeth were chattering and, for the second time in a week, she was almost numb with cold.

George found she was standing halfway up a hillside. The only route off that she could see was to walk slowly down the incline. That seemed to lead beneath the old railway track.

Several thoughts came to her. Firstly, her own car, containing a change of clothes for the evening and her Explorer map, was still in Bridgerule; she'd had a lift here from Sheila. But she would be amazed if the woman was still around. Which meant that she had a walk ahead of her, in one direction or another.

But if she was finding her way in the gloom, could she use the old railway track to lead her towards Marhamchurch? That might be easier to follow without a map than some cross-country path to Bridgerule from Merrifield.

She wondered if her phone was still working. When she went walking she usually kept it in her bum-bag, inside a waterproof bag. That was mainly to protect the phone from heavy rain, but the package had fallen in the bath before now and survived. If, by some miracle, it was working after her swim, she could ring Maxine again to seek help.

Or even Marcus? There'd been no time to meet him properly last night, but she gathered that he was a man on his own. He might not mind driving out to pick her up. After all, he'd already come out once to help rescue her. And then tried to invite her for a meal.

She felt a great deal warmer toward him than she ever had towards Edward Gabriel.

CHAPTER 44

For the first time in this afternoon's horrific nightmare, something positive happened to George.

She had made her way slowly down the canal incline and scrambled onto the old railway track, then worked out which was the direction for Bude (no way was she ending up in Holsworthy). Her wet clothes were clinging to her body and the sharp wind was exacerbating the cold.

She was about to start her trek when she noticed a high-visibility, orange safety jacket, lying on the edge of the track. It wasn't obvious who it belonged to. Last week there'd been a gang doing roadworks on the main road nearby: perhaps it got left behind by accident? Or it might have blown away when someone took it off during a tea break.

But for George, shivering with cold, it was a godsend. For now, at least, it belonged to her. She was still cold from tip to toe, but at least her body could be protected from the wind. She peeled off her sodden sweater and tee shirt, pulled on the jacket instead. It was a much larger size than she would have chosen, designed for a burly man and reaching well below her waist, but it was dry; and best of all it was windproof.

She was still wearing her socks and walking shoes, both sodden. It would have been a lot worse, much more painful, if she was barefooted.

For she had quite a way to go – several miles. And the old railway track appeared to be considerably overgrown, especially when it ran through wooded cuttings.

But it wasn't quite as bad as it first appeared. For although the cuttings were all overgrown with thorn bushes, when you got close you could see that keen walkers had developed narrow paths to cut through them.

George had turned away from Holsworthy, was just about to tackle the first cutting out of Merrifield, when she heard a shout behind her.

Glancing back, she saw there was a tall, shabbily dressed man standing on the top of the incline. He was waving at her with a stick. Then he started to hobble down the incline.

Was this the figure who had chased her round the cavern? Thinking back, she couldn't be sure. The cavern had been extremely dark and she had only seen it at some distance, kept as far away as possible. It might not have been an animal after all. Even so, she wasn't going to risk meeting the man again, least of all at close quarters. Quickly she turned and headed into the cutting.

Probably her high-vis jacket caused enough confusion to make the man unsure: was she the person he'd already chased? Or was it someone else? For he turned and disappeared back inside the cliff, at the place where the canal had last been visible.

George wasn't stopping for anyone. It had turned out that her phone, though faltering, wasn't completely ruined after all. She'd had a short phone call with Marcus: he was already out with Maxine, doing research around Bridgerule. "Grassroots GCHQ", he called it. She explained that she was being chased. Asked him to drive to Marhamchurch, then follow the old railway line up towards Merrifield. All being well they'd meet somewhere along the route.

The thought of a strong man walking towards her, a man committed to her safety, was a considerable comfort. That beard of his was enough to frighten anyone. Though it was a pity the light was starting to fade. Dusk was falling early this evening.

George kept going as quickly as she could. The movement seemed to keep the damp inside the high-vis jacket in check. If anything, she was starting to feel a little warmer. Though her legs rubbed continually against her sodden walking trousers. She was far from comfortable.

But she knew that feeling sorry for herself wouldn't do anything for her morale. She tried to switch her mind to other things. Who did Marcus remind her of?

She had gone perhaps half a mile when she heard another shout behind her. It was that man again. And despite his limp he seemed to be gaining on her. Possibly this was a more familiar route for him? Was she on his usual way into Bude?

She started to jog but that made the rubbing of her wet trousers on her legs even worse. She glanced back again. It didn't look like the man could jog, anyway. Overall their speeds stayed about the same. The gap between the two kept roughly constant as the miles went slowly by.

The railway line went under several bridges. Beneath each there was no sound of traffic, so George assumed there must be little-used minor roads overhead. But underneath a forest of wiry bushes, many covered with brambles and thorns, seemed to have expanded to fill the whole area under the bridge.

It was getting dark now. Not easy to see the narrow path that had been forced by walkers through the Cornish jungle. At least, not easy for George. Her chaser must know this route better: he caught up a little of the distance between them at each bridge.

George's advantage had shrunk to less than a hundred yards when she saw something completely unexpected ahead.

There was a pair of stone-built walls, fifteen feet apart,

running exactly parallel away from her. It looked . . . well, it looked like the top of a viaduct.

Had her mind finally flipped? What was it?

It was almost dark now, but her eyes had adjusted as darkness fell. Fortunately, she hadn't seen any bright lights in the last half hour.

It was a viaduct. The railway line must have had to cross a valley. One that was too wide – or too deep – to be handled by a standard embankment. She couldn't see the depth, but it was certainly quite wide.

Fortunately, the viaduct itself had some protection – five-feet high stone walls – on either side of what had only ever been a single-track line. They'd had some safety concerns, even a century ago. There was no danger of her falling off.

But the man behind had closed the gap as she'd been staring. He was now only fifty yards behind. And gaining fast.

George turned away. But looking more carefully ahead, she saw there was a reason for what had looked like an evil grin. For the track didn't just run straight over to the other side of the valley. There was an obstacle in the way.

The farmer who owned the land on either side of the viaduct must have had problems with his cows wandering from one side to the other. In a tidy world he would just have put gates at both ends. But being pragmatic, he had simply constructed a barrier halfway across. Unfortunately, it was made up from many of the prickly bushes that grew only too profusely beneath the nearby bridges. Making it almost impassable, either to an ambling cow, or to a fleeing woman.

She was trapped. All her last few hours' effort, swimming and diving, walking and jogging, had been in vain. She gave a cry of anguish and despair.

CHAPTER 45

Marcus and Maxine had had a profitable day in Bridgerule. Then Maxine had gone home. 'I need to spend some time with my family,' she explained. 'After all, you'll be seeing me again this evening.'

So Marcus was on his own when the call had come from George. 'I'm being chased,' she'd pleaded. 'Can you come along the old railway line to help me?'

For a second, Marcus wondered if George had turned into a fantasist. Paranoid, sensing danger everywhere? But he'd seen her, helped rescue her, from the Bridgerule church tower: that had been a real problem. She might have continued trapped in that tower for days. Almost certainly, then, this new threat was equally real.

In any case, Marcus had nothing else planned for his afternoon. Driving over to Marhamchurch and walking up the old railway line to meet her would be as pleasant as anything else. And it would give him some time on his own with George.

Fortunately, the security man was also a map fanatic. He saw that he didn't need to go as far as Marhamchurch, could park lower down at Helebridge. Where he got out, the start of the railway line was unclear. Then he saw a faint trail, running across the field beyond. Once he'd got over a small stream and onto the trail, it became clear that this was part of the old railway line. The line became clearer as it reached the higher fields.

At one point Marcus noticed a footpath running under the old line, running, his map said, from the hamlet of Helscott over towards Marhamchurch. But that was no use to him today. He pressed on.

Worryingly, it was starting to get dark. He had his torch with him – after all, he was security man – but the line wasn't always easy to pick out as it curved across the grassy fields. After all, it hadn't carried trains for sixty years. But he needed care; it would be a disaster to lose the railway track in the fading light.

Then the line started to bend the other way.

It was still climbing steadily. There was no clue on his map of anything unusual ahead. It was too dark, now, to see very far at all.

So it was as much a shock to him as it was to George, coming the other way, when he came to the viaduct. And saw the thorn-bush barrier, built halfway along it by a determined farmer.

Marcus went forward and examined it carefully in the gloom. For a tall giraffe, he thought, it would have been easy. But for a mere cow or even a human, it wasn't easy to get through or over.

Away from Cleave Camp he wasn't wearing his security jacket, nor was he carrying any weapon. Maybe he should wait here for George to reach the other side?

It was ten minutes later that Marcus heard the cry of anguish. That sounded like George. There couldn't be that many women being chased along the old railway line on this chilly November evening.

He peered over the top of the barrier. He could just make out a small woman in a high vis jacket with curly hair that looked like George. No more than twenty yards away was a ferocious-looking man. It was time for drastic measures.

While he'd waited, Marcus had examined both sides of the barrier. On one side the thorn bushes spilled right over the via-duct wall and the route looked completely impassable. On the other side, though, there was just a chance – at least for someone who was prepared to balance on the wall.

Marcus had also done his best to see how far it was from the viaduct down to the valley below. It was hard to judge by torch-light, but he feared it might be eighty feet. He didn't fancy balancing on the wall, especially in the dark. But he was prepared to sit on it, facing inwards, and to shuffle along with his legs amongst the thorns. If he was going to fall anywhere, it needed to be inwards.

'George, come over this side,' he shouted.

George jerked her head round and saw him. Relief flooded her face: she wasn't alone. In her fear, she had almost seized up. But now she stumbled across and, with some effort, clambered onto the wall like him, with her legs facing inwards. Started a slow shuffle, past the tangle of bushes towards him.

But the ferocious man saw what was happening and came after her. He had more of a struggle to clamber up than the agile woman, but then he, too, was seated on the wall. Then he reached towards her and grabbed her jacket by the neck. Pulled it really hard, trying to force George to lean backwards, causing her to fall off the viaduct to a likely death far below.

But as has already been said, the jacket was far too big for George. Not tight-fitting at all. It slid upwards, right over her head. The man was caught off balance, wobbled, and then fell backwards off the wall. One minute he was there; the next he had disappeared from view.

Meanwhile a frantic Marcus had slid along, grabbed the half-naked George around the waist and clutched her towards him. 'Don't worry, I've got you now,' he muttered.

There was a pause. But now the man had disappeared there was no need for hurry. They could shuffle, slowly but safely, past the bushes to Marcus's side of the barrier.

A moment later he had reached the Marhamchurch end of the bush-barrier and jumped down onto the main viaduct. Then he was guiding the shocked, partially clad woman down towards him. Opening his cagoule and pulling her gently inside it, he gave her the tightest of cuddles. After all, she was looking very cold indeed.

A few minutes later, Marcus stood back, retrieved his spare sweater from his backpack and handed it over. 'It'll be too big for you, but it should keep you warm,' he advised. 'Are you OK to walk? It's a mile and a half back to my car. All downhill.'

'Just about. I like the sound of "downhill". What about -?'

'I'll handle it. Don't you worry.' As he spoke, he took his phone out of his pocket and dialled a number.

'Hello,' he began. 'I've just seen a nasty incident.'

A pause. Clearly, he was being asked for details.

'A woman was walking along the old railway line across the Trelay Viaduct. She was being chased by an older man. There's a thorn-bush barrier halfway across the viaduct which blocks the way. The woman managed to struggle past it, but the man didn't. He fell over the side.'

Another pause. More details were obviously being sought.

'I think he might be seriously injured, but he's down in the bottom, it's too dark to see. Or to get down to.'

There was a pause. Then he spoke again.

'The woman? She's suffering from shock. Also half naked, I've no idea why. I'm about to take her somewhere warmer.'

There were a few more comments from the other end. This time Marcus scowled at the phone.

'She doesn't need police attention at this moment, officer. I'm sorry. I'll be in touch again later.'

Marcus turned to George. 'Bloody policeman. Wanted far

too many details. Their first priority has to be to see if the man is still alive. Ours is to get you safe and warm. Come on.'

They started walking steadily down the line. It didn't go under any more bridges or through any more woods, so there was less undergrowth and no bushes to surmount. George walked slowly but she kept going.

Marcus was desperate to know how George had come to be in the situation where he'd found her. But it was doubtless another long story. And he had to wait for her to tell him. That wouldn't be till she was sheltered and warm.

But the talk of making sure she was safe pricked his conscience.

'George, when we get back to the car, I think it'd be a good idea to take you to the hospital for a check.'

'What on earth for?'

'Well, hypothermia, for a start. That high-vis jacket hardly kept you warm, even before you lost it. And the lower half of you is soaked.'

'I'm starting to warm up a little, though.'

'On top of that, I wonder what you've drunk. Smells to me like you've been in stagnant water. But what else was in there?'

George gave a whimper. 'I don't want to go all the way to Truro, Marcus. Or Barnstaple.'

'Neither do I. But there's a small hospital in Stratton. We could try there.'

Half an hour later they had reached the car and were setting off for Stratton Hospital. Which, when they got there, was a model of efficiency. It was still only six o'clock so not too busy. George could be seen almost straight away.

The casualty nurse was sympathetic to George but insisted that Marcus sat outside, in the waiting area. George gave a short resumé of her afternoon's adventures. 'I fell into the old canal at Merrifield. That's when all my clothes got soaked. Then, after I climbed out, I had to walk back to Marhamchurch.'

'My, George, you've been a busy lady. No broken bones though? That's something. Firstly I need to take your core temperature. Then we'll measure your blood pressure and pulse rate. Once we've finished all that, we'd best give you some time in bed to warm up and recover.'

'What about my . . . partner?'

'Shall I send him home?'

'No! I need him to get me back to my car. And we're meant to be going out for a special meal this evening.'

'Right.' Something was going on between these two. The nurse resolved: she wouldn't stand in the way if she could help it.

Two hours later Marcus was still sitting patiently in the waiting area. He had made a couple of phone calls and checked his emails. After that he had amused himself watching later arrivals. Then he spotted the casualty nurse.

'Excuse me,' he said, jumping up to accost her. 'Can you tell me anything about George? Is she OK? I was the one that brought her in earlier.'

The nurse recognised him but knew she had to respect patient confidentiality. 'Ah yes. I'm afraid I can't say anything. Unless you're a relative?'

He sighed. It was time to show his hand. He had been silent for far too long, but now he no longer had any choice. 'But George is my wife.'

'And what's your name?' asked the nurse. People were always trying to beat the system. It was best to check.

'I'm Mark Gilbert.'

275

'OK, Mr Gilbert. I'll just need to check a few things with the patient.'

He went back to his seat. Emotions a-jangle. She returned a few minutes later.

'George Gilbert says she married Mark Gilbert many years ago. Even told me the date of the wedding. But she's been widowed for years and years.'

'That's what I'm trying to tell you. We were married on May 15th, 1993. Happily married with one daughter: Polly. I was almost killed in a plane crash in Iran in 2009. Word came back to the UK that I was dead. In fact I wasn't. I'd lost my memory, had no idea who I was for over a decade. But now I've been restored, I'm whole again. And I'm desperate to see her. Please.'

The nurse disappeared again. This time for longer. Mark Gilbert had played his last card. He could only wait to see the response.

CHAPTER 46

It was nearly half an hour before the nurse returned from talking to George. But she had a broad grin on her face as she beckoned him to a quiet corner of the waiting room.

'George says that she first encountered the "new you" late yesterday afternoon. Since then she reckons you've saved her life twice and tried to invite her to dinner once. She hopes that in the future there'll be a lot more dinners and that she'll need far fewer rescues.

'Now, while she was resting and warming up, I put her in a room on her own. The aim was to protect her from the hustle and bustle of hospital life. Would you like to visit your wife in there? Remember, if you do, that she's barred from all excitement. Or would you rather take her home – wherever that happens to be?'

The nurse smiled. 'Her test results are all fine, by the way. And her temperature's back to normal. She can leave as soon as you both like.'

Mark's face took on a look of rapture. 'I think I'd like to take my lovely wife home. We've got a lot to talk about. There's a missing twelve years for a start.'

George was looking almost as pleased as Mark when he finally got to her hospital room. 'Nurse tells me, darling, that you can go home now. Your tests are fine. But she says we mustn't have too much excitement all at once.'

'Mark! I can hardly believe this. Even though you're standing

277

in front of me, larger than life. It's going to take a while for it to sink in.'

A moment of panic crossed her face. 'Trouble is, I promised to take you and Maxine out for a meal this evening. To tell you what I was doing up the tower and see if we could make any sense of it. And today there's a whole new chapter to add. That's plenty of excitement on its own – and there'll be even more when we start the analysis.'

Mark grinned. 'As I was waiting and saw the time slip by, I could see that a meal tonight was never going to work. I rang Maxine, we agreed to reschedule the meal into lunch tomorrow. Then I rang the pub in Stratton, got them to book us in for a meal then instead of now. I hope that's alright?'

George smiled. 'That's wonderful. Just what I would have done. Right, Mark. Shall we go to your flat here in Stratton? Or would you like to see my cottage in Treknow, on the edge of Tintagel?'

Mark took a nano-second to decide. 'You know, George, I'd rather like to see this cottage in Treknow. It sounds more appropriate for a second honeymoon than my rather dismal flat. But if you don't mind, I'll do the driving. We'll take my car. By the sound of it you've had an extremely busy day.'

Mark suggested they could go straight to the Treknow cottage. 'George, I assume you've got a spare toothbrush? I can manage without pyjamas.' He thought he might as well make his preferences clear.

George specified her own rules as they set off. 'Let's agree, Mark. We're not going to mention anything about our various ongoing enquiries this evening. Nothing at all. There's plenty to say but we'll keep it for lunch tomorrow. It wouldn't be fair to Maxine to start without her.'

'On the other hand,' she continued, 'I do need to know what really happened to you after that dreadful plane crash. And what on earth are you doing working as a security officer at Cleave Camp? That doesn't sound like you at all.'

So, as they drove down the A39, Mark went back to his last, disastrous flight into Iran. 'It was just an innocent business trip. The person in the next seat was called Marcus Tredwell. I didn't know then, but he was with British Security.

'He was doing something on his phone when there was an almighty bang – it was a huge explosion – and the plane fell out of the sky. It was on the edge of Iran. I was lucky – I was blown out of the blazing aircraft as it hit the ground. I think I was the only survivor. Along with Marcus Tredwell's phone. But I had completely lost my memory. So they mistook me for him.'

'It was a remote spot. Took several days for any news of the crash to reach the wider world,' recalled George. 'Then we were told there were no survivors. A policeman came to the door, told me that my husband was dead. Gave me a number to call at the Foreign Office. Polly and I could hardly believe it. She was just fifteen; I don't think the poor kid ever really got over it. She was unsettled, emigrated to New Zealand soon after she'd graduated. She wanted to be as far beyond reach as she could. That'll be a big challenge for both of us in the days ahead.'

There was a moment's silence, but this wasn't the time to take this further.

After a pause, Mark continued his story. 'I couldn't tell them who I was. I really had no idea. But they had the phone. And they knew about Tredwell. Somehow or other they already knew he was in British security. But they wanted to find out a lot more. Which of course I couldn't tell them. I was also a full-blown medical emergency. Badly burned, broken bones, innards half defunct. There was conflict between the doctors who

279

wanted me left alone to recover and the interrogators who wanted me to talk before I keeled over.'

There was silence in the car. For the first time, George started to realise how much Mark must have suffered. 'I don't think I can take in too much more detail this evening, darling. Not tonight, anyway. You poor, poor man. But tell me, is that dreadful beard you've acquired just there to cover some hideous scar? Or the result of torture? Or is it a fashion accessory?'

It was a bizarre choice: torture-legacy or trend-follower? Mark started to laugh. George wasn't sure why, but she started giggling too. For fully five minutes their relief, that this hideous conversation belonged firmly in the past, overwhelmed them both.

'I don't suppose you have a man's razor in your cottage?' That started them off again.

'There's a late-opening supermarket in Tintagel,' she replied. 'We'll call there on the way. Come to think of it, d'you fancy fish and chips from Camelford?'

'Hey, is that place still open? D'you remember, we would always call there on our way back from Polzeath. Those meals were always special.'

'They were open a week ago, Mark. "Peck'ish", they call it. I'm not cooking this evening, anyway. We've too much to talk about.'

Later, as they started on their well-heated Peck'ish fish and chips in Ivy Cottage, Mark glanced around appreciatively. 'This is a really homely cottage, George. When did you buy it? Good job I'd taken out that life insurance.'

George giggled. 'To be honest, Mark, I didn't use that here. No, all this was from your late uncle, Uncle Bill.'

Mark looked shocked. 'Gosh. I didn't even know that he'd died.'

George recalled the occasion. 'That was my first solo adventure. After you disappeared, Uncle Bill knew I was struggling, emotionally and financially. He arranged some consultancy work for me in Padstow. A gang of locals hoped to give the place an upgrade. I was their advisor, staying in his cottage. But we got tangled up in a murder. A headless, armless, legless body that was found in a pool behind St Edward's slate mine. That's just up the road from here.'

'That sounds like another tale to tell at length round a well-lit stove. Does this one work, by the way?'

'Oh yes. Why don't you get it started while I have that bath. There are plenty of logs in the basket. It'd be nice to get the cottage really warm. Then we can cuddle down, either here in front of the stove, or upstairs in bed. Which would you prefer?'

CHAPTER 47   Sunday Nov 21ˢᵗ

The call came at half past nine on Sunday morning.

'George, it's Maxine. Peter's just told me: his friend Brian Southgate has invited us to lunch. I had to tell him I was already committed to a meal with you. Peter said not to worry, he and Rosanna would go on their own. To be honest, Brian's desperate to see our little one. I think she's the star attraction. So, I was wondering. Could we start our conversation earlier – say, over coffee. I haven't checked that with Marcus yet, mind.'

'I'll ask him.' There was a pause before she replied.

'Mark says that sounds ideal. We'll see you at the Stratton Arms around, say, eleven? Bye.'

It was only as she put the phone down that George realised that she'd given away more than she'd intended. But she wasn't planning to keep much secret now. Twelve years of assumed widowhood was long enough for anyone.

The Kings Arms had a comfortable lounge at the rear. Maxine had already claimed three soft chairs in the quietest corner when George and Mark arrived. She had to look twice to be sure it was him.

'I'm glad to see the end of the beard, Mark. I didn't like to say anything, but it really didn't suit you.'

'I'll order the coffees,' offered George. She'd give Mark a few minutes on his own with her old friend. This "back from the grave" business raised more questions of etiquette than she'd realised.

When she got back to the lounge, ten minutes later, the two looked at ease with one another. It was only later she learned there'd been talk along these lines between them a few days earlier.

'Right. I think that stage one is making sure we each know what's happened to each other so far. No attempt to unravel anything. Let's give that an hour. Then, stage two, we need to see how much of our two enquiries – one in Cleave and one around Bridgerule – overlap. Are they completely distinct or do they have something in common? Finally, stage three, we need to identify suspects and pick out the criminal. If, indeed, we think there's been any crime committed at all.'

The arrival of the coffee gave rise to a short pause before their conversation could resume.

'I'll go first,' offered Maxine. 'It's all to do with the Camp. I'm afraid there'll be parts where I'll have to suppress the detail. Most conversations I have within the Camp are covered by the Official Secrets Act. Fortunately, there's only one crime that I'm aware might have happened. That took place before security was an issue at all.'

George frowned as she raised her mug. How could security not be an issue? Then she realised. 'You mean, during the Second World War? That's a cold case that's gone past freezing. Wow. Please, go on.'

Maxine had a sip of her coffee before she responded. 'For reasons I can't tell you, I was asked to research some aspects of the Camp's history. Which took me back, eventually, to its use as an airfield. It had a role during the war training anti-aircraft gunners. The gunners had to shoot at targets that were dragged behind the aircraft – sometimes at night. It was potentially dangerous and at one point, in July 1944, one of the planes was brought down by the gunners. It went down as a case of "friendly fire".

'Now, as a separate line of inquiry, Mark and I had been exploring some tunnels deep below the Camp.'

She paused to drink more of her coffee. Mark seized the chance to contribute. 'Yes. Very old tunnels. They went down and down. In the end one of them came out partway up the cliffs over Stanbury Beach.'

George opened her mouth to speak, she recognised the name. Then she remembered their agenda. Unravelling and linking up came later. 'Go on.'

'On our way back we found a cavern. With many barrels, all unmarked. They probably held some kind of spirit. We also found a full-length tow rope.'

'That was in a tunnel that went under the airfield,' said Maxine, taking over once more. 'Which made us suspect that the "friendly fire" wasn't as accidental as had been supposed.'

It took George a moment to make the link. 'Ah. You mean, if someone had shortened the length of tow rope being used, the target would be much closer. The chance of a gunner hitting the towing aircraft by mistake would be so much greater.'

'Two men were in the aircraft that was brought down,' Maxine continued. 'One was an American called Chuck Colson. One theory was that, in the cauldron of war, he might have stoked fierce resentment in his English colleagues. The other casualty was a local called Bert Pearce. He lived in Bridgerule.'

Mark barged in again. 'Yesterday Maxine and I tried to contact some of Bert's relatives, to see if they could tell us more. He had a younger sister, Amelia, who died in 2015. But she had two daughters, who still live in the village: Mary and Martha.'

Again George started, but she managed to stay silent. Then she realised that the others had fallen silent too.

'That's a summary of our efforts, George,' concluded

Maxine. 'So what's been happening to you?'

After a short comfort break George started her debriefing. She began by unfolding her map covering the area round Bude. 'I'll point to this as I go. The geography might be important.

'All this really began,' she said, 'with the disappearance of Daphne Gabriel. She's a woman in her seventies, wife of Sir Wilfred, the owner of Merrifield Manor. That's here, about a mile south of Bridgerule. It happened during a firework party they'd put on for the village.

'As it happens, I was there. I'd met the Gabriels' son, Edward, on the train to London, a couple of weeks earlier. He asked me to help him sell tickets at the gate. But I'd left the Manor before I knew there was any problem.'

George went on to summarise Inspector Peter Travers' attempts to find Daphne; and his conclusion that there was "no evidence that she had been harmed".

'At that point I agreed to help Edward in his search. If Daphne had left of her own accord, what on earth was she looking for? But we fell out badly when he realised I was open to the worst case scenario: namely, that his mother had been killed.'

George described her visit to Barnstaple Record Office to consult the diary of the long-lasting vicar of Bridgerule; and the odd discovery that there'd been two births on the same wartime day at Merrifield Manor.

Then her investigation of the St Bridget bellringers, culminating in her adventures in the bell tower. Her listeners nodded sympathetically at this point. This was where they'd all come together.

She also outlined her trip with Martha to Stanbury Beach, and the bitter cold experience of swimming naked from that beach. Mark's eyes were bulging at this revelation, but he managed to hold back his comments.

Finally, she sketched the outline from her historian friend, Emma, and how the notion of a priest hole had led to her quest, with Daphne's friend Sheila, into the stables of the Manor; the discovery of the underground canal; the encounter with the creature; her escape beneath the wall; and her subsequent, terrified chase along the old railway line.

'Which is really how I encountered Mark,' she concluded, turning towards him. 'Goodness knows, darling, what would have happened if you hadn't been there.'

'I did report the whole attack to the police,' Mark admitted. 'I rang them again this morning. They told me they'd searched the area beneath the viaduct but found nothing at all. Though, they said, the ground was soft and marshy and there were plenty of trees. It was just possible that someone could have landed on one but slithered down it and managed to walk away.'

By now it was just after twelve. 'I'm going to order us more coffee,' said Maxine. 'Let's all take a five-minute break. Then we can start afresh, listing all the connections between us. I reckon there'll be more than one.'

'I've got the first,' said Mark. 'That's the small barrels, or kegs. Maxine and I found some deep under Cleave Camp. While George has seen two lots – one hidden in the bell tower at Bridgerule, the other stacked in the secret wharf beneath Merrifield Manor. That can't be three independent lots of the same secret hoard, surely? There must be a connection between them.'

'We'll come back to that in a while,' said George. 'It sounds really important. Something that will bind all this work together. What else is there?'

'I've got a pair of dates,' said Maxine. 'It may be just a coincidence, but I noticed the "friendly fire" took place in July 1944, while your double births happened, you said, in April 1945.'

'Come on. It's not that odd,' protested Mark. 'Wartime! Lots of things happen in wartime.'

'But look at the interval between them. July one year and then the following April. Nine months later. Couldn't that be significant?'

'It could be,' agreed George judiciously. 'Is there anything else?'

'I've got something,' claimed Mark. 'Stanbury Beach. That was where Daphne decided to go searching and later my lovely wife went skinny-dipping. But it's also where the underground tunnels below Cleave Camp emerged. That can't just be a coincidence. Surely?' He glanced at the two women for support.

'Well, linked in to that there's something more,' said George. 'Martha appears in both our narratives. She was the friend of Daphne that took me to Stanbury. Froze with me in the sea. But unless I'm much mistaken, she's also a niece of Bert Pearce.'

There was a reflective silence. Playing "Only Connect" from two independent narratives wasn't that straightforward.

'I've got one more thing,' said George. 'We've both mentioned the notorious pirate, Cruel Coppinger. One of her friends told me Daphne was reading a biography of him, written by the Revd Robert Hawker. She'd found a copy in the Merrifield Manor library. But his name was also mentioned by my friend Emma.'

'I came across it at Morwenstow as well,' said Maxine, 'on a lunchtime visit. They'd lend you the book to browse as you ate. Mind, I think there was a lot of poetic license in what he'd written.'

There was another pause and then Mark spoke. 'We've also heard the name of Sheila mentioned several times this morning.

The holder of the key to the tower. She's the only reason we found the priest hole. And the only witness to the phone call that took Daphne away from Merrifield Manor.'

'Which brings me to something else,' he continued. 'Take a look at George's map. She's marked the track of the old railway line from Merrifield to Bude. But look. Both of Inspector Travers' pieces of evidence that Daphne had run away were found on that route too.'

Maxine leaned forwards to see where he was pointing. Then she noticed another highlighter marking, in central Bude. 'What's that, George?'

'Oh, it's the Olive Tree, where I went for coffee with the Canal expert. That was the first I'd heard of inclines and how they worked. I also had words with the lifeguards. Martha used to go there for coffee with Daphne.'

'Did she now. Did you glean anything?' asked Mark.

'Well. Daphne asked the lifeguards about swimming at Stanbury. She was told it was almost impossible to get down there. But they were a friendly bunch – even invited me to have lunch with them.'

'Locals, I assume?'

'Mostly. One was from Australia. He said he liked the Cornish scenery but thought the weather was awful. You can't blame him, really. November's not exactly warm.'

'Right,' said Maxine, with as much authority as she could muster. 'Guys, we're in danger of wandering. Do we have any more links? If not, we need to go back to what we've found and see what they tell us. Where are we going to start?'

CHAPTER 48

'I'd say the most surprising connection we've found is the kegs. Exactly the same size, in three different locations. All old. Whatever's going on?' Maxine was the one posing the question, but for once she had little idea of the answer.

There was a long pause as the matter was considered.

'The only thing I can think of,' said Mark, 'is that these kegs are smuggled goods. I mean, the ones we found at Cleave could have been brought in by sea. Left on that isolated beach at Stanbury, then hauled up the cliff, one by one. Loaded over a period of years, maybe. But what about the ones at Merrifield?'

'I'd say that's obvious,' replied George. 'They'd have come in via the Canal. Then moved on to the bell tower by horse and cart. From where, possibly, they could be shipped on to paying customers.'

'So what era are we talking about?' Maxine was always wanting fresh ideas to be based on hard facts.

'The early nineteenth century was the time for pirates, Maxine. Coppinger was a key one in those days. Could they have all been to do with him? The Canal was here and working by the 1820s.' George was pleased for a chance to impart her smattering of history.

'But Coppinger was famous as a pirate. That's not the same as a smuggler.'

'Well, he was a man with ideas – bad and good. Perhaps he could see piracy was over and decided to take on smuggling instead. Or maybe he saw the new Bude Canal being built and decided to exploit it. After all, it was mostly carrying sand and lime to help inland farmers.'

She paused, letting the ideas develop. 'It'd be easy enough to hide a keg inside a large crate of sand. Revenue would never think to check. All he'd need would be a docile manor owner, somewhere along the Canal, to keep ordering more sand.'

As she said this, George started to realise where this argument might be taking her.

'But if the kegs came through Bude, George, they'd be easy to check in the harbour, before they ever got loaded onto the tubs.' Mark was seeing the process from a business point of view.

There was a moment's silence. Then George continued to develop her theory. 'You know, there was one weak point I noticed about Bude's publicity: it leaves out the rest of the planet. No-one seems to have asked what else might have been happening in those years on the lower Tamar.'

'Was there anything?' asked Maxine.

'I looked it up. At the time they were building the Canal here, South Cornwall was building other ones nearer to Plymouth. Up and down the Tamar. I mean, that's tidal up as far as Morwellham Quay. One canal reached Launceston from the south in 1817. Now, remember, Coppinger came here from France. That was where you got the best spirits. I looked that up too. Someone invented absinthe around the time of the French Revolution. It was a very high-value product. D'you think it would be beyond him to set up a trading scheme to bring it to Cornwall from France? One that came as far as North Cornwall: up the lower Tamar to Launceston and then on via the Bude Canal.'

A further thought came to her. 'From that point of view Merrifield Manor would be an ideal storage point. It's built practically on top of the Canal. That might well account for what's still left in the wharf.'

There was silence as the idea was evaluated. It was radical but then Coppinger had a reputation as a radical man.

Mark could still see a problem. 'That explains one lot of kegs. But if Coppinger came up with this scheme, why would he bother with ships leaving kegs on a wild, remote shore at Stanbury – ones needing to be hauled up into a remote cellar beneath Cleave Manor?'

George thought for a moment, then came up with an answer. Dates were once again the key.

'Mark, might it be like this? Coppinger came to Cornwall around 1800. At that time there wasn't a Bude canal. It was just a gleam in a local's eye. But if by some skulduggery or other, he became the owner of Cleave Manor, then using the tunnels below it to receive smuggled goods – maybe kegs of the newly invented absinthe - would have seemed an obvious ploy.'

Maxine recalled the readings from the Revd Robert Hawker at Morwenstow Rectory tea-room and started to see where she was going. 'Perhaps that would explain why Cleave Manor has disappeared so completely. There's no trace around the Camp at all. Most people – even our Commanding Officer – have never heard of it. And the Ordnance Survey have left it off the latest Explorer maps. No trace at all.

'But suppose that the Revenue learned who was living there. They would come in great secrecy to capture him and destroy his manor. Maybe set the whole place on fire. Coppinger might have got out, say via the tunnel to the cliff and then down a rope to Stanbury Beach. But he'd have had to leave the kegs behind. Which is where they've been ever since.'

There was silence: one could even claim, a satisfied silence. Nothing had been proved but some plausible arguments had been developed. Best of all, the presence of kegs in different locations had been accounted for.

It was at that moment of triumph when the waitress came to tell them that their lunch table was ready.

CHAPTER 49

Settling themselves for lunch, deciding which kind of roast dinner each would have (beef, lamb or pork?), and choosing an appropriate bottle of wine to accompany the meal gave them a few minutes respite from deeper thought. But no-one wanted to lose momentum.

George started them off. 'Our second most intriguing connection, I'd say, concerns the same-day births at Merrifield Manor and the "friendly fire" deaths at Cleave Airfield, nine months earlier.'

Maxine pressed her. 'Have you any cause to be suspicious about the births themselves?'

'I've been trying to get my head round it. Might be a happy coincidence. Coincidences can happen. But it's more likely, surely, to be because the babies were in fact twins? And if so, why pretend otherwise? What does it imply? Remember, this isn't ancient history we're talking about. These two babies grew up to be the owner of Merrifield Manor, Wilfred, and his recently disappeared wife, Daphne.'

Maxine was more up with genetics and heredity than Mark. She'd had time to read them up in the days before Rosanna arrived. Though she hadn't looked at the books since.

'OK. Let's suppose they were – are – twins. That needn't affect the inheritance. The pair might not even know. Their parents might have stuck with the story they told your long-life vicar, told the same thing to Wilfred and Daphne as well. Maybe shifted one of their birthdays by a few days so the possibility was hidden. Apart from the midwife present at the birth, who would actually know?'

'But there is one problem, Maxine. Their son, Edward, would be a child of incest.' Mark was up with some parts of marriage law. 'That might give Daphne a reason to worry, if she thought the truth was about to emerge. For a start, it might make it hard for their son Edward to inherit.' He shrugged. 'It would at least make it open to challenge.'

George pondered. 'That's certainly one way to explain why Daphne might have become anxious in recent days. Less keen, maybe, to spend time with her husband Wilfred. How would she feel if she knew the man she was living with, sharing a bed with, was actually her twin brother?'

'It would certainly make her a bit less keen to share her worries with him,' observed Mark.

This was all very interesting and might be important, but Maxine was eager to pursue the Cleave Camp aspect and the nine-month gap that she'd computed.

'But of course, it could all be a lot worse,' she said. 'What if the father of these twins wasn't the current owner of the Manor at all? The real father might have been a gung-ho American pilot, reacting to the pressures of war. Like, say, Chuck Colson. That would really widen the picture.'

Their meals arrived at that moment and gave them a few minutes of diversionary activity. And time to think. Mark filled their glasses with Cabernet Sauvignon, they clinked thanks for families old and new before starting on their roast dinners. But they were still musing on possibilities.

'How ever would an American pilot, based at Cleave airfield, come to know a household at Merrifield Manor?' asked Mark. 'It's wartime, remember, and they're ten miles apart.'

'That's easy,' replied George. 'What d'you think happened

at all the functioning manors in the war years? Edward mentioned it when we first met. These places provided quarters for the forces at the airfield. I bet, if anyone had kept the records, we'd find that Chuck Colson was one of many they put up there. But Chuck was a long way from home. If anyone was going to roam about the place looking for female company, it would be him. No wonder someone wanted to shoot him down.' She stabbed a sprout angrily.

For a few minutes all three concentrated on their meals, which they had to admit were very tasty.

'But even if all this was true, it happened a long time ago. How would it come to light in recent days?' asked Mark.

'I don't suppose you found out anything about the Merrifield midwife during your investigations?' It was a long shot, but Maxine was desperate for hard data.

George smiled. 'I did, actually. North Cornwall is a small world. She was the mother of Martha and Mary. I even asked Martha if her mum had said anything about Merrifield. Martha said she was a professional nurse, wouldn't ever talk about her patients. And her daughters ditched all her records after she died.'

One-time businessman Mark was always looking for a loophole. 'No doubt that's all true. But they could still have glanced at the records as they shredded them; especially to see any mention of a place like Merrifield Manor. Either woman – Martha or Mary, or even both - might know what really happened. That could be the start of the rumour.'

George was inclined to believe the best of her skinny-dipping companion on Stanbury Beach, but she had to admit Mark had found a potential gap in her testimony.

They continued thoughtfully with their meals.

Maxine was still after data. 'So, George, can you give us any time frame for Daphne's worries? Any clue on when they began?'

George puzzled for a moment. She'd heard odd snippets from one friend of Daphne or another but not tried to put them in chronological order.

'Wilfred and Daphne went to see Wilfred's younger sister, Alicia, in Australia. That was a few years ago – 2016. Edward described it as their "holiday of a lifetime". They'd never been before and I doubt they'll go again. Someone I've talked to in the last week – I can't remember who – asserted that Daphne started to be anxious soon after they came back. So she's been bothered for several years.'

'Did Edward go with them?' asked Mark. He, too, was taking his data gathering seriously.

'I've no idea. Why would that matter?'

'Well, if he was there, he might have heard, or overheard, whatever made Daphne anxious. If there was any suggestion that he was a child of incest, that would give him a strong motive to do away with one of his parents.'

There was a pause as the others considered this.

'Remember, George, he stopped using you as an investigator once you started questioning what had happened to Daphne. Threw you off the case, you said.' Maxine had a good ear for descriptive detail.

'And note that incest could be proved by DNA. Comparing samples from them both would show if Wilfred and Daphne were brother and sister. But, of course, that'd be much harder to prove if Daphne was no longer alive.'

George started to argue but Maxine continued. 'These days, George, they can get DNA from dead bodies. Exhume the coffin and take a sample. But they can't do that if the body has vanished beyond reach.'

'So Edward might be our strongest suspect so far,' concluded Mark. He seemed rather pleased with this outcome.

George looked from one to the other and then back again: this was her husband and her best friend. Looked again. But she could see that they weren't joking.

Which in turn made her desperate to move the conversation on.

'But now we are talking about Australia, there's one more suspect to add to the list,' she claimed.

Maxine thought back to George's account earlier. Surely it had all been local? How had any Australian been mentioned? Then it came to her.

'Ah. You mean the Australian lifeguard? That's a bit far-fetched, George, isn't it?'

'Well. I recall Edward saying to me that his Australian aunt had a couple of children – they would be his cousins.'

'So what?' It seemed Mark was already casting Edward as the guilty party. Didn't trust a word he'd said.

This felt like hard work but George persisted. 'Suppose this younger sister knew about the possibility that Wilfred and Daphne weren't her siblings at all, she was the legitimate heir. Might not bother her, she's happily married to an Australian on the far side of the world. But it might matter a great deal to her children. One might have decided it was worth a punt to come to Cornwall. Being a lifeguard in Bude might be one way to do it. After all, we know that he spoke to Daphne – he knew who she was. They had a conversation about Stanbury Beach.'

They'd all finished their main course by now. The waitress came to offer them the dessert menu and various items were chosen.

The short interruption gave them the chance to regroup.

'If we are trying to make a complete list of suspects, there are two more people who I'd like to add,' said George.

'Go on,' said Mark.

'Well, one of the bellringers. Someone must know the secrets of the bell tower. The man who led me up the tower was the same man that had previously guided Daphne. He was called Henry.'

She could see her companions were unconvinced. 'He might simply have been the friendliest, or the most fit,' retorted Mark. She tried again.

'There's also Sheila: Daphne's so-called best friend. If anyone knew Daphne's secrets, it would be her. I'd no suspicion about her until we reached the wharf beneath the Manor and met the fearsome being. I'd gone inside, she was still in the doorway. I shouted a warning and she was very quick to slam the door shut from the other side. Maybe it was just an instinct for self-protection, but it left me alone with the being. I've not asked her about it yet but I certainly intend to.'

'Now you mention that, there's one more,' said Mark. 'That's the creature himself – also known as the tracker on the train-line. He was out to get you, George. It's a pity he got away. Actually, of all of them, he's the most obvious. He was certainly brutal. But who on earth was he?'

The arrival of their desserts halted their discussion and gave them something else to think about. They were making progress. Indeed, they were starting to have a profusion – if not a confusion – of suspects. But they were a long way from finding hard proof of anything. Or even from pinning down the crime.

More evidence was still needed.

CHAPTER 50   Monday Nov 22nd

It was Monday morning. They'd done plenty of thinking and arguing; now it was time to assemble whatever hard evidence they could find.

Maxine and Mark were due back to work at Cleave Camp. George, though, had no immediate commitments, so was free to continue her self-appointed quest of searching for traces of Daphne – alive or dead.

George and Mark had spent their second night in Treknow. Little of their chat was about the case, they had plenty of more personal things to talk about. On Monday George dropped her husband outside Cleave Camp, on her way to Barnstaple. She wanted to start her day with a return visit to the North Devon Records Office.

She knew it'd be open: it had been exactly a week since she'd spent the whole day there, examining the Revd Kingdon's diary.

The same curator was on reception and recognised her face.

'It's Mrs Gilbert again,' she began. 'I've come about the Kingdon diary.'

He looked slightly put out. 'I wish you'd called earlier,' he began. 'We've a lot of stock in here. We only lay out an item when we know someone is coming to examine it. It'll take me a while. Which year are you after?'

'I don't need to see it. What I was after this time is your visitor book. And your memory. Who else has been to see it in the last few months?'

This time he looked surprised. She continued, 'You implied,

last time, that I'd had a predecessor. I wondered who it was?'

The curator frowned. There was such a thing as data protection. But it was early morning and he had no other visitors yet. And Ms Gilbert – or Mrs Gilbert, had she secured a husband in the past week? – was a serious-looking person. She wasn't here on a whim.

'Actually, I remember her quite well. An older lady. She came in early September. She was very clear what she wanted to see. I don't recall her name, but I've a feeling it wasn't that different to yours. Let's have a look at that visitor book.'

He seized the book, which was open on the desk, and turned back the pages. 'Ah, yes. Please note, Mrs Gilbert, that I'm not saying anything. But it was that lady here.'

George smiled as she left the Record Office. It had been an hour's travel for a two-minute conversation; but it set her on her way.

George had no more business in Barnstaple. Her next conversation would take place in Bridgerule. She phoned Sheila before she set off, to make sure she'd be in.

Sheila looked troubled as George knocked at her door. No doubt she was feeling guilty about the way she'd slammed the door, leaving George locked in with the creature in the cavern.

'George! Still in one piece. Thank goodness. Did it help, me turning the light on? It took me a few minutes to find the switch.' She looked fearful at the thought of recriminations.

But George didn't want to start the meeting with an old grievance. Saturday seemed an age ago. There was something new on her mind, prompted by her visit to Barnstaple.

'Sheila, something is really bothering me. And for all our sakes I need an honest answer.'

Sheila looked even more worried now. 'I'll try, George.'

'I'd like to go back to that evening two weeks ago in the Merrifield kitchen. The police gained the impression that you and Daphne were both in there for the whole time, up until the time she got the phone call. But I don't think that was strictly true. What really happened?'

For a moment Sheila did not answer. She looked George straight in the eye and saw this was not a casual question: she was deadly serious. Sheila had carried the truth lightly in the past, but this required a complete answer.

'You know something, don't you?' She saw George nod and sighed. 'Well, I guess it was bound to come out in the end. Everyone assumed that Daphne and I were beavering away in the kitchen right through the evening. That was what Sir Wilfred thought, and what he told the police. But in fact we'd done most of the cooking beforehand. And we made it clear that we'd bring the food out: we didn't want it to be collected. We wanted to keep the kitchen as our private sanctuary.'

'So what time did Daphne really leave? The police thought it was some time around nine thirty.'

'It was a "time around nine thirty". "Around" is such a sloppy word, you know. My watch might have said it was half past seven. But I was busy, couldn't be sure. I mean, I didn't look at it very often.'

'So what time was the phone call?'

'What phone call, George? That never happened. It was just a tiny fib that Daphne asked me to tell, to confuse the overall picture.'

George said nothing, but somehow managed to keep the surprise out of her face. There was a pause as she considered her next question.

'So really, Sheila, you had reason to think she was leaving. It wasn't such a shock. You had an inside track on the whole thing.'

Sheila gave a long sigh. 'I knew that Daphne was very upset about something – I didn't know what. She told me she hoped to vanish from the scene – to go beyond reach. I didn't know exactly what she was going to do. But I'd hoped to hear from her before now – if she was still alive. I do hope she still is, somewhere. But I'm afraid, I've no idea where that might be.'

George did not choose to stay for coffee. Elements of the case were starting to fall into place. But there was still a lot that was missing.

In Cleave Camp, more facts were being assembled. Maxine had been back to the Camp Commander's office to re-borrow a few of the airfield wartime logbooks. Following her weekend conversations there was something else she needed to check.

On her previous read-throughs, she hadn't taken much notice of who was in the sin bin. That couldn't be much to do with a shot-down aircraft, surely? But something she'd heard now made her want to know if anyone was in the bin on the dreadful night of the "friendly fire". And, it turned out, there was.

A man whom the Commander of the time dubbed "Dennis the Menace". A very tall man, who was widely believed to be at least slightly crazed. Dennis Saunders was one of the regular pilots, at least he was when he wasn't suspended. And then, in the small print, Maxine spotted the crucial fact. He was usually partnered with Bert Pearce. Dennis had been scheduled to fly on the night when Chuck Colson had been drafted in as a late replacement.

If shortening the tow rope was intended to get at anyone, it certainly wasn't Chuck Colson. He wasn't meant to be there at all.

It was a vital breakthrough for Maxine. A clear response, a

rebuttal to the long-standing rumour which had so poisoned trust between the British and the Americans over the years. Friendly fire had indeed killed the American. But it wasn't intended for him at all.

Maxine made sure she'd written down all the key details in her notebook. At last she had something positive to tell Bill Oakshot.

Mark had taken some ribbing when he'd arrived at the Camp that morning without his mega-beard. He'd accepted it in good heart, he knew why he'd chosen to remove it. But he decided to remain known as Marcus for the rest of his stay here; he expected that would not be for too long.

Maxine had contacted him mid-morning, giving him the name of the man in solitary confinement on the night Bert Pearce and Chuck Colson had been killed. He was keen to take the information back to Bert's nieces, Martha and Mary.

They had spoken of Uncle Bert's rough diamond friend but not divulged his name. Claimed it was "a long time ago and they'd never been told". But Mark suspected they wouldn't be able to deny the name once it was presented to them.

In the meantime he had more research to do.

Mark had worked regularly on his days at Cleave Camp and was due the occasional half day. This was one time he claimed the privilege. A call to George and she came for him at one o'clock.

'There's somewhere I'd like to take you for lunch,' she told him. Twenty minutes later they had parked on the canal-side car park in Bude and were walking beside the canal for lunch at the Olive Tree. George was glad to see the lifeguards were once more lunching there. She wanted to show off her husband.

'This is Mark,' she told them. 'He's my long-lost husband.'

In turn the lifeguards introduced themselves and George listened carefully, noting all their local accents.

'You've lost someone,' she observed.

'Oh yes. Larry's gone home. Said he couldn't take the cold weather any longer. Some of these Aussies are wimps.'

'Better not let his cricketing mates hear you say that,' said Mark. 'Wimps or not, they're hammering us at the moment. Like they did last time. And the time before.' That opened the way to an animated discussion of sporting events on the far side of the world.

George left them to go inside and place an order for their lunch. Where she also, by "chance", picked up Larry's surname. Though it was not one she recognised at the time.

'Where now?' George asked her husband, once their lively lunch was over.

'I'd like us to go and visit the epicentre of this affair. Martha and Mary.'

'That's handy. I was hoping to go there myself.'

The sisters were at home and invited them in. It wasn't their first visit. Mark and George had each been inside their cottage before, but it was the first time they had appeared together as husband and wife. Mugs of tea were offered and accepted.

George was the first to speak. 'I went to Barnstaple Record Office this morning. Looked at the visitor book for early September. Daphne Gabriel had been there before me, looking at the diary of the Revd Frank Kingdon. In particular his entry, made at the time, that Daphne and Wilfred had been born on the same day in 1945.'

Their hostesses were starting to look guilty.

'I think it's inconceivable that, after she'd seen it, Daphne wouldn't have asked about your mother's recall of that day.

After all, she was the midwife. Her professional pride would stop her saying anything. Her own records were destroyed. But Daphne was your friend. Didn't you notice the mention of Merrifield as you destroyed them?'

There was a pause. The two sisters looked at one another. Then Martha answered.

'You're right. As you suspected, Daphne and Wilfred were twins. Daphne was the older. She was devastated as I confirmed that when she asked me. You see, it made Edward a child of incest. And meant that her younger sister's suspicions, whispered to her on their only visit to Australia, were correct. It was no wonder she wanted to get away.'

While they were in a mood to confess, Mark also had a challenge. 'Maxine and I found the old airfield records at Cleave this morning. Your uncle's friend was called Dennis Saunders, known as "Dennis the Menace". But he wasn't killed by friendly fire, he lived on around here till well after the war. Did he have any children? They'd be about your age.'

Again there was a pause. Martha and Mary glanced at one another. Telling full-on lies to a well-informed questioner was harder than casual evasion.

This time Mary answered. 'Dennis had one son: Neville. "Neville the Devil", the locals called him. We could all see he was unhinged, the doctors said he was clinically insane. Neville was sectioned, spent half his life in the mental unit attached to Stratton hospital. When that was closed in the 1990s, he found an abandoned railway carriage in a cutting and turned it into his home. But he continued with his medication; social care nurses came to check from time to time.'

'The medication made him more manageable,' added Martha. 'Mary and I would take him out for a walk occasionally. Daphne sometimes came too. I think she sometimes took him out on her own.'

'And did you learn any more about his background?' asked George.

'Neville would sometimes tell us tales from his dad,' went on Mary. 'We never knew if they were true or false. He said his dad spoke of deep tunnels, far below the surface. With kegs of a wonderful spirit: absinthe, I think he called it. Claimed it was the drink of Oscar Wilde, which his great, great, great grandfather had brought over from France. Martha and I assumed it was pure fantasy. I've no idea what Daphne made of it.'

George and Mark looked at one another. They could have asked more. Had Neville encountered Daphne as she made her escape from the firework party through the cavern? Had he caused her to drown in the Canal? And whatever the story on Daphne, it seemed to them likely that Neville, bereft of medication, had been the one who had terrorised George, chased her along the old railway and almost pulled her off the high viaduct wall.

But there was no point in suggesting any of this to Martha and Mary. It wouldn't help them now. Better that they continued to take a well-behaved Neville (however badly bruised) for his regular outings. Their ignorance might be his bliss.

The four parted company a short while later.

CHAPTER 51

Maxine had refused to join Mark and George for a celebratory case supper at the Falcon Hotel, its dining room overlooking the lowest reach of the Bude Canal. After four sessions out in the last few days, she knew her husband and child had to come first. But she had been able to come out for a post-bedtime drink, once Rosanna was asleep.

In the meantime the reconnected couple had plenty of questions of their own: could they request a wedding reaffirmation, for example? Did the Church of England offer any Lazarus-like service to welcome people back from the dead? Which aspects might need referring to lawyers?

On Monday evening the lounge was quiet when Maxine joined them. Mark already had his Doom Bar bitter; hot chocolate drinks were ordered for the women. Their various data discoveries of the day were first shared.

'So where does that leave us?' asked Maxine.

'We've got a firmer time-line now for Daphne, on what we know or strongly suspect,' answered George. 'It goes like this.'

She took a deep breath before starting her account.

'I'd say the whole thing started with the death of Martha and Mary's midwife mother, Amelia, in 2015. They chanced on her entry about Merrifield Manor as they destroyed her notes. Now they'd been good friends with Wilfred's sister, Alicia; she was almost the same age. One of them relayed the item to Alicia in Australia.

'In turn, Alicia whispered it to Daphne when they visited a year later. But though the midwife was clear that she and Wilfred were twins, she couldn't confirm the father. It might be Francis Gabriel. Or the twins might be illegitimate, with no legal claim on Merrifield Manor at all. That was the nightmare which Daphne returned with – that was her core problem.'

'So over the next few years, Daphne tried to dig deeper. She asked Wilfred, and later Sheila, if they knew anything about her early childhood. But neither could tell her anything.

'She also started researching the notorious North Cornwall pirate, Cruel Coppinger, from the biography she found in the Manor library. Was there any treasure left from his piracy? There was a cave where he was supposed to keep it. She started searching for it in places like Stanbury Beach.'

'How would that help?' asked Maxine.

'Well, it wasn't to make her rich. But she worried about what would happen to Edward, wanted to leave him a legacy.'

'OK. I can accept that. But how did she move on from searching remote beaches to looking beneath her own Manor?' asked Mark.

'As one of her bellringer friends told me, she had a new lease of life after Australia. One new activity she took up was taking Neville Saunders for walks, and she too heard his burbles. But whereas Martha and Mary thought it was nonsense, Daphne suspected there might be an element of truth.

'She wanted to climb the St Bridget's church tower: was it in sight of the Manor? Could messages be sent from one to the other? Then, like me, she spotted the hidden cupboard on the middle floor. With the kegs and bottles, and the equipment to transfer spirit from one to the other.'

'She might also have looked up Oscar Wilde from Neville's chatter,' suggested Mark. 'That'd tell her the spirit was absinthe.

I looked it up. It's highly alcoholic – 70% proof – and very valuable.'

'Right,' George nodded. 'But the key step was when she went to Barnstaple in early September and read the Revd Kingdon's diary. That hardened up the "twin" rumour. And it also told her the Canal used to run almost under the Manor.

'Now she was close. She didn't know yet about the passage down from the stables. But she had Neville's burbles and Kingdon's observations. She lived on the spot. I reckon she'd look for the Canal incline, and where it went into the hillside.'

'Ah. That's why you wanted to go back there this afternoon,' said Mark. 'Tell Maxine exactly what you found.'

'I saw the tunnel where the Canal disappeared, at the top of the incline. And a half-hidden doorway – that must have been how Neville managed to continue the chase, after Sheila put a light on. I'd say that's how Daphne first got into the cavern and found the kegs beneath the Manor. And once she'd confirmed some of Neville's memories, she had to accept the rest. The kegs had been left there by his three-times great grandfather.'

'So what really happened to Daphne?' asked Maxine. 'She knew now that she had been "married" to her twin brother; her son Edward had become a child of incest. But she couldn't even be sure of her father. Was there anything left to live for?'

'You think she'd be driven to an elaborate suicide?' asked George.

'Wouldn't you?'

George looked across at her rediscovered husband and smiled. 'I hung on when Mark seemed "beyond reach". And it's turned out for the best.'

Maxine smiled. She was pleased for them both. Then she repeated her question. 'So what did happen to Daphne?'

George smiled. 'I rang Sir Wilfred this afternoon and gave

him a suggestion. That he should ring his sister in Australia – allowing for the twelve-hour time gap, of course. I don't think he rings her very often, the two aren't that close. He rang back while Mark and I were having supper. Told me that Daphne reached Australia two days ago. She's not dead after all.'

Maxine gave a sigh. 'Well, that's a relief. Peter was right to drop the case after two days. No crime to investigate.'

There was a pause. George pursed her lips. Maxine and Peter were among her closest friends. But, even so, she had to offer a challenge.

'You can get the right answer without the correct working. We both know that from mathematics – Fermat, for instance. His "famous last theorem" was correct; but it took three hundred years more to prove it. By a Cambridge educated mathematician, incidentally.'

'So what did he miss? My husband, I mean.'

'For a start, why weren't the twins the usual joy to their parents when they arrived? Why all the subterfuge? Why couldn't they just announce Daphne as Wilfred's sister?'

Maxine nodded. 'That's right, you know. You'd need an overwhelming reason to separate any pair of twins at birth.'

Mark had finished his beer and listened hard. Now he made his first contribution. 'Was it because Daphne was the older? Was their father into male primogeniture? Couldn't stand the thought of his daughter taking over the family name?'

George shook her head. 'It couldn't be that simple, Mark. If that was all, they could surely have reversed the reported order of the twins' appearance.' She shook her head. 'No, I've got a deeper explanation. I think it was because Francis suspected – or maybe knew – that neither child was really his.'

Maxine's and Mark's instinct was to reject the idea. 'Why ever would he do that?'

'Well. There was one other detail I noticed in the Kingdon Chronicles, but I didn't realise its importance till today. The name Gabriel also came up much earlier in the diary: the same vicar baptised the infant Francis in 1894.

'Right,' said Mark, doubtfully. Where was his wife going now?

'That's a long time ago. So by 1944,' George continued, 'Francis was fifty years old, Matilda not much less; and they were childless. Which was no doubt a source of continuing anguish to them both. Then came the turmoil of war, with all those Air Force troops billeted at the Manor.

'I'd say that one of three things could have happened. Firstly, the household cook, unmarried, could have had a fling, willingly or otherwise, with one of the airmen, got herself pregnant. At which point Francis and Matilda intervened to hide her disgrace. When she bore twins, they offered to take the boy off her, leaving her to bring up the girl. It would be one situation where splitting a pair of twins made some practical sense.'

Maxine nodded slowly. 'Yes. That's just about plausible.'

'Or secondly,' George continued, 'Matilda had a fling with one of the troops and got herself pregnant. When he was told, Francis suspected that he wasn't the real father, but was eager at this late stage to claim the chance for an heir.'

This time Mark was the one to offer support. 'If they'd been trying for years and years, Francis might not be that fussy.'

'Or thirdly,' George concluded, 'Francis could have taken a last chance to see if he was the one who was infertile, by having a fling with the cook. Either secretly, or with Matilda's agreement. So he was pleased when the cook got pregnant – even more so when it turned out she had twins. And, in that case, splitting the pair would have some logic behind it.'

'If the father was an airman, aren't we back to Chuck

311

Colson?' asked Maxine.

'Possibly. But remember, Chuck was an arrogant American, but not the man anyone was trying to kill. The real menace was Dennis Saunders. He was a persistent troublemaker, regularly inside the airbase sin bin. Wouldn't he have been a far more plausible surrogate father?'

Maxine blinked. 'Gosh. I hadn't thought of that.'

'If it was him, it gets worse,' continued George. 'There was a genetic aspect. His son Neville was also unhinged. Spent years in a mental hospital. Mark and I think it was one time when he'd no medication that he tried to put me beyond reach, first inside the cavern and then over the viaduct.

'But remember, Neville would burble on about his three-times great grandfather. His dad talked of tunnels and kegs of spirit. So I'd say, given all else we've found out, and the genetic disorders, that the Saunders could well be direct descendants of Cruel Coppinger.'

A pensive silence followed this suggestion.

Mark was taking his wife seriously. 'Was it Daphne who showed Neville the cavern below Merrifield Manor?'

'It had to be, Mark. No-one else knew it was there. Perhaps she was checking Neville out, see what else he might recall.'

A horrible thought came to her. 'Hey, was that how the man got left inside?'

There was a further pause for deliberation.

'It would have mattered less if he'd kept having his medication,' observed George. 'It was missing that which made him so wild. Maybe Daphne left him some, but he finished it?'

'Or maybe it fell in the Canal?' mused Maxine.

Mark was thinking hard now about the situation his wife had found herself drawn into, inside that cavern. Very hard indeed.

Then an even worse notion came to him.

'D'you suppose Daphne meant Neville to be found at all? Might she hope he'd never be discovered in that long-hidden cavern, that he'd go mad . . . or die slowly from starvation?'

It was an awful thought. Took them some time to evaluate.

'Why ever would she do that?' asked Maxine.

'Well, suppose Daphne found the cavern, put bits and pieces together and suspected that Dennis was her real father. That meant Neville was her half-brother – and also Wilfred's. Suppose that ever came out: say, a rumour sweeps the village. The effect for the Gabriels would be devastating – ruinous. Daphne had to make sure it never happened. Removing Neville from the scene was one way to achieve that.'

It was a possible motive. There might be others.

'I think our friend Peter Travers needs to take this further,' said George. 'We haven't proved anything yet, just constructed a plausible time line. But if it's true, attempted murder is very serious, even if it's not as bad as murder. I'd say he needs a police search team in that cavern. Is there any trace of Neville's medication, for example? Or any desperate message?'

Mark had other ideas. 'I'd say the police first need to find Neville's home. Martha knows where that is. Has Neville found his way back there? Is he badly injured?

'Also, Peter needs to talk to Daphne Gabriel. On Zoom, maybe, via an Australian police station. What's her account of it all? Some aspects of this case may be settled, but there's plenty more to go at. If she left of her own accord, why did she go to the trouble of leaving all those "clues" on the old railway track? Those absinthe kegs in the bell tower would be worth examining as well.'

Maxine Travers sighed. She could no longer allow her husband to drop the case. It was too crime-ridden to ignore.

EPILOGUE   February 2022

There was excitement at Auckland airport. A 27-year-old woman, with a small daughter and Kiwi husband just behind her, was eagerly awaiting the next planeload of arrivals.

George saw her amongst the crowd as she came down the escalator. 'Polly,' she cried. 'My lovely daughter. It was so good of you to invite us over. And this must be Rowena. Here, let me have a cuddle.'

Behind her, Mark was even more emotional as he saw his daughter for the first time in thirteen years. He and Polly were both crying unstoppable floods of tears as they embraced.

'Dad, I was certain I'd lost you. This is amazing, beyond belief. Welcome to New Zealand.'

Polly's husband surveyed the moving scene for several minutes before he spoke for the first time. 'Hey, welcome both of you, George and Mark. I'm Harrison, Harrison Crombie. We've booked a holiday home a short way down the coast. I guess we'll have plenty to talk about.'

One week later, George received the email from Martha.

Dear George and Mark,

Greetings from Bridgerule. It's bound to be warmer where you are than it is here. I've not been tempted to swim again. But we've had a hothouse of excitement these last few months.

In late November, Inspector Travers came to see me and Mary. At his request we took him to Neville's railway carriage and introduced them. Neville was in a bad way; he had fallen off

314

the viaduct! But he was back on his medication, couldn't remember exactly how it had happened.

After that, various things occurred that we didn't know till afterwards. Travers likes his secrets! But they can't compete with the village grapevine, egged on by the Bridge Inn landlord.

First, Travers talked to Daphne, over in Australia, via Zoom. I don't think it was an amicable discussion – it turned out she was responsible for all the disappearance clues; there was talk of prosecution for "wasting police time". But it put Travers onto the cavern under Merrifield Manor – I gather from Sheila that you've been there? But it was only when his team explored it with searchlights that they found the big surprise.

There was an upturned tub in the far corner. And hidden beneath it was a skeleton! And what a skeleton it was. It was a big bloke, almost seven foot tall.

Except that he wasn't that big when they found him. He was in two halves, you see. Split across the middle. The general belief is that he must have been split in two when a cable snapped on the incline. Which meant he had died while the Canal was fully operational, in the 1800s. Which would certainly be a less dramatic demise, if it really was Cruel Coppinger.

Did you know, George, that these days they can get DNA from a skeleton? By now Travers wasn't feeling friendly towards Merrifield folk, so he did. He also got DNA from Sir Wilfred himself – just to see if there was any connection. His aim was to identify the skeleton, see.

If I was a scriptwriter I'd close this email here, make you wait for the result – like we had to. But you're a friend, so I won't.

Roll of drums . . . it turns out that Sir Wilfred is a direct descendant of the skeleton!

But Travers doesn't give up once he's got started. Straightaway he got a DNA sample for Daphne from her hairbrush; after all, she lived in the Manor too. Bingo. She was a direct descendant of the skeleton too. And also the sister of Sir Wilfred.

The Merrifield couple were twins, as my mum knew. Which makes poor Edward a child of incest. It's not clear to the village that he can inherit anything. Anyway, he's trudged off back to London. Where we all hope he'll stay.

But, did you know, incest is only a crime if the couple knew it when they married – which in this case they obviously didn't.

So Travers couldn't take that tangle any further.

Instead he turned to the bell tower and the kegs and bottles hidden within. No doubt you knew about that, too?

He had one bottle's contents analysed by forensics. It was top-quality absinthe, very drinkable. Imagine the joy in the laboratory as they consumed the rest of the bottle! Each keg was worth several thousand pounds. Someone had been taking them out of the cavern and into the tower. Then bottling the contents and moving that on, a few at a time, to some far-distant wine and spirits dealer.

Now Travers started making enquiries. Who, apart from the vicar, had keys to the church?

One was our mutual friend, Sheila. But it couldn't be her. She simply wasn't strong enough to haul up the kegs – I gather each one weighed about sixty kilograms.

Somehow or other, Travers found out that there was one other church key, held by the tower captain, Thomas Vardy. You might recall him: the man with the bow tie. He's currently in Bude police station and being questioned.

I'm sure there'll be more to come. I'll keep you posted.

In the meantime, George, make the most of the New Zealand summer. And enjoy swimming in that warm sea! You'll find it much colder when you come home.

love, Martha

AUTHOR'S NOTES

This work of fiction is set in real locations with historical arte-facts. But I've made up Merrifield Manor and its link to the no-torious North Cornwall pirate, Cruel Coppinger. I've also en-hanced the fabled manner of his death.

For security reasons little is published about Cleave Camp. The fuel shortage and the tensions between British and Ameri-can staff are my invention. There was a Cleave Manor, but it's no longer on maps. My links to Coppinger are also fictional, as are the Camp tunnels and the "friendly fire" incident in 1944.

Two of my sources, Revd Robert Hawker and Revd Frank Kingdon, did minister in the locations specified. Kingdon's di-ary is held in Barnstaple Records Office. Of course, it contains no observations on life at Merrifield Manor.

Mike Smith is the real postmaster of the Crescent Post Office and gave me his own memories of the Bude railway. His friend Chris Jewell briefed me similarly on the Bude Canal. I am grate-ful to them both. These are the basis of the chats on pages 35 and 222. Some dates I've suggested are only approximate: inter-net sources don't always agree.

I am grateful to Anthony Grills for access to the Trelay Farm viaduct (shown on the front cover). He told me that his father used to run along the top of the viaduct wall as trains passed along. I wasn't sure my characters were brave enough to do this, so I invented a thorn bush blockage halfway along instead.

Thanks too to Doug Beaumont, Tower Captain at St Peter's Caversham, for inviting me to a bellringing practice and the subsequent visit to the nearby Griffin pub. I don't know if there are bells in St Bridget's, the church was closed on our visit. But there are many other bellringing teams at churches in the area.

As with my earlier books, I am grateful to friends and relatives for wise comments on early drafts, especially Simon and Karen Porter, Les Williams, Chris Scruby, my wife Marion and daughter Lucy Smith. Dr Mike Pittam made some acute observations on the plot and corrected some medical inaccuracies. Angela Bamping was a highly efficient copy editor. All errors, including those remaining, are mine.

If you have enjoyed this book, please tell your friends and consider putting a one-line review on Amazon to encourage others to read it. If you have any detailed comments – or ideas for future conundrums – please contact me via the website below.

David Burnell   *website: www.davidburnell.info*
May 2022

Trelay viaduct, viewed from the meadow below

Set around Padstow, Delabole, Looe and Trelill

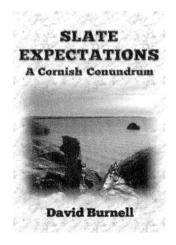

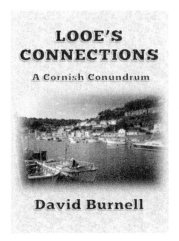

CORNISH CONUNDRUMS 5-8

Set around Bude, Lands' End, the Lizard and Truro.
The 9th Conundrum, Brush with Death, is set in Delabole.

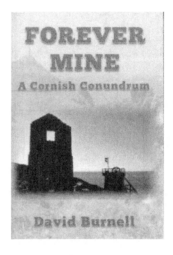

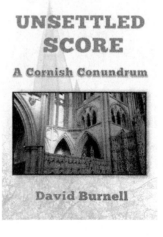

Printed in Great Britain
by Amazon